LUCY IN THE SKY

BOOK TWO

HART'S RIDGE

LUCY IN THE SKY

Lucy Gray doesn't always start trouble, but it's sure to be t
when she arrives. This time, when she runs from the towr
thinks is too small for her big dreams, she's determined to
her biggest mistake yet and finally hits some good luck. B
sister Taylor has always told her that if it looks too good
true, it probably is. This time, she might be right.

Deputy Taylor Gray grew up wanting to solve crime,
never dreamed of taking on a case that could change he
forever, either bringing them together in a healthier dy
shattering any hope of ever fixing the many fracture
With this one, there's no other option—she *will* get to th

The Hart's Ridge series features Deputy Taylor Gray
woman carrying the world on her shoulders as she do
to solve mysteries and piece her fractured family back

Lucy in the Sky is book two of the new Hart's Ridge
mystery series, written by Kay Bratt, million
selling author of *Wish Me Home* and *True to Me*.

ALSO BY KAY BRATT

LUCY IN THE SKY

Lucy Gray doesn't always start trouble, but it's sure to be there when she arrives. This time, when she runs from the town she thinks is too small for her big dreams, she's determined to undo her biggest mistake yet and finally hits some good luck. But her sister Taylor has always told her that if it looks too good to be true, it probably is. This time, she might be right.

Deputy Taylor Gray grew up wanting to solve crime, but she never dreamed of taking on a case that could change her family forever, either bringing them together in a healthier dynamic or shattering any hope of ever fixing the many fractures within. With this one, there's no other option—she *will* get to the truth.

The Hart's Ridge series features Deputy Taylor Gray, a young woman carrying the world on her shoulders as she does her best to solve mysteries and piece her fractured family back together.

Lucy in the Sky is book two of the new Hart's Ridge small-town mystery series, written by Kay Bratt, million-copy bestselling author of *Wish Me Home* and *True to Me*.

LUCY IN THE SKY

A Hart's Ridge Novel
Book Two

Printed in the United States of America

First Printing, 2023

ISBN: 978-1-7363514-9-9

Red Thread Publishing Group

Hartwell, GA 30643

www.kaybratt.com

Red Thread
PUBLISHING GROUP

*L*ucy couldn't imagine that her current location could be any more opposite from the small-town scene she'd left three days ago. Unlike quiet little Hart's Ridge, here, she could feel the energy from the city—much more visceral than she'd ever even imagined.

Like Atlanta on steroids.

The air around her pulsed with sights, sounds, and all the people rushing about as though their destination was the most important one on the planet. Since leaving the bus terminal in Midtown, Lucy had spent the day walking all around the city.

She'd watched people's outfits and attitudes shift drastically every few blocks, depending on the zip code. Midtown was full of tourists, Washington Square Park had students, and there were too many rich folks trying to look like paupers walking around the Upper East Side.

The evening found her wandering around Central Park, exhausted and waiting for morning to come so she could get a good look at the Dakota building. Luckily, she'd run into Margot, a nice woman who had offered her a spot in her tent. At first,

Lucy was reluctant, but finally, exhaustion and Margot's hospitality and motherly worry for her safety won her over.

Lucy had slept fitfully but enough to keep her going.

Now, she sat on a bench across the street from the Dakota, watching the coming and going of the elites who slipped in and out of the building. The two bellmen worked like a well-oiled machine, the younger one stepping up to open doors and carry packages and the much older one doing most of the greeting and other small gestures.

She marveled at how nonchalant the residents were, moving about in their pampered way, not even realizing that just yards from them were humans trying to stay alive from one night to the next. All Lucy's life, she'd wanted to see the famous building, and when she'd decided to run from Georgia again, heading to New York had been a no-brainer.

She'd made it—with no clue about what to do next. Really, there was only one major thing to get done now that she'd left the judgmental laws of the South. And as soon as she could find the right place for the right price, she could knock that off her list too.

Her load was light, and that made things easier. All she had was a backpack containing her few clothes, a pack of bologna, a loaf of bread, and a bag of chips she'd nabbed that morning with a five-finger discount. She had to admit, stealing it had scared her half to death. In the old days, she had been able to shoplift anywhere and anytime with nearly no fear of getting caught. Now, with all the surveillance and Big Brother over everyone's shoulders at every second, she wasn't as smooth as she used to be. Her stint in the dreary Atlanta jail cell a few weeks back had proved that and made her ever so much more wary.

Jail was not fun. That was one reason that she did everything she could not to look homeless. Her youth and, yes, she hated to admit it, but her beauty, too, helped her with that. While some of the residents of Central Park looked haggard and used up, life on the run wasn't yet showing on Lucy. She always found a way to get a shower, whether it was by a stopping into a local gym and talking her way to a free one or going to a truck stop and paying a few bucks.

That reminded her that she also had Taylor's police own money, and the guilt burned through her. She would never have stolen from family if it wasn't important. Taylor should've given it to her when Lucy asked. Then she wouldn't have had to take it.

She patted her pocket, making sure for the millionth time it was still there. She had to keep it safe, and it couldn't be wasted on bread and bologna and the like.

She had to admit, she wished she'd stayed in Hart's Ridge a bit longer. There was something to be said for having a dependable roof over her head and the safety that Taylor provided by being the protective big sister, even if it did get old fast. Lying on the ground the night before, with her feet and hips aching, she'd thought of her last bath before she'd left town, the steaming water and tons of bubbles, and wished it had been a bit longer.

Now, Lucy's living quarters consisted of a small patch of grass near the Central Park Reservoir. Her roommate was a woman named Margot, who, if what she said was fact and not fantasy, had once had her own penthouse and a trust fund before heroin had ruined her. She was clean now, at least off drugs, but she had an alcohol dependence.

Lucy liked her, though. Margot was smart and had seen Lucy wandering around the park her first night and offered a small piece of her own setup for protection. She had a private-school education, but better than that was her four-year degree from the school of hard knocks. Those were the kind of people Lucy wanted to stay near if she was living on the outside. They'd show her the ropes of where she'd landed and keep her safe or at least as safe as she could be.

The only problem was that Margot was a talker, especially after she'd started on her second bottle of the day. And Lucy, though she'd also been considered quite gabby over the years, could only take so much ranting about the system, the government, and everyone else who had brought Margot's house of cards tumbling down.

Lucy had to get away from her as much as she could.

Now, she sat staring at the Dakota building and all the lookieloos around it while she again wallowed in the deep sadness of the loss of a legend.

A small group of Japanese tourists, all wearing matching red visors and carrying umbrellas to keep the sun off their faces, stopped in front of the gates and began taking photos.

The black lantern the Dakota kept on at all hours in memory of John Lennon was visible from where Lucy sat. Of course, he'd been gone for decades, but that didn't make Lucy's sadness any less palpable.

The building was magnificent. The first of its kind, even. When it had been built, apartments were not even a consideration for the elite. The rich lived in large, single-family homes, while apartment living was reserved for the poor.

Lucy knew every detail of its fascinating history, from its tall, gothic-style gables to the striking arched entrances. The builder, Edward Clark, had known he'd have to do something different to get people to share his vision, so he'd made the Dakota more lavish than anyone could imagine, like a luxury hotel. It employed full-time manservants and maids and included a private dining room that even offered room service.

He had built it around a central courtyard because the carriages had to have room to pass through with their precious cargo of residents, many of them quite famous over the years.

Black iron gates led into the courtyard. John had been just about to walk through them that night and stop by home on his way to dinner so he could tell his son goodnight.

And then some psycho had taken him out.

Lucy watched the two doormen. One was doing some squats.

The other was older and very dignified. She wondered if they even knew they were standing on hallowed ground. Did they <del>i you listen to the music?</del> Know who John was?

Originally, the top two floors had been the quarters for all the hired help, and that was where Lucy imagined hers<del>i ll to have</del> lived. She never made grander dreams, somehow always knowing her life was meant to be one of strife and struggle.

Honestly, she would've been happy on that top floor, slinging a mop and dumping chamber pots. It would've been just fine for the small-town Georgia girl she was. Just rubbing elbows with the famous would've been enough.

It was morbid, but she couldn't help the lifelong attraction to who he had been, the music he had made, and the life he had lived.

A legend. Someone who had only wished for peace and unity.

Such a shame.

Suddenly, a man dressed in a suit emerged from the Dakota. She could see the irritation and stress on his face all the way from her viewpoint across the street. In one hand, he carried a brief-case, and in the other, he held the leashes of two French bulldogs, which were straining as hard as they could to go somewhere.

The man pressed the leashes and something else that Lucy couldn't see into the doorman's hand then looked out over the traffic and pointed across the street.

Straight at Lucy.

The doorman nodded, and the businessman got into a black car at the curb.

Then the doorman crossed the street with the dogs, coming right at her. He looked irritated too. What was it about the two dogs that made two men scowl? Lucy thought they were cute enough, as much as pug-nosed critters could be considered cute. They were dressed in matching outfits. The bigger one wore a brown Coach jacket, and his collar was black with spikes. The smaller dog matched him, though her attire was pink.

"Hey—you were supposed to meet him at the door. Mr. Banfield isn't too happy with you, so you might not be working for them for long," the doorman said. Then he tried to hand over the leashes of two dogs that were, by now, madly trying to enter the park.

She saw the name tag on his jacket said Oscar.

Lucy held her hands up. "Whoa. You got the wrong girl. I don't work for him."

He squinted down at her. "You ain't the new dog walker?"

"No, I'm not."

He thought for a moment. "Do you want to be? Someone was supposed to show up today after the missus fired their last one. I have a fifty for you if you're doing the walking. We can split it today."

Lucy looked at the dogs then back at him. "Those dogs are worth a lot of money. You're going to hand them over to just anyone? Are you crazy?"

"You look honest to me. Anyway, if you take off with them, that's on him, not me. But you wouldn't get far. Everyone from twenty blocks around knows who they belong to. Anyway, he told me to bring them over to you. Listen, I gotta get back over there. I'm missing my tips. Just take them this once and bring them back in half an hour. Please."

Lucy sighed. "Fine. But I get the whole fifty."

Oscar laughed. "Now you're looking street-smart. When you return them, you'll get it. This is Bentley and Bailey. Don't say it in front of the Banfields, but the dogs will answer to Bent and Bae and don't need all the fuss. But for God's sake, don't let them get dirty."

He left her standing there, holding as tight as she could to the leash because Bentley—or Bent—was still straining. They looked at her, surprisingly unalarmed that a stranger was about to take off with them, and she laughed.

"Fine. Let's go."

6

"Go" must've been the magic word because at that, the two took off as if she'd set their butts on fire. Lucy nearly lost the leashes, but she got them under control. She wondered when they'd last been walked, but no one else could literally feel the excitement and joy coming from them as they trotted along, sniffing every blade of grass they could find.

Bent hiked his leg at least half a dozen times before they'd gone twenty yards. Bae squatted a few times, much more demurely than her brother. Lucy had to admit, the two of them were showstoppers with their shiny fawn-colored coats and squishy noses. She was getting irritated at how often people were stopping them to ooh and ahh and try to pet the dogs.

"Stop for a second, you two," she said to them and reeled them in like big fish at the end of a line.

Bent sat down, his body contorting to a very strange position as he stared up at her. The effort pushed a pillow of gas out of him, and it squeaked out of his butt, making him jump up and turn around to see what the offending noise was.

Bae gave him a look as though he were an idiot.

Lucy laughed. The two were hilarious together. Clumsily, she wrestled the couture jackets off them, almost losing Bent in the process. She tucked them into her backpack.

"Now, you are a little less adorable. Maybe we can have some peace." Once they'd walked about ten minutes, she turned them around and started back.

When she got back to the bench, she hesitated.

The dogs could be sold for thousands.

All she had to do was make a quick—*very quick*—disappearance, jump on a Greyhound bus again, and relocate somewhere that wouldn't be looking for the Banfield pooches.

She looked at the dogs. It would be a lot of work to keep them hidden until off-loading them. And the owners would probably hunt her down relentlessly. Obviously, they had the money to do it too.

She waited for the light then stepped into the street. It wasn't the fear of the Banfields that had her taking the dogs back, though. She might be a petty thief, but she wasn't heartless. Who knew? Perhaps the pups loved their owners and would suffer emotionally. Or could be that Mrs. Banfield needed them for her mental health. As she crossed the street, she thought of Taylor and Bernard. Now, he was a special one. Nothing fancy about him but so darn intelligent. She wondered if he missed her.

The older bellman saw her first. "Great job, young lady. I must tell you; you handled getting them critters across the street like a boss."

Lucy smiled up at him. He didn't care that she didn't smell like a million bucks. His kindness was for everyone.

"You're back!" Oscar said as he turned, smiling broadly. He plucked the bill from his pocket and gave it to her. "Go ahead and deliver them to the apartment. The housekeeper will get them from you. It's apartment 99 on the fourth floor."

Lucy stood there open-mouthed before her common sense kicked in. She was going to get to see inside the Dakota, and no one would throw her out! Well, she hoped no one would. She tried to calm herself and look like she was supposed to be there.

The dogs guided her, and they stepped inside.

It was gorgeous. Even beyond her expectations. The marble staircase alone looked like something out of a vintage movie. The ceilings looked to be at least fourteen feet high.

It just smelled like money. Old money, to be exact.

Lucy almost expected to hear angels sing or at least hear "Over the Rainbow" playing through the halls, considering Judy Garland had once lived here. Lauren Bacall had also lived here, among other well-known names, though none could compete with her beloved John.

She paused for a second, and the dogs strained at their leashes. If she went slowly enough, maybe Yoko Ono would come out of her apartment. Or at least someone famous.

When no such miraculous moment happened, Lucy let the dogs lead her to an elevator. She wished she could go to the top floor and see it as it had once been, with servants' quarters, a playroom, and a gymnasium. Those were no longer there, since that floor had been converted into apartments.

The elevator stopped at the fourth floor, and when the door opened, Bent and Bae rushed down the hall, Lucy holding on behind them for dear life.

Bent got to the apartment first and used his paw to scratch. Lucy cringed at the sound of his nails against the thick mahogany door, but it opened right up, and she was staring into the face of an older woman holding a dust cloth in her hands.

She snatched the leashes from Lucy's hands. "You're five minutes late, and Mrs. Banfield is very upset. She already called the police to report her dogs were kidnapped."

Lucy held her hands up. "Yikes. My apologies. I didn't know it was that tight a schedule." She didn't add that she didn't know anything at all because she wasn't their dog walker!

The housekeeper sighed. "Why can't we ever get someone that understands protocol?"

"There's a protocol for walking dogs? Wow, lady. You need to loosen up. They had a great time. Golden showers on every piece of grass they could find and a half dozen head pats from strangers, and now they're back safe and sound. I call that a success but whatever. Have a nice day."

Lucy turned and left. She didn't need the drama, even if she would've liked to have a chance to step inside and have a look around the apartment. If the housekeeper was that stressed out, she sure didn't want to run into the missus.

Rich people weren't worth the effort.

She took the same route out of the building, careful to be quiet and mind herself so that no one would think her an intruder and call the authorities.

When she stepped back out of the building, she saw Oscar in a huddle with two other men. Something was going on.

"Please, Mr. Johnson. It will never happen again," the older bellman said, his hat held to his chest in earnest.

"Yes, I know it won't, Edward. Because you won't be here any longer," a thin, red-faced man said. He wore a blue suit that looked nearly as stiff as he did.

Oscar looked angry and bent toward the man, using his finger to punch the air in front of his chest for emphasis. "You know damn well that he can't help it."

Johnson wasn't moved, his face set like a stone.

Edward's was crimson. "Let it go, Oscar. I don't want you to lose your job too. They've already made up their mind. I'll collect my things peacefully."

"No—I'm not letting that happen. You need this job, Edward. I don't. I'll quit, and then they'll have to keep you on."

"No, we won't," the dude named Johnson said. "I can get two new employees in a snap."

"What's going on?" Lucy said.

They saw her standing there, and Edward mumbled something then charged past her and headed into the building. She saw tears in his eyes.

"He's embarrassed," Oscar said. "He had a little accident, and one of the residents reported it. Now they want to fire him. Edward needs every penny he can get to just keep a roof over his head. A shabby one at that."

"He's had a lot of good years here," Suit Guy said. "It's time for him to step down and let someone younger take his place."

"Tell that to Mrs. Linder, who comes down every morning for the hot cup of chai tea that Edward brings her from the café around the corner, rain or snow. Or her husband, Ronald, who looks forward to talking to Edward before every horse race. Edward is greatly loved around here, and they aren't going to take kindly to you getting rid of him for something he can't help."

"Can I ask, what's the issue?" Lucy said. It distressed her, too, thinking of the old man losing a job that he loved and that so many loved him for.

"It's not something to discuss in front of the ladies," Johnson said then turned his back on Lucy.

"Oh, for heaven's sake," Oscar said. "He had a little wet spot on the front of his trousers no bigger than a dime. It's not like he bagged the scullery maid in the grand pantry."

"This is not the first time," Suit Guy retorted. "It's a recurring issue."

Lucy pulled on Suit Guy's sleeve to get his attention.

"Are you telling me that because a senior citizen would dare to have a wet spot on his trousers, you'd relieve him of the job that is probably barely putting food on his table? Shame on you. This is exactly what is wrong with America today. No one cares about anyone anymore. There are so many other compassionate solutions to this problem, yet you take the coward's way out by just disposing of him like he's nothing! Did you enjoy pushing him to the edge of despair? Making him beg for his job? I bet you will never have to worry about senior-adult poverty. You'll never have to go without heat in the winter or decide whether it's cat food or medicine for the month. You should be ashamed. I hope you can live with yourself."

When she took a breath, she noticed everything around her had gone quiet. She looked around and saw that a crowd had formed.

They applauded.

Johnson was livid. "Just who the hell do you think you are? And more importantly, do you know who I am?"

Another man stepped forward out of the crowd.

"Relax, Johnson. You're the building manager, not a long-lost Kennedy. But I agree. I'd like to know who she is too." He directed the question at Lucy.

Oscar cleared his voice. "Mr. Banfield, that's your dog walker."

Bentley and Bailey's dad looked down at Lucy and frowned.

Now what? Had he already been told she'd been five minutes late returning them? Like, what was five minutes? Did the dogs have such a tight schedule in their little dog lives that not a minute could be spared? Were they both now laid back in a lounge chair, getting little dog facials and fancy pedicures?

"Hi," she offered. "Your dogs are cute."

Then she felt like an idiot. *Your dogs are cute?*

"What is your name?" he asked, a slight accent in his tone that she couldn't quite recognize.

"Lucy."

"Last name?"

"That's restricted information."

That made him laugh.

He turned to Oscar. "I forgot my glasses. Can you run up and get them?"

Lucy remembered the little dog clothes in her bag.

"Wait—here are the outfits the dogs were wearing earlier. I forgot to hand them over." She rummaged in her backpack, pulled them out, and handed them to Oscar.

"You took their clothes off?" Mr. Banfield asked, raising his eyebrows at her.

"Um—yeah. Why? Are clothes required for dogs in Central Park? I assure you, they didn't feel a bit naked. They seemed happy to be free of them. You should've seen those tiny butts swinging back and forth."

The building manager glared at her. "You shouldn't have done that."

Banfield laughed. "Oscar, hand those to the housekeeper, and let's pray that Suki hasn't noticed they came in undressed."

"Yes, sir," Oscar said. "I'll go up now."

There was an awkward pause.

"Wait a second," Banfield said, looking at all of them. "What's going on out here, Rudolph?"

Lucy rolled her eyes at the name for the building manager. It was a perfect fit.

"We've relieved Edward of his duties, sir."

"For what reason?" Banfield asked, suddenly stern.

"Because he—well, um..."

"He had a tiny wet spot on the front of his trousers," Lucy broke in. "He's an old man. Maybe he didn't get his break fast enough. Or it could have been he had a little leak. So what? It happens. But your guy Rudolph, here, has no compassion."

Banfield looked at Rudolph.

"Is that true?"

"Yes, sir. But this isn't the first time it's happened, and there were complaints from a lady. We can't have that here. As you know, we are a reputable establishment."

"I am very aware that we are a reputable establishment, since I'm on the board of directors," Banfield began. "But are you aware of the Employment Act of 1967, which protects employees over the age of forty from discrimination on the basis of age?"

Rudolf sputtered. "I—I..."

"Has Edward had any complaints about how he conducts his position with the Dakota?"

"No, sir."

"Is he always on time and showing up for his schedule?"

"Yes, sir."

"Everyone loves Edward, Mr. Banfield," Oscar said. "Well, except one resident, and I'm sure you can guess who it was that made the complaint."

Banfield nodded. "I sure can. Probably the same one who complained that residents shouldn't be allowed to come and go after eight o'clock at night and that dogs should be against the tenant rules. Yes, she's been walking around this building for more than a decade, trying to find anything and everything to be mad about. But this goes too far. Rudolph, do you want to be the one representing us in an ageism lawsuit?"

"No, sir," Rudolph said, his face and nose suddenly matching his namesake.

"You will reinstate Edward immediately, with a generous raise and an apology. You'll also make it clear that he's allowed a short bathroom break whenever the need arises. And get him a damn stool to sit on when no residents need him." He turned to Oscar. "Thank you for standing up for your friend. Loyalty in this current world is rare and priceless."

He pulled a bill from his pocket and held it out to him.

Oscar shook his head. "No, thank you, sir. I don't want a reward for doing the right thing. Edward's more than my friend. He's my mentor."

Banfield smiled. "Then maybe I should give it to this little spitfire." He held it out to Lucy, and she plucked it from him and tucked it into her pocket. She didn't need a tip for doing the right thing, either, but times were hard.

"Thanks." Satisfied that she'd made even more money and that Edward still had his job, she turned to leave.

"Are you coming back later today for their evening walk?" Banfield asked.

Lucy hadn't planned to come back. She figured that the dog-walking company would figure out its mistake and send someone new, and that would just make her look as if she'd done something shady if she showed up too.

"No, I think they're sending someone else."

He looked surprised. "You don't want the job?"

"No. But thanks."

Behind him, Oscar was giving her an exaggerated dumbfounded look and nodding his head. But Lucy had things to get done while she was in the city. Or at least one thing. Then, when it was over, she was leaving. New York was far too expensive to try to make it on her own.

Now Banfield looked determined. He obviously didn't like to

be told no. "You don't have to be just the dog walker. We really need a dog nanny."

Lucy burst out laughing, and he scowled.

"I'm serious," he said.

She couldn't help herself. Rich people were so ridiculous. "Oh? And what does a dog nanny do exactly? You want me to wash and powder little Bentley's plump butt every time he dares to leave a Tootsie Roll? Dress Bailey in frills and bows? Play tea party with them while your wife is otherwise busy at her charity functions?"

Now Oscar was backing away from them as though he didn't want anything to do with Lucy.

"Well, now that you mention it," Banfield said, "Bentley could use a bit of powder on his butt. Might help those raunchy farts of his."

Lucy smiled. She loved a man who could take a joke.

"But seriously, Suki has been having some, well... issues. The housekeeper is too busy to give the dogs the attention they need, and the dog walkers keep quitting or getting fired. That leaves Suki nagging me all the time to step in. They're okay, don't get me wrong. For dogs. But I have a lot on my plate."

He almost made her feel sorry for him. He knew how to use his deep brown eyes to his advantage, that was for sure.

"I'm really not sure how long I'll be here in the city."

"Room and board? And a salary. You can bank the pay. Come on, you must be a dog lover, right? So do it for the dogs."

Lucy really wasn't that big on dogs, but she still considered it. After all, even seeing the Dakota had always been a dream of hers. Now she was getting the opportunity to live in it for a while. Even if it only lasted a few weeks, it would be something she could remember for the rest of her life.

And what if, by some spark of synchronicity, she ran into Yoko?

Lucy stuck out a hand. "You've got a deal. When do I start?"

CHAPTER 2

*B*ack in Hart's Ridge, Taylor sat at her dad's table while he remained in his recliner, sullen and silent, Diesel lounging at his feet. She felt sick to her stomach. Possibly in shock. The talk—or *interrogation,* as her dad had called it—hadn't gone well, and he'd clammed up and refused to say another word. An hour earlier, she'd called the prison to get a name to go with the inmate number on the money order receipt she'd found in his mail. The mail that, yes, she'd sifted through so that she could pay his utility bill, which she didn't think he could afford.

The mail that showed her exactly why he couldn't afford it.

Because he was sending money to someone in prison.

Her shock when they'd stated her dead mother's name as a current inmate was indescribable.

Now she needed answers.

"Why aren't you at work?" he finally said.

"I'm on vacation. Now, let's start talking. Before I decide to completely shut you out of my life, I'm willing to give you a chance to explain yourself. That chance expires when I walk out this door."

"Then walk."

Damn, he is stubborn.

She wasn't on vacation. She was on unpaid leave. She still had a job, but the sheriff had torn her a new one about the Meyers case. Shane had relayed to him what had gone down when they went to serve the search warrant, including how Taylor had taunted Meyers and provoked him to take his life.

It wasn't fair. The piece of crap had been ready to do it anyway, just so he wouldn't have to face the shame of being caught. Sure, she shouldn't have told him about the evidence against him, because if he had lived, he would've known the case they were building, but she wouldn't go so far as to say it was her fault.

That wasn't how the sheriff saw it, though. Fortunately, their long relationship counted for something, because he'd quietly reprimanded her, given all the credit for solving the case to Shane, and told her to do better. He'd reminded her that there was a consequence for getting too emotionally involved.

He was always trying to teach her a life lesson.

As for Shane, he was such a jerk. She was done with him and hadn't spoken to him since the press conference in which he had gotten all the credit for solving the case.

She dreaded going back to work and facing him.

Before that happened, she had to get some things straight with her dad.

He was going to have to start talking, or she'd start walking.

"All these years, you've lived a lie," she said. "And you've made us live it with you."

He finally turned to her. "It was your mother's choice. She demanded it and claimed if I told you girls, she'd kill herself."

Taylor shrugged. "Well, since we already thought she was dead, I guess that wouldn't have been a stretch."

The statement made her feel guilty on top of her anger. It was her own mother they were talking about. Not dead. Not killed in a fire with her little brother. Alive and well but rotting in prison for arson and murder. It was almost too much to comprehend.

"And Robert?"

"Dead. Like, really dead." He said it flatly, as though he wasn't talking about his only son, the little boy who had been the joy of their family for the few short years they'd had him. But she spied a sudden wince before her dad buried it underneath a stoic expression.

"How did I not know that Mom made it out of the fire alive? How is it even possible that you were able to do this? To keep this all secret? We didn't ask you questions."

"Cate was taken to the hospital and then air-lifted to the burn center in Idaho. She was bad. The doctors really didn't think she'd make it, so I told you all she didn't. She spent three months in the burn unit at the hospital before she recovered enough to be transferred to jail. After she was found guilty, they transferred her to prison. She never came home. All three of you accepted that she and Robert didn't survive because I didn't tell you any different. I'm pretty sure you were all in a state of shock and accepted what I said without question."

"Oh, God. Please tell me you didn't have a funeral for her."

"Nope. Didn't have one for either of them. Got your brother's ashes, and we spread them on the lake, just like your mother told me to do. But I said they were the ashes of them both."

Now she remembered that. Why hadn't she remembered until now?

She shook her head. It was unbelievable. Like something out of a movie. Her father had played the part well. She would've never thought he had it in him to be so deceptive.

"Do you think she did it?" she asked, though she didn't want to. She didn't want to imagine that the mother about whom she had nothing but fond memories could've done something so heinous, so very evil.

He sat up and glared at her. "Hell no, she didn't do it. Your mother loved Robert with every breath she had! She loved all of you kids. That's why she wanted you to believe she was dead. Cate said no child should visit their own mother in prison, and she wouldn't have you girls troubled that way. She said you'd heal faster if it was all buried and done. She insisted we move out of Montana, where the talk wouldn't get to you."

"So that's why we're here in Hart's Ridge. Because Mom said so."

"Cate picked this town for you. It was all her, and she wanted me to get you girls as far away from that place as I could afford."

"And Lucy? Anna and Jo? They've never suspected?"

"No. And you would've never known, either, if you weren't so damn nosy," he said. "I've never given you permission to take my mail and go through it. What were you thinking? Now look what you've done. You've opened Pandora's box, and your mom is going to be devastated."

That lit her fuse, and she let him have it. "*She* is going to be devastated? Wow, Dad. What about four little girls who grew up thinking their mother was dead? Who needed a mother figure so desperately they cried in their sleep for many years? Three girls who grew up with big-time issues because they didn't have that mother in their life?" She didn't add that those same three girls had had to watch him nearly drink himself to death in their mother's absence.

"It would've been worse on you all to visit her through prison bars."

"You don't know that. We should've had the choice."

He hung his head and looked ashamed.

It was a good time to get more details out of him.

"Take me through it. What happened that day?"

She didn't really expect him to tell her. She'd asked before once a few years had gone by, and she'd tried to put the pieces of those childhood memories into an adult's mind, to have them make sense. But he would never speak of that day with her—or anyone, for that matter.

He began, and she held in her surprise. He spoke slowly, as though every word was painful to get out. "We had a family fishing day planned, but Robert had come down with a bug the night before. It was cold, and Cate wanted me to cancel the trip. I didn't want to, so she decided to let the rest of us go, and she'd stay home to let him sleep in."

Taylor had no memory of fishing that day. The flames were all she remembered.

"How did the fire start?"

"The only thing she could figure out was that it was the kerosene heater. We used one in the living area to help us keep the power bill down. Cate saw us off then went to sleep on the couch. When she woke up coughing, she said she jumped up and saw the fire and tried to get to Robert's room, but the flames were between them."

"So she left him and saved herself?"

He looked her straight in the eye, and this time, she saw anger. "Don't you ever say something like that again, Taylor."

"Go on."

"Cate ran outside and around to his bedroom window. She threw his tricycle at the glass, shattering it. By then, someone had called the fire department after seeing the smoke from the road, and they got there as your mom was trying to climb through the window. They pulled her back and held her down to keep her from going in."

"But they went in, right?"

He nodded. "They did, but it was too late. He was already gone."

"But if they saw her trying to save him, how could they convict her of murder?"

"Damn state arson investigator. His testimony sealed her fate. The jury convicted her. Cate went to prison. End of story."

But it wasn't the end of the story. Taylor couldn't believe that they had given up so easily, but she composed herself. "At least now I know where your money has been going. I thought it was all vodka."

"Oh, I'm no saint. I still buy a lot of vodka. I don't send her much money, but I do what I can. She didn't want me to even send anything, but I've heard how hard it is in there without someone on the outside helping."

"And her family? My grandparents? Is this why you said we never knew them?"

"That's true. You girls didn't know them. After your mom married me, they wanted nothing to do with her. They never met any of you."

Taylor could only imagine what a hell-raiser her dad must have been back then for them to disown their own daughter for marrying him.

"Where do they live? Do they see Mom?"

"They used to live in Florida, and the old man died. After that, your grandmother saw the news about Cate and reached out. She tried to help."

"Does she have money? Could she help fight the charges?"

"She used to have some money, and she tried. All kinds of petitions and appeals, all of them shot down, and then the year was up."

"What year?"

"In the state of Montana, you only have a year from the date of your guilty verdict to present new evidence of your innocence. In Cate's case, she didn't even have any evidence, but after the year, it was too late anyway."

"That doesn't make sense. Sometimes, the new evidence can't be found for much longer than two years."

He shrugged. "Tell me about it."

"I can't. I don't know anything."

He gave a snort. "And that surprises me coming from you, our little family detective. Every year, I've imagined this would be the one where you did your own investigation and figured it all out. With the pain-in-the-ass internet as it is, a few clicks could've led you to her."

"I never tried. I wanted to remember Mom and Robert as I last saw them. Not imagine them through photos of a charred home." She supposed not looking for information was a form of self-preservation. She'd needed counseling. They'd all needed it.

"I wish I had that same luxury," he said. "I still see the scene that we drove up on after our day on the lake. The house sitting there like a dark skeleton with the black smoke curling up to the sky. The police barriers and firemen everywhere. It's all soldered to my brain."

"Tell me about the trial, Dad. What kind of defense was launched for her?"

He shook his head. "I don't know, Taylor. It's complicated, and I just can't go over this all again. Please—I'm begging you to let it go."

Taylor tapped at the table, pausing before her next words.

"I hate to tell you this, Dad, but the justice system works. She is probably guilty."

He dropped his head. "Please, Taylor, don't say that. I don't have the energy to kick your ass out of this trailer, but if you keep it up, I'll find it."

She stood up, went to the refrigerator, pulled out some eggs and butter, and set them on the counter. She checked the bread box, but it was empty.

"I'm going to fix you some eggs and then go get some groceries. My God, Dad. You can't keep living like this. You barely eat. You never go anywhere. You don't take care of yourself."

Suddenly, it occurred to her.

Her father was punishing himself.

She turned to him. "You think it was your fault, don't you?

You are holding yourself responsible for Robert's death and Mom being in prison. You think if you'd canceled the fishing trip that day, he'd still be here. Is that what this shitty life you are living is all about? Drink yourself into oblivion, starve your body, and refuse to let yourself experience any joy in life because of a tragedy that happened when you weren't there?"

He didn't answer. At least not vocally. The one lone tear that slid down his cheek told Taylor all she needed to know.

"Dad, whether it was an accident or murder, it wasn't your fault."

Guilt. It was something she struggled with herself, even though she knew guilt was an emotion that fed on itself, every bite getting heavier and heavier for the person to carry.

She didn't want anyone to be unfairly burdened with it. More reason for her to figure out what the hell had happened that day.

TWO HOURS LATER, Taylor was home and had a wet washcloth pressed to her forehead. She'd already made one run to the bathroom, retching the contents of her stomach up after reading through the first few articles she could find about the fire and Cate's conviction. Everything she thought had been buried about the trauma of coming home to their house to find nothing but a charred frame and the chaos of what happened afterward had come rushing back.

But she had to get through it. She needed to be armed with as much information as she could find before she made that visit to Montana. She knew now that the key to saving her dad was proving to him without a shadow of a doubt that Cate was where she should be.

That was going to take more research than she could do from her kitchen table.

She clicked on the next article.

Catherine Leigh Gray receives life sentence for arson and felony murder

She read further, taking in every detail of the report the state arson investigator had filed. He'd concluded that the fire had started in two places, on either end of the home, and that a liquid accelerant had been poured across the living room floor and also to the front door, then used to start the blaze.

A forensic analyst had also testified that he had identified a petroleum distillate in the floor samples taken from the living room and the bedroom in which Robert had died.

Exactly what her dad had told her.

From beneath the table, Diesel whined.

It looked cut and dried to her. Cate was guilty.

Taylor looked at the clock and was surprised to see that she'd been sitting there for three hours, trying to find all the details.

"Fine," she told Diesel. "I'll fix you something. I can't take any more of this anyway."

She stretched, noting the pain between her shoulder blades, before she went to the refrigerator and took out the concoction she'd put together to pour over his kibble. With more time on her hands, she'd done some reading about the dietary needs of dogs and how kibble alone—or at all—was not good for their system.

"You know, I'm still going to figure out how to find out where your dad is and see if we can arrange a meet-up. First, let's get you looking shiny and strong so he doesn't think I'm a horrible pet owner."

Samuel Stone.

She poured some of the broth into a bowl and slid it into the microwave. Diesel liked it just a bit warm.

Sam Stone?

Or even maybe Sammy Stone.

Not Sammy, please. That sounded wimpy.

The microwave dinged. She pulled out the broth and poured

it over a bowl of salmon-flavored kibble and set it down in front of Diesel.

He dove in ravenously

A name was all she had to go on, but as soon as she had a free minute between getting her butt chewed off at work and finding out her dead mother was alive and kicking in a women's prison in Montana, she meant to backtrack Diesel's path and try to locate Samuel Stone.

CHAPTER 3

The next afternoon, Taylor and Diesel headed to the Bear's Den and were passing Hardee's when she saw that a cruiser had pulled into the parking lot behind a car. The officer had the driver spread-eagled over the hood and was searching him.

It was Deputy Kuno, McElroy's replacement. He was a rookie.

She almost kept going, but when she realized it was Mr. Diller's car and that he was the person bent over the hood, she pulled in and parked her truck behind the cruiser.

"You stay," she said to Diesel, ignoring his pleading eyes. He hated for her to leave him behind.

Kuno had Diller's hands behind his back and was snapping handcuffs on him by the time Taylor climbed out of her truck and walked over.

"What's going on?" she asked.

Kuno jerked up on the handcuffs. "Stand up."

Diller continued to lean over the hood and groaned. A crowd had gathered, and the buzz spreading among the onlookers was getting louder.

"Let him go," someone yelled.

Taylor looked around and saw Chipper Dayne, the firewood guy, and he looked angry. She turned back to Mr. Diller and leaned around to get a look at his face. "Are you okay?"

His eyes were closed, his face ghostly pale and shining with a sheen of sweat.

"He's going in for driving under the influence," Kuno answered for him. "He was swerving all over the road before he pulled in here. Then he stopped the car over three parking places. He's drunk."

Taylor saw red. "He's not drunk, you idiot. He's diabetic and in hypoglycemia. He was probably trying to get inside and get some juice before he blacked out!"

"I'll go get it, Taylor," Chipper Dayne said from the crowd then took off for the restaurant doors at a jog.

"What are you talking about?" Kuno asked, looking suddenly nervous.

"Just what I said. Get these handcuffs off and get him to the back seat before he faints and goes into a diabetic coma."

Kuno didn't argue. He looked scared. He quickly unlocked the cuffs and slipped them off then got under one of Diller's arms and helped Taylor guide him into his back seat.

"Juice is coming, Mr. Diller," Taylor said. "Wake up. Don't you dare close those eyes!"

While she patted his cheeks firmly to wake him, Kuno jumped into the front seat and used the radio to call in the emergency.

Taylor talked to Diller until Chipper returned with the juice.

She held it to Diller's mouth and poured in little sips at a time. He swallowed without opening his eyes, but he did reach up and cradle his forehead and moan about his head pounding.

She didn't want to leave him, but she also didn't want to be there if Alex arrived first with the fire truck. She was under enough stress without dealing with him.

"Mr. Diller, can you open your eyes and look at me?"

He finally did.

"Taylor. Thank you, young lady," he mumbled.

She heard Kuno's sigh of relief behind her, and internally, she seethed at his stupidity. *Traffic 101: First, be sure the driver behaving erratically is not having a medical emergency.*

"You gave us quite a scare," she said, embarrassed at his gratitude. "Why did you let your sugar get so low, Mr. Diller? This could've ended much worse."

He shook his head. "I need to get some groceries. Been feeling under the weather, and my pantry is low. Haven't picked up my pills either."

Taylor made a mental note to find out if Medicare could have someone stop in and check on the old man a few times a week. Mr. Diller was too independent for his own good.

"I need to stop by Beards and Shears to get a shave when I get out of here," Diller mumbled.

"No, that can wait. You need to go straight home and rest, and Officer Kuno, here, is going to take you, and you'll be sitting in the front seat. I'm going to call dispatch and tell them to send Penner to get your car then on to the pharmacy for your medication and to pick you up a few groceries. He'll bring your car and everything back to your home, and Kuno will take him back to the station," Taylor said.

"I don't have time for—" Kuno began.

"Or we can get the sheriff to help," Taylor cut in, instantly shutting him up. He also needed a lesson in seniority.

Kuno glared at Taylor over Diller's head then spoke through gritted teeth. "Yes, I'll take you home and wait with you for Penner to bring your meds."

"I'll be glad to go get his meds and pick up some things from the store," Chipper said, coming closer to the car. "I've already delivered all my firewood. The rest of my day is free."

Taylor turned to him. "Thank you, Chipper. That'll be great. Just come over to my truck for a minute."

She said goodbye to Diller, and she and Chipper walked to her truck.

Diesel was panting excitedly as she reached in and took her wallet from her console. "Use my debit card. Get him some, get him some fresh fruit and a few microwave dinners. That's what he lives on. Make it the healthy ones, though."

"Oh, I can get this, Taylor," Chipper said. "I'd be happy to, and I know my wife would box my ears if she thought I didn't try to help."

Taylor hesitated. She truly was low on funds. Especially after Lucy's little snatch and grab.

"I insist," Chipper said, waving away the card.

She slipped it back in her wallet. "Okay, fine. Thank you. Now, I need to get going. I'm not officially on duty, and I don't want the sheriff pulling up and giving me what-for."

He waved her off as she climbed in and started the truck. He was a nice man—maybe a little too cheerful for her taste with all that smiling and whistling, but he tried hard to fit in and be one of the locals, a feat not easy for people who hadn't been born and raised here. Even though Chipper had been a Hart's Ridge resident for nearly ten years and knew just about everyone, he was still considered a transplant.

For the rest of her drive over to the Den, she couldn't stop thinking about Cate. Wondering what she looked like. What she did with her free time. And whether prison had hardened the soft personality that Taylor faintly remembered her having.

She was already in the Den, seated at their booth with Diesel at her feet, when she looked at the time on her phone and realized Cecil was late. He was never late. She hoped that tonight of all nights, he wouldn't have to cancel.

She really needed him.

A few regulars were lined up at the bar, including the fire chief, Alex. Since the altercation they'd had a few weeks back, he had pretended she didn't exist. Taylor wasn't proud that she'd pulled her gun, but it couldn't be undone now, and after all, he'd deserved it. She'd genuinely felt worried for her life.

She thought back to that evening and remembered the comment he'd made about her family running away from Montana and what he knew about the fire. Turned out he hadn't been spouting lies. Now she wondered how many people he'd run his mouth to. Just thinking of the possibility made heat rush up her neck. She'd spent decades trying to be a good example to the town. Trying to outrun the stigma of growing up poor and the assumption that low-income status meant someone wasn't good people.

Cecil arrived and slid in across from her. After a night to process things, she needed his counsel and was glad it was time for their weekly meet-up.

"Sorry. I had a flat tire."

"Oh no. Why didn't you call me? I could've helped," Taylor said. She could see the sweat still glistening across his forehead, and she felt terrible as she thought of him out there in the heavy Georgia humidity.

"I'm old, Taylor. Not dead. I can change a tire just fine." He winked at her and took a long sip from his glass. Then he reached down under the table and patted Diesel. "How's this big fellow doing?"

"He's okay. Still acting a bit melancholy. I've decided I want to try to find out who his original owner is and see if I can connect. I think it might do Diesel some good."

Cecil raised his eyebrows. "Gonna give him up?"

"Don't know. Maybe. If he'd be happier with the other guy."

"Guy?" Now Cecil's eyebrows shot to the ceiling.

Taylor laughed. "Yes, guy. He came from some guy named Samuel Stone. I just want to find out if maybe the guy has had second thoughts. I don't want to give him up, but my gut keeps telling me not to let this go."

"You and that gut. Seems to me it's usually right."

She shrugged. "Sometimes. But it sure didn't lead me to what I'm going to tell you next."

"Hmm… I'm intrigued." He raised his eyebrows and made a series of lines dance across his forehead.

Taylor would've laughed at his expressiveness, but with the subject matter being what it was, she was still feeling overwhelmed with the situation. She hoped that Cecil, her longtime confidant, would be able to help her work through some of her bitterness about it.

Sissy arrived at the table, her pad and pen out. "How're y'all doing?"

"Okay—whoa, wait a minute," Taylor said, noticing the glimmer on Sissy's hand. "Don't tell me he finally asked."

Sissy beamed and gave them a better view of the modest diamond. "Sure did. He wants to make an honest woman out of me. Finally!"

"Well, that's just wonderful," Cecil said.

"Congratulations," Taylor agreed. She was happy for her. Payton was a good guy with a great reputation around town, and Sissy had waited long enough. Taylor knew she wanted their relationship to be official for their daughter's sake. Taylor would've cut him loose long ago, but Sissy was in love and had waited him out.

"Thanks. We haven't set a date yet. Payton said he wanted to get used to calling me his fiancée first before we took the next step. But anyway, hopefully, it'll be before Hayley turns eighteen and our money will have to be spent on college instead of a wedding." She laughed. "Are y'all ready to order?"

"We sure are, sweetheart," Cecil said. "I'll take my regular."

"Pimento grilled cheese sandwich and fries for me," Taylor added. "Thanks, Sissy."

"And I'll bring the handsome boy something too."

When she was gone, Taylor took a deep breath. "Cecil, you've known my dad a long time."

He nodded. Their relationship had begun when Cecil had been appointed a sponsor for her dad in Alcoholics Anonymous. Taylor's own friendship with Cecil had developed after Dad had relapsed and refused to go to meetings again. Then she'd needed someone to talk to. Someone who could help her navigate his addiction and avoid enabling him. Cecil had fallen easily into that role, and they'd become close. It didn't matter to her that he was decades older and that they came from two very different backgrounds. It was the way he listened to her with no judgment and the easy feeling she got around him. Like a salve to her soul.

That kind of friendship was rare.

"Well, you know about us leaving Montana after our house fire that killed my mother and little brother."

His face went somber instantly. "What's this about, Taylor?" He lifted his glass to his lips for another drink.

"My mother didn't die in that fire. She's in prison for arson and murder," Taylor whispered across the table.

He put the glass down with a thump. "Say that again?"

"You heard me right. She was convicted of setting the fire that killed my brother. Dad said that she made him a deal—she wouldn't kill herself if he wouldn't let us girls know that she was alive. She didn't want her daughters visiting a mother in prison or having the rumors hanging over us. She thought it would be better if we thought she was dead."

Cecil looked shocked. "I don't even know what to say. I mean, are you sure? That's just crazy."

She nodded. "I'm sure. I got Dad's mail so I could pay his utility bill, and I found a statement from the women's prison in Montana. It only had an inmate number as a reference, and I thought maybe he'd found himself a girlfriend. Someone who was taking advantage of him for money. I called, and they gave me the name. It's her, Cecil."

Cecil sat back in the booth, suddenly looking all his advanced years. "I'm so sorry."

"Yeah, me too." "Sorry" wasn't a big enough word.

"What the hell were they thinking? Has he any idea what you girls have gone through without a mother? I can't believe that even through the haze of alcoholism, he couldn't see how wrong that was."

"I know. It's probably why he has just about drunk himself to death. Either the guilt of what they've done or from missing her. One of the two."

Or the way he used to abuse her mother, she didn't add.

"About a month ago..." Cecil started, and Taylor could see he was going to say something very serious by the way he lowered his head and his voice. "I made a meal."

She raised her eyebrows at him. She supposed he made quite a few meals.

"This was a special one. I made linguini pasta from scratch, set it off with a secret pesto recipe I found, and baked a loaf of bread straight from my own oven."

"Impressive. Who was visiting?"

He looked away for a moment, and when he looked back at her, his eyes were glistening. "Not a damn soul. That was the meal I used to make for my wife on every anniversary. I felt like doing it, and when it was done, I set me a plate, lit a candle, and bawled my eyes out. Then I tossed every bit of it in the trash."

Taylor couldn't swallow past the sudden lump in her throat. "Oh, Cecil." He'd never shared anything about his wife with her before.

"I tell you that, Taylor, not for pity for me but maybe a bit for your dad. The loss of a good woman will do crazy things to a man's soul. You need to let this play out a bit and give him whatever mercy you can find."

Sissy returned with their food and set it down on the table.

Diesel came out and wagged his tail.

"Here you go, handsome." She set a small paper plate of sliced steak down on the floor in front of him.

"Thanks, Sissy," Taylor said.

When Sissy stood, she looked worried. "What's going on? You two look like you've lost your best friend."

"No, we're okay," Taylor assured her.

Cecil was her best friend. Her parents—well, that was more complicated.

"Let me know if you need anything else," she said then walked away.

"Do you think she did it?" Cecil asked, getting back to the subject.

That was a hard question. The investigator in Taylor wouldn't let her make that call yet. Not without more digging. "He says she didn't. That she wouldn't."

"He's loyal."

"Seems that way. But maybe he's protecting her."

"Or he can't grasp that she could or would do something so horrible," Cecil said. Then he immediately looked aghast. "Oh, I'm sorry. I'm not saying that she—"

Taylor held her hand up. "It's fine. I know you aren't. And she may have done it. A jury found her guilty, after all. The evidence must've been compelling. You know I believe in our justice system, Cecil."

The words were out before she remembered seeing poor Mr. Diller spread-eagled over the hood of the car, falsely accused of driving under the influence. But that was different.

Cecil let out a long breath. "Wow. So where do you go from here?"

"I really don't know."

"Are you going to try to see her?"

She thought about that before answering. The little girl in her had wanted to run out of her dad's trailer and go straight to Montana to see the mother she remembered. The angry adult in her felt like shutting the door and letting Cate rot for what she'd done.

Taylor was somewhere in between. "I want to investigate first."

"I figured you would. Are you going to tell your sisters?"

"▓▓▓ ▓▓▓▓ I ▓▓▓▓▓ ▓▓▓▓, B▓▓ ▓▓▓'▓ ▓▓▓, ▓▓▓▓. I'▓ ▓▓▓▓▓▓▓▓▓ ▓▓▓▓ thinking about it. And I'm hungry. Getting hangry, actually."

He smiled at her and picked up his fork.

They got through lunch with no more talk about her parents. Taylor was relieved. Even though Cecil couldn't solve her problems or tell her the best avenue to take, just being with him had settled her spirit enough to give her the energy to keep going.

In the parking lot, he walked her to her truck. She opened the door and let Diesel jump in.

"Taylor," he said.

She climbed in, shut the door, and opened the window to see what he had to say.

"You'll be fine."

She leaned her head back against the headrest. "I hope so, Cecil. Sometimes, though, I'm tired. Just tired."

He put his hand on hers, and the warmth flowed through her. "You were given this life because you were strong enough to live it. Never doubt that for a moment."

"Or maybe I'm just dumb enough to try." She tried to laugh, but it came out as a croak.

He smiled like a father indulging a child.

She started the truck and pulled out with him watching her go.

AT HALF PAST MIDNIGHT, Taylor sat at her laptop and finished the last of her chocolate milk. She'd spent the last three hours falling down the tunnel of researching Cate's case.

She still didn't know enough, but at least she knew more.

Catherine Gray, guilty of arson and felony murder by a jury of her peers.

Taylor doubted very much that they were her peers.

According to testimony of the arson investigators, there were two separate fires. One was in the south bedroom along the south wall and was found to have been caused by a liquid accelerant that left traces behind.

Taylor wondered what Cate had used. Gasoline? Lighter fluid?

The second fire had originated at the doorway and had traces of accelerant determined to be in a path from that bedroom doorway, through the living room, and to the front door. Where, obviously, they thought Cate had exited and left her son to burn alive.

Cate had received a sentence of sixty years for murder and fifty years for arson. She'd been up for parole twice and rejected both times.

Taylor felt as if she was searching for a needle in a haystack, except if it had been, at least she'd have some idea what she was looking for.

After looking to see if Lucy had sent an email yet, she switched over to a search for Samuel Stone. Facebook was the best place to look, but it brought up seventy-seven profiles.

That didn't mean one of them was his.

She quickly surfed through profiles, skipping over the ones that looked too young or too old. The ones who didn't fit the bill of someone who might enlist. She was generalizing but using her gut to do it.

Just as she was getting ready to pass over one elderly Sam Stone, something in his profile picture caught her attention. The man was holding a framed photo of a younger man in uniform. She clicked on the photo, and it read, *So proud of you, Sam.*

Taylor sat back. Did that mean the photo was a memorial shot? Or could it be the father was simply proud he'd enlisted?

Either way, really. And it might not even be the right one, anyway.

She shot off a private message and attached a photo of Diesel.

At least she was making some effort to appease her gut, which told her Diesel was pining for his first owner. She didn't want to admit it, but something was making her feel guilty. As though she'd stolen someone's dog. That was silly, considering she had gotten him from the shelter after he'd been bounced around several times.

He lay at her feet, releasing a long sigh every so often. Impatience or sadness. She wasn't sure which.

"Okay, I'm done, Diesel. Let's go take a walk."

She led him outside, and they hit the path to the lake. She loved being outside late, when everything was quiet and sleeping. She didn't want to think. She didn't want to wonder. Or obsess.

"Let's just breathe and think about nothing for fifteen minutes, boy."

He turned and looked at her then focused on a noise in the leaves ahead.

Taylor saw the hair on his back rise, and he ran back to her, stood in her way, and began to growl.

"What is it, boy?" She wished she'd grabbed her sidearm before leaving the house. "C'mon, let's go back."

He didn't want to turn around, but finally, he obeyed, though he did keep turning his head to listen.

"It was probably just a squirrel."

When they got back to the house, Taylor led Diesel inside.

"Wait—something's off."

She looked around the kitchen, where they'd come in, then let her eyes rove around the room to settle on the table.

Her laptop was open.

She stared for a moment, swearing she'd shut it before going on the walk.

Or was that another time? Was this one of those moments when she thought she'd put on deodorant but didn't know if the memory was from the day before? Absentmindedness at its best.

She went to pick up her gun, and when she stepped through the living room, she smelled something strange. Cologne.

Diesel showed up beside her, hair up again and growling.

"Go see, boy."

He ran through the house, sniffing corners and going crazy until he'd checked every square inch. There was nothing there that shouldn't be.

Except for the whiff of cologne.

"I really need to invest in some cameras. As soon as we have the money," Taylor muttered to Diesel as she went through the house and closed all the blinds. More than likely, she had nothing to worry about, but the peculiar smell and the dog's concern gave her pause.

She went back to her computer with another thought on her mind.

Why would Cate even *want* to kill Robert? And if she had wanted him dead, then why not all her children? And the man who had abused her?

Then again, it was always a mystery why some women killed a child.

Or all of them.

She googled *women who kill their children*.

In 1983, Diane Downs, a twenty-seven-year-old divorced postal service worker, told police that a "bushy-haired stranger" had flagged down her car and shot her three children on a back road near Springfield, Oregon. Later, one of the surviving children testified that it was Diane and not a stranger who had gone on the murderous rampage.

Then there was Susan Smith, who had buckled her two little

boys into their car seats and then let the car roll down a ramp and into a lake in South Carolina, drowning them both. She'd claimed hijacking, too, before she finally confessed.

Chris Watts had smothered his daughters and then strangled his wife, all to pursue a new life with a mistress he'd only known for a month. He'd claimed an evil spirit made him do it. Taylor refused to look at the photos along the bottom of the story. She remembered the children's faces well enough from when it had been on the news.

Then she clicked on Andrea Yates from Texas and felt even more sick to her stomach. Yates had methodically drowned her five children, one after the other, in their bathtub, laying their bodies side by side on the bed for her husband to find. She'd claimed that Satan ordered her to do it, and she was saving them from eternal damnation. Reading further, Taylor saw that Yates had always suffered with mental illness and had made multiple attempts at suicide before she became a mother.

Her gaze landed on the photos before she could look away.

Those poor children. Noah was seven, and his little brother, John, had been just five. Paul was three. Then there was Luke, dead before he could even graduate the terrible twos, and the six-month-old defenseless baby, Mary.

The photo of the mother, Andrea, was confusing because she was young and at least semi-attractive and looked so—so *normal.* Well, except in a few of the shots in which her eyes looked creepy as hell.

Taylor clicked to close that window and opened a new one without heartbreaking photos and descriptions of children. There were too many stories and no way to make sense of any of them. Taylor wanted to know why or how mothers could do it.

New internet search: *Why do mothers kill their children?*

One hit really piqued her interest:

"Altruistic filicide, the most common motive, where a mother rationalizes that killing her child is in the child's best interest."

Had Cate decided that Robert shouldn't grow up witnessing the abuse of his mother by his father? Had she been planning to kill herself and take Robert with her, but something didn't go right? Had she suffered from depression and mental illness?

Taylor needed to know more about Cate. And the case. For so many years, she'd let it all lie dormant in her mind, never pursuing the details. But that had been when she thought Cate was dead.

Now the questions burned inside her. Was Cate a killer?

Taylor thought again about going to Montana and facing the woman who had abandoned her duties as a mother, asking instead to be considered dead.

She could just come right out and ask her.

Did you kill my brother?

That way, she could look into Cate's eyes and see if she was guilty or not.

She remembered that she now also had a grandmother. One who probably knew more about Cate and her inner self than anyone else did.

Since Taylor was on paid leave from work, now was the perfect time for a road trip.

Look out, Grandma. You're about to get an unexpected visit.

CHAPTER 4

*L*ucy leaned back just in time to miss getting her nose clipped by the top of the bottle that Margot waved in front of her face. One more night, and then she'd be staying in the Dakota and taking care of two dogs instead of living in a tent. It felt a bit surreal to even fathom.

"Do you want some?" Margot asked, her words slurred.

"No, thank you." Lucy put a hand on her stomach then removed it quickly.

"Why are you hiding that bump?" Margot asked.

"I'm not hiding it."

"You keeping it?" she asked.

"Do you want a sandwich?" Lucy asked, pulling her backpack around. Margot was giving her shelter, so the least she could do was feed her. But she didn't have to answer her questions.

"Nah." Margot took another swig of the wine.

"I really think you should eat something." Lucy hadn't seen the woman eat anything all day.

"Deflection."

"What do you mean?"

Margot settled down onto her butt, leaving her squatting

stance. "Causing someone or something to deviate from an intended purpose. You don't want to talk about the baby, so you are deflecting."

Lucy didn't speak.

"I was pregnant at twelve years old," Margot said.

"That's terrible."

"You aren't going to ask, are you? I'll tell you anyway. Yes, I had the baby. My parents were strict Catholics, and an abortion was out of the question. They told everyone I had the mumps, and my seventh-grade teacher sent my homework home every day with my brother."

Lucy couldn't imagine being pregnant in the seventh grade. She hadn't even had her period when she was that age.

"Were you scared?"

Margot's eyes widened. "Oh, yeah, I was scared. Terrified. I had no idea what was going on inside of me. That it was a little human hadn't been explained, and the changes happening in my body made me think I was dying. Then, in the middle of the night, during one of the worst storms I've ever lived through, I went into labor. My mother tied my arms to the headboard because I was going wild with pain and trying to fight her—fight what was coming out of me. I probably should've died, but I didn't."

"No doctor?"

"Hmmph. Having a doctor come would mean someone would know our secret. They'd rather that I die than that their reputation be tarnished."

"And the baby?"

Margot looked away. "I named her Grace. She came out with a halo of blond hair that felt softer than anything I'd ever felt then or since. She was beautiful. I'd never held a baby before, and I was so scared I'd hurt her. But after years of being sexually molested by my father and my brother, I was emotionally closed off and didn't know what to feel."

Lucy swallowed past a lump in her throat. "I'm so sorry."

Margot shrugged. "It's okay. It's my burden, and I'll carry it, not you. For years, I refused to let myself think of her, I pushed her out of my mind. No one told me I should grieve for her, or showed me how to grieve. I was a kid. I forgot all about her, and no one has spoken of her for more than thirty years or more."

"But you remember her now."

Margot's eyes filled with tears. "I sure do. When my father died—for I think that was who planted her inside me—I was flooded with her memory. I could see her face again for the first time. Even smell her. I remembered the sounds she made, like a kitten mewling as she snuggled against me, looking for milk. I remember how she breathed, and it felt so strong. She trusted me. Wanted me. Not my mother. Then I went to sleep one night with her against my chest, and when I woke, she was gone. My mother had taken her away. She said I suffocated her by accident between the mattress and me. I never got to tell her goodbye."

Lucy put her hand out and touched her arm, but Margot jerked away and took another drink.

"I'm ashamed that I didn't love her then."

"You were young," Lucy whispered.

"Yes, I know. I didn't even know what the word meant. Even my own mother didn't love me. She envied me because I had my father's attention. Then my brother's favor. But I didn't want it. Any of it. I hated it with every fiber of my being." She looked out beyond the span of grass.

"They were monsters."

"They never touched me again after that," Margot said. "I wasn't the innocent little girl anymore. My body was spoiled for them when they saw the blood and everything that came with the birth of Grace. I can thank her for that, you know. She stopped them. They never spoke of the abuse, and they never owned up to it, but they knew what they did. We all knew."

Lucy put a hand back on her belly. Her heart hurt, but at least

Margot could find purpose in the birth of her lost child. It always amazed her how people who shared the same blood could hurt one another so deeply. Now it made more sense why Margot had ended up living in Central Park. She wondered if Margot's mother and brother were still living, but she wouldn't ask.

"I wish I had something of hers from the days I knew her," Margot said. "Anything. Just a scrap of the blanket she was swaddled in. Or even one of her cloth diapers. Just something to hold while I remember her."

"She's in your heart."

Margot nodded, but her expression was still hard. "Yes, she is. And I know that I love her now. I miss her." She looked at Lucy. "Can you miss someone you only knew for five days?"

"Absolutely, you can. She was your child."

Margot didn't say anything more.

They sat there in the silence, both lost in their own thoughts.

LUCY WOKE six hours later and gathered her things then crawled out of the shelter. It had been a late night filled with more talk, though no more of the lost child or the one that Lucy carried. Instead, Margot entertained her with stories of life in the park— the madness and the good times.

Lucy listened open-mouthed when Margot talked about the concerts she'd seen by Garth Brooks, James Taylor, and even Diana Ross. She had a particularly funny story about Elton John when he'd nearly fallen off the stage while dancing.

Some of the other stories were sad, like the evening she'd survived Hurricane Ida when Central Park got more than three inches of rain in just under an hour. She and some others had fled the park and taken refuge under different scaffolding around the city but were still bombarded with wind and rain. Even the subways had flooded, sending thousands of people who usually sheltered there for the night escaping up to the streets.

Around nine o'clock, just as Lucy was getting tired, a few of Margot's friends came by, and they sat in a circle, singing songs to a guitar picked by a man named Mike. He carried a tattered canvas camping chair with him, and when he pulled out a needle, Lucy thought he was doing drugs.

Margot explained that Mike was a diabetic and had tried the shelter system, but it was too rough for him. He'd applied for the Safe Haven housing that the city provided to people who couldn't stay in the shelters because they were too fragile (and the violence too rampant), and they'd told him he had to be on the streets for at least a year to qualify.

"You have to do a whole year out here, even in the brutal winter, so they can say you might be eligible?" Lucy asked him.

He'd nodded. "If I make it, that is. My feet hurt me so bad, some days I don't think I'll last another day or two. I'm sixty-two years old, and I feel about eighty. But I just take it one hour at a time."

Mike had stopped talking then and begun singing. Margot whispered that she thought his music was the only thing keeping him alive. Lucy had to admit, he did a wonderful rendition of John Legend's "All of Me." She'd really enjoyed it.

The more that Margo talked and interacted with her friends, Lucy could see how smart and compassionate she was, as well as intelligent. It was a travesty that a woman like her was living the life she was, and it made Lucy think she probably needed to start working on getting her head straight. She didn't want to be Margot in ten years. Yet she also didn't want to conform to the way that society—and her sisters—thought she should live her life.

Just as they were getting ready to call it a night, another dude wearing a hard hat and a neon-green cape came by, took one look at Lucy, and screamed at her. "Buy me a coffee, Ass-Face!"

It had shocked them all into sudden silence. Then Lucy laughed at his boldness, and soon, everyone else was laughing, too, even the lunatic.

Margot finally explained to him that Lucy was like them.

Lucy didn't contradict her. She hadn't the heart to tell her friend she wouldn't be staying there or that unlike the rest of them, she was hoarding a grand in her beat-up backpack. It also felt wrong somehow to know that by daybreak, she'd be walking across the street and staying in the lap of luxury while Margot kept one eye open at night to keep safe.

Now she walked quickly to the public restroom that opened at six. She hoped she wouldn't run into any park police. Margot said they'd called a truce long ago, and the officers no longer bothered her, but Lucy was on her own and sure didn't need to get a ticket for encroachment.

She reached the small brick building and slipped inside, washed up and changed her clothes, and was on her way to the Dakota fifteen minutes later.

When she crossed the street, Edward was the only one there, and he tipped his hat to her.

"I heard what you did for me, missy. Thank you very much for helping to keep me out of the soup kitchen."

"You can call me Lucy, and you're very welcome. The building manager had no right to treat you so disrespectfully. Anyway, that's done. Do you have any pointers for my first day on the job as the dog nanny?" She grinned.

He laughed. "These people are something, ain't they, Lucy?"

"I'm sure you've seen a lot, Edward."

"Oh, you ain't kidding. I can't tell you how many hours I've had to sit through listening to people's problems about their health or relationships. They want my advice too. Sometimes, I just want them to go on up to their apartment or about their business, but it's hard not to get caught up and try to figure out a way to help. I think Johnson should give me a couch and a timer. Let me start charging per hour."

Lucy smiled at that. She could imagine Edward was a very good confidant.

He returned to stand behind the podium and leaned over it. "Well, you go on up. It's about time for the Banfield babies' first walk of the day. You don't want to be late," he said then opened the door.

"Want to give me any insight on Mrs. Banfield?" Lucy could only imagine what she would be dealing with. Upper-crust, rich white woman living in a million-dollar apartment—that was enough said. She hoped her job with the dogs wouldn't spill over to being anyone's gofer. If she were her sister Anna or even Jo, it wouldn't be a problem. But Lucy had never been able to kiss up to anyone. It wasn't her nature.

She hoped that Mrs. Banfield wouldn't be one of those self-absorbed people who looked right through her as if she was invisible.

"I rarely see her, so I couldn't really tell you much about her, other than she stays to herself and rarely leaves the place. I'll let you get your own impression," Edward said.

Lucy took a deep breath and waved goodbye. Then she entered the building, rode up the elevator, and approached the door.

On the first knock, the dogs erupted into barking, and the door opened.

"I'm Carmen. Next time, use the service stairs, not the elevator," a dark-haired woman said as she bent to grab the dogs. She was the no-nonsense kind. She was at least fifty years old but as fit as Lucy or more so, dressed in a black T-shirt and black leggings, her hair tied up in a loose bun on the top of her head.

"Oh, hi. I'm Lucy." *And thanks for the kind welcome*, she nearly added.

"Unless you have the dogs. Then use the service elevator."

"Got it," Lucy said.

"You'll only be in the west wing. I'll show you their room," Carmen said, shutting the door while using her foot to keep the dogs from bolting.

Their room. Wow. The dogs had their own room.

"Mr. and Mrs. Banfield have separate bedrooms, one on each side of the penthouse." Carmen chattered as she led Lucy through the small foyer and then into a long room filled with huge paintings. "This is the gallery. Never touch the art."

She led Lucy into a hallway that ran parallel to the living area.

The dogs followed, sniffing at Lucy's heels. "I'm here to clean until two o'clock every day but Sunday. Make sure you don't let the dogs get dirty, especially after I've left for the day. They can play with their toys but only one toy at a time for each. Don't let them drag it all out."

Lucy took in the opulence of the rooms as they went by. The floors were some sort of black wood, and expensive rugs were layered everywhere. The ceilings looked to be at least twelve to thirteen feet high, with huge windows that faced Central Park. Other than the wood-burning fireplaces and mahogany pocket doors throughout, the style was more modern than she'd expected, considering how old the building was.

They went through a den that was done in cool grays, creams, and whites, with a zebra area rug as the focal point, then a library before they entered a small room to the left of the main living area.

"This is the service room. You can take your breaks in here."

She saw a washer and dryer and a small kitchenette with a table and two chairs. Off that was a tiny bedroom. It was simple, nearly stark, with just a twin-sized bed and a bureau and two small dog beds made to look like four-poster beds, complete with matching satin bedding. There was a wicker basket full of dog toys. Leashes in different styles and lengths hung on wrought iron hooks on the wall.

Bentley immediately jumped onto the garnet-colored bed and looked up for approval. Bae sat at Lucy's feet, her eyes begging for a rub. Lucy caved.

Carmen gestured around. "This is the maid's room, but I don't stay here, so you'll have it. There's a half bath for you to wash up in too." She opened a door, reached in, and flipped the light on, showing the toilet and sink in a closet-sized room. Then she opened another door that showed a closet.

"If you have clothes, you'll share this space."

Sharing a closet with canines was new, but whatever. Lucy peeked in. The closet was full of many different dog sweaters and coats. Baskets along the top held different collars.

"I won't need much room," Lucy said, though she didn't elaborate. Carmen's judging eyes kept Lucy from wanting her to know she only had what she carried in her backpack.

The whole room felt very impersonal. It sure didn't have the welcoming feel that Margot's tent and presence did. But it was shelter. Safe and warm. She could live with it until she figured out what her next move would be.

"Bailey has severe allergies, so don't wear perfume or hairspray. They both have dry eyes and need their faces cleaned then drops three times a day. Bentley has hip dysplasia on the back left and will need a massage each evening before bed. I'll show you how to use the laser machine."

"Laser machine?"

Carmen squinted at her. "You do know you will have complete responsibility for their health and well-being, right?"

"Yes. I get that. I just didn't know I'd be playing *Star Wars* with the backside of a dog."

Carmen didn't laugh. "If you don't pay special attention, he'll get a slipped stifle, and you'll really be in trouble."

"I'm afraid to ask."

"Means his kneecap will slip out of place. Just be sure to give them the right amount of exercise. Not too much and not too little. Don't let them near any ponds because they'll sink like little cannonballs."

"I thought all dogs could swim."

That won her the darkest scowl yet.

Lucy moved her gaze from Carmen and looked down at Bentley. He tilted his head at her. She hoped he'd make it easy on her. Bailey was busy licking her butt, though in a very prima donna way.

"No swimming. Got it."

"No feeding them anything off their diet either. They both have an endless reserve of natural gas that keeps a constant stench of death around them if they have anything they shouldn't and sometimes no matter what. It's brutal."

Lucy laughed out loud at that.

Carmen crossed her arms. "It's not funny. They both also vomit a lot because of the deformity of the esophagus in their breed."

"Great. Lots of farts and vomiting. Anything else?"

"So much more. But basically, from here on out, you oversee making sure these little creatures keep their hair, drool, vomit, feces, and gas clouds out of every room of this apartment but this one. If—and I do mean if—you succeed in that, then you will make my life so much easier, which will, in turn, benefit you."

Lucy frowned. "I thought this job was going to be a breeze. Now you've got me scared."

"You should be. They are a lot of work."

"Do you take care of the entire place yourself?"

"Sure do. Four bedrooms, four and a half bathrooms, living room, den, library, kitchen, and an office. Oh, and a small salon. That's why I need to get busy."

"Am I going to meet Mrs. Banfield?" Lucy asked. She was ready to get it over with.

Carmen shook her head. "No. Not today. She's in her room,

and don't ever disturb her. Even if you hear strange noises coming from there."

Lucy narrowed her eyes. "What kind of strange noises?"

Carmen shrugged. "Any noises. She's sleeping now. Just leave her alone and focus on the dogs. I'll make enough lunch and dinner for you each day, but you'll be taking over doing the final supper clean-up. Right now, you need to get these dogs to the park before they mess on my floor."

"Yes, ma'am," Lucy said, saluting Carmen.

"One more thing. Mr. Banfield is very regimented. I've made out a schedule for the dogs, and you need to follow it to the letter."

"Oh. I thought it was the missus who was the master of the pooches?"

Carmen frowned. "And don't be thinking you'll be bringing any sass in here either. Keep to yourself and do your job, and we'll get along fine."

"Sorry. But I have an appointment today that I can't break. I'll walk the dogs and bring them back then take off and be gone a few hours."

"So be it, but don't make a habit of messing with their routine. Now—I have a floor to mop while you're gone."

Lucy ushered the dogs out into the hall and quickly found the service stairs.

"Let's go, you ferocious wolverines." She opened the door and barely got it wide enough before the two of them were competing to wiggle through it. They were serious about their walks. She couldn't blame them. Two dogs in a fancy penthouse with nothing but a housekeeper and a sleeping beauty had to be bored out of their minds.

Today they were sailor twins, obviously.

"Hold up." She pulled on the leashes, and they had no choice but to stop. Quickly, Lucy undressed them and tossed their matching navy, white, and red outfits—emblazoned with anchors, even—into her bag. She considered yanking the bow from Bae's hair, but since she wasn't sure how it was even in there and if she could get it back, she left it alone.

Once the dogs looked like dogs and not furry little children, Lucy followed them down the stairs, out the service door, and through the courtyard, and then they made their way across the street to the park.

The park was already getting going, and Lucy made fast tracks with the dogs. They passed face painters and a snow-cone stand then a dozen women dressed in fancy spandex and doing Zumba to the beat of "I Will Survive" by Gloria Gaynor. The dogs paused for a moment, curious at the intense expressions as the hips bounced to the left and right, but Lucy urged them along just as the chorus hit the crescendo and the women followed their leader into a spin that would've made a normal human throw up their breakfast. She would have bet a dollar that most of them had never had to survive anything but the stampede of an end-of-season Macy's clearance sale. Let them spend a night or two huddled on a bench in thirty degrees or hiding in a park's public bathroom, hoping a raving meth head didn't break in and try to rape them. Then they could sing it with more passion.

"No, *I* will survive," she muttered as they passed. "Y'all get back to carpool."

As they walked, she realized that if she wore a certain expression—her "don't mess with me right now" face—no one had the courage to approach and ask to pet the pups, and she wouldn't be stopped half a dozen times. She kept that up, and by the time they'd circled back and were crossing the road again, Bent and Bae were huffing, and she was certain they'd sleep the next few hours away.

They had only been gone half an hour, but when she entered the apartment, Mr. Banfield had returned, and Lucy could hear him yelling from his wife's room. She quickly dressed the dogs again in case it was about her. She didn't need any drama.

The schedule said to give them fresh water and treats after their walk, so she did that. Once they were settled in their room, she went to hers and gathered her backpack.

She was almost out the door when Mr. Banfield slammed out of the bedroom and stomped down the hall. "Carmen," he shouted. "I need my blue suit steamed."

The housekeeper appeared quietly, as though she'd been summoned from a genie bottle, and she headed toward his room. As she passed Lucy, she put her finger to her lips.

"I didn't say anything," Lucy whispered dramatically, earning a scowl back from Carmen. "And I'm leaving."

Before she could get through the door, Banfield was there amid a flurry of cursing and handwringing and a red face that made him look like a toddler throwing a tantrum. "You." He pointed at Lucy. "I need your help."

"Oh, sorry. I was just leaving for an afternoon appointment. I'll be back, though. Can it wait?"

He looked her up and down then back up again. "No. I mean, like—I need you for the evening. Carmen will help you get ready." He turned and yelled for the housekeeper.

Sometimes Lucy couldn't believe the gall of the uber-rich.

"No. Whatever it is, I can't," Lucy said. She truly needed to get something scheduled before it was too late, and the first step was to find a clinic.

Carmen came around the corner.

"Carmen, please get her ready for a cocktail party by six. I need a plus one, and none of my usual are available. Suki won't do it," he said, rolling his eyes in the direction of his wife's room.

She nodded and gestured to Lucy to follow.

"Hello? Earth to Mr. Banfield," Lucy said. "Can you hear me talking, or have I suddenly become invisible? I am not going to any cocktail party. Not tonight or in this lifetime."

Banfield was about to turn on his heels and head the other

way, but Lucy's statement stopped him. "But I need you," he said. "You work for me."

"Correctamundo. But as the dog nanny. Not your personal escort. That wasn't in my job description. And do you need glasses? It's not like I'm cocktail party presentable." She didn't mention she hadn't had a proper bath in nearly a week. That would be far too humiliating. She was lucky she'd been able to put herself together enough to even land this job.

"I'll pay you an extra day's pay," he said, putting his finger to his lip as he studied her. "I think Carmen can do something with your hair. Carmen will find a dress you can wear."

Lucy was starting to get irritated.

"Look, I know that you think most people *like me* would be thrilled to be Cinderella for a day. Dress in your wife's couture clothes and maybe even wear some jewels and pretend to be fancy for a while. But that's not me. I don't like fancy. Will never be fancy. And I'm not interested in pretending." She opened the door and stepped out, giving him a forced smile. "I'll stick to the dogs but thank you for offering."

"I'll pay you a thousand dollars in cash at the end of the night." He stared her down. "And I swear, it's just for show. All you must do is stand with me and try to look smart."

Carmen raised her eyebrows at her challengingly.

Lucy paused for a moment, considering her pride and how much she'd love to tell him to shove his grand up his rear end and that he couldn't have everything he demanded.

But *people like her* didn't have the option to be proud.

She stepped back in and closed the door behind her.

"Fine. But I draw the line at heels. And I don't wear lipstick."

CHAPTER 5

*S*o, this was what the elite did for fun. Lucy felt as if her ears would bleed if she had to listen to one more boring conversation or nod at one more painting that simply looked like a kindergartener had found a craft closet and gone ballistic.

She moved to the other side of the room, where a different type of painting caught her eye. It was in a different style than the others, the colors bleeding through the canvas in a muted design of doodle-like drawings. Eyes, hearts, and even random kitchen utensils. The mellow pale pinks, browns, and greens blended in a comforting creative stew that made her curious to see more from the artist.

The tag said *Christoph Dione, expressionist.*

A guy in a lavender paisley-patterned suit next to her stepped closer. "I find it difficult to connect emotionally with this work, but perhaps it would be different if you lived with it."

"Hmm," Lucy offered up, afraid to say much.

"Good thing I can't afford it," the guy laughed. "I'm not at the right place in life to pay twelve grand for a piece yet."

She laughed nervously.

They continued to stare at it until he spoke again. "It reminds me of the work by César Collazo from Uruguay. That's probably what Dione is going for. I've heard that Collazo's work fetches seven figures now, and it's very limited. He's definitely one to emulate."

He put a heavy sarcastic emphasis on *definitely* and sounded pretentious.

Lucy held no doubt that she was earning her thousand dollars. Every penny of it.

The man moved on, and Lucy worked her way over to Ian.

She'd thought of her sister Anna a few times and tried to channel her. Anna hadn't been born into money; she'd married it. But this type of environment would fit her like a glove. Anna was comfortable in all the hoity-toity settings because she loved being a part of *high society*.

She would've pulled the charade off flawlessly.

Banfield—Ian, as he'd urged her to call him—looked very interested in the young woman who stood across from him. She swirled her little olive-on-a-toothpick-thingy and vomited pretentious garbage conversation to him. She was really going for the intellectual look, her Chanel reading glasses hanging from a gold lanyard around her neck, no cleavage to be seen in her totally respectable navy pantsuit, her limp brown hair tucked behind her ears.

The only semblance of feminine effort was the close-toed black heels she wore.

She must be a poser.

Ian had explained to her the different types she'd run into there and stressed to her not to waste too much time on posers or art snobs. He needed to listen to his own advice.

"When you really think about it," this woman lectured, "people think that dogs are treated as companions, but they are technically in a class of beings to whom basic rights are denied."

Ian's eyebrows came together in an interesting V. "Oh? How so?"

"It's simple, really," she droned on. "The relationship is an unbalanced symbiosis of dominance that adds to the deconstructive process between an animal and a human."

Lucy thought of Bentley and Bailey and wondered if the woman knew that they existed and were treated better than most human children.

But she said nothing.

Ian had given her a very simple set of instructions. And straightening out a dumbass at the cocktail party wasn't part of them.

He was thrilled that she could speak with a decent fake English accent, because with him, she was going to be Lucia Leighton, a British friend from his college days, and she was visiting from her home in Martha's Vineyard, where she'd recently moved from after leaving Southwold, a small sea town in Suffolk County in the United Kingdom.

Lucy had been surprised that Martha's Vineyard happened to be an island in Massachusetts and not just a winery, as she'd always assumed. He had quickly educated her about Cape Cod, as well as a few facts about her fake hometown in England. He had told her she was single, had a master's in fine arts, and in addition to her accent, spoke with a lisp, making her undeniably shy and reluctant to engage in conversation.

He was pretty good at spinning a fictional background. She had to give that to him. And ironically, she had indeed once had a lisp. Her sister Taylor had gone to bat for her with the school guidance counselor, insisting Lucy have school-sponsored speech therapy even though all the slots were full for her third-grade year. When Taylor was intent on making something happen, nothing could stand in her way, and by the end of her fourth-grade year, Lucy's lisp was gone. Well, except when she got drunk. Then it snuck in like an alley cat on the prowl.

Ian had also instructed her that she had a two-drink limit.

Lucy wasn't drinking anyway. Alcohol wasn't something she

craved right now. It wasn't as if she was trying to protect the thing growing inside her. She just didn't feel like drinking. And especially not when she was supposed to be following a strict script.

While her thoughts were wandering, Ian had ended the conversation with Animal Analyst Annie, placed his hand on Lucy's elbow, and guided her away to a corner, where they were alone.

"I had to end that conversation when she started telling me that people were not morally entitled to use dogs for their entertainment or safety and that calling them pets was disrespectful."

"That sounds intriguing. So can we leave yet?" she asked, batting the ridiculous eyelashes that Carmen had pasted on her eyes. The furry things were a compromise after Lucy refused to have foundation makeup spackled on like paint. Lipstick was allowed too. But no eyeliner or shadow.

Carmen had finally agreed that with just the eyelashes and lip color, as well as the simple yet obviously expensive little black dress that barely showed her tiny bump and the solo diamond pendant placed around her neck, Lucy looked classy.

Oh, and the updo.

It seemed that dear Carmen was a Jane of all trades. She'd sent Lucy straight into the shower—the best part of the whole damn deal—and when Lucy emerged smelling like roses, with her hair blessedly clean for the first time in what felt like ages, Carmen had dried and coiffed it into a very professional-looking French twist and secured it with a pearl-encrusted barrette.

"I have four daughters," she said proudly when Lucy complimented her skills.

Lucy looked good. Surprisingly so.

But the heels were a problem.

Lucy hadn't yet seen Suki, but the woman must have been all of six feet tall or more, because she wore a size ten shoe, and they'd stuffed tissue paper in the toes and heels of Lucy's borrowed footwear. With every step Lucy took, she was afraid she really was going to be like Cinderella and leave a slipper behind. It would be embarrassing, but it would also trigger a whole lot of questions about who she was and why she was wearing shoes four sizes too big.

Banfield would melt in place.

That made her smile, and he gave her a strange look. "What?"

"Nothing. I asked if you were ready to go yet. My feet are killing me." She was also dreaming of the clean bed she was going to get to sleep in.

"No, Lucia," he enunciated sarcastically. "I told you that I must stay until I get a chance to talk to Jorge Vanzo. I heard he's going to be here."

"But you've talked to half a dozen people. Can't that be enough?" She knew she was pushing her luck, but at this point, she'd rather be sitting in a circle of her old friends in Central Park, listening to Mike strum his guitar, than perched on Banfield's arm like a tiny pet bird, chirping at his anything-but-engrossing conversation.

"Jorge Vanzo is an artist from Uruguay who is as yet undiscovered. I only know about him through a friend of a friend. Discovering artists and making them relevant is my specialty. Do you know that I once sold a painting by an undiscovered forty-two-year-old Russian artist at auction for more than ten times its high estimate? I make dreams happen. For them and for me. Now, be quiet and look interested. I'm paying you enough that you should want to be the belle of the ball."

Banfield had also schooled her on what it was he did for a living and the difference between an art advisor and an art dealer. He was the latter, and he made his money by selling the works of the artists he represented. Like a movie star's or author's agent, he got a percentage of each sale. It was imperative that he watched for artists who were currently unrepresented and especially undiscovered.

A loud cackle of laughter caught their attention, and they both looked at a woman who stood in the middle of the room, commanding it with her presence. Those who weren't at her feet gazed at her from afar and looked as if they wanted to be.

"Damn, she's here," Ian said. "I hope she doesn't get to him first."

"Who is she?" Lucy had to admire the way the woman effortlessly held the attention of everyone within three feet of her as she regaled them with a tale about her latest trip to Europe and all the amazing art just waiting to be discovered. She was overdressed but in a way that she pulled off effortlessly with the long, pale-rose gown she wore. Diamonds—and big ones at that—sparkled from her ears. They were the only jewelry she wore and were expensive-looking enough to be all that was needed. Her hair was platinum blond and cut in a bob from which not a single hair dared to step out of place. She stood confidently on six-inch heels, their spikes lethal enough to take out a jugular vein in seconds.

She could see that the woman had power.

"My nemesis, Jackie Schafer of the Manhattan Schafers. She's the ultimate art queen curator of the area, and everyone wants her attention. She also thinks I stole a collection out from under her a few years ago, and since then, she's been out to get me. Did I mention she was a royal pain in the ass? She's probably already sniffing around Vanzo."

"So, once you've spoken to him, we can go?"

"It's not that simple. I need to hook him. Convince him to let only me represent his work."

Lucy was never arrogant about it, but she knew she had a way with men. They saw her as small and feminine and wanted to be her hero. She'd used it to her advantage many times over the years, though she'd never needed or wanted a hero.

"Let me have a crack at him first," she said. "What's he look like?"

Banfield pulled out his phone and brought up a photo of Vanzo. It showed a man in his late twenties or possibly early thirties. Deep, dark eyes and a shocking cap of black, wavy hair. He was attractive, fit but not obnoxiously so.

She could work with that.

"I got this. I'll get him to a corner alone, and when I think the time is right for you to swoop in, I'll give you a wink. Just don't crowd me."

"If this works, you've earned yourself a bonus for tonight."

"How much?" she asked. Being mistaken for a dog walker was beginning to resemble winning the lottery. Lucy was going to end up with more money in her pocket in the next weeks than she'd had altogether in years.

"We'll see. Get busy."

He walked away, and Lucy stayed in place for a moment, surveying the room. Once she'd seen all the faces she could from her position, she dumped her drink into the nearest potted plant and then went to the bar, where she could get a different viewpoint.

He found her before she found him.

Whether because of synchronicity or just luck, he walked right up beside her at the bar and quietly asked the bartender for an old-fashioned.

"Oh, I'm sorry," he said, turning to her. "Were you waiting first?"

"It's fine. I just need a water with lemon."

He raised an eyebrow. "Not a drinker?"

"Sometimes," she said politely. "Not tonight."

When the bartender handed over their drinks, he gave her his full attention. He wasn't overly bold, and she sensed a shyness in him. She was going to have to make the first move.

"I'm Lucia," she said with just the slightest lisp on the end of her accent. She held her hand out.

Instead of shaking it, he leaned forward and grasped it then held it to his lips for a second.

"Jorge. Jorge Vanzo," he said softly. He appraised her for a moment then whispered under his breath, "*Qué bellez.*"

"I don't speak Spanish."

"I say you are quite a beauty. And, I add, a sight for sore eyes."

"Why is that? There are plenty of pretty women strolling around here, some of them prime for picking by a handsome guy like you."

"I've not seen even one who I can look into her eyes and see her soul like I can yours. You—you are fragile but strong. Unpretentious but proud. And so very real."

Lucy was struck silent. He was right. And wrong. And perhaps not as shy as she'd first thought. She could see why women fell for artists. They sure had the words. She'd never felt her pulse pounding in her ears like it was now. She was going to have to be careful around him. It was business, not another short fling.

"I—I'm not sure what you mean," she said, finally finding her footing. "Are you a collector of art?"

He looked thoughtful. "Hmm. Yes, I guess you could say that. I have many pieces."

She felt frustrated. He was playing with her.

"Are you also an artist?"

"Let's talk about you first," he said, with not a trace of the arrogance or eagerness she expected from a struggling artist. "Where are you from? You didn't say your family name. I want to know all about you." He took her elbow and led her across the room to a set of French doors then out to a terrace on which they were alone.

They leaned on a railing and looked out over a courtyard, watching water bubble up and cascade down a fountain with a Greek god posed at the top. Jorge was too close, and Lucy scooted over a foot or so, hoping that would help her relax. She had a part to play.

"Not much to tell. I'm Lucia Leighton. I come from the Suffolk area of England, but I haven't been back there in ages. I'm somewhat of a wanderer and have lived in a few different places, always open to adventures." At least the last part was the truth, and Lucy didn't have to feel guilty about telling another lie, though why she would, she wasn't sure. Lies had never bothered her before.

"Leighton? Are you related to Sir Frederic Leighton? He was a famous artist in the late nineteenth century. I believe he was a baron too."

Hmm... that was a very good connection to know about. Thank you, Jorge...

"Somewhere down the line, yes," she said. "But I'm not much on family history. I chose to make my own way, which has made my success that much sweeter."

He studied her, and she wondered if he was seeing the untruth in her eyes.

"I'm glad to hear you are successful. What do you do?"

Crap—Banfield hadn't told her what her job was! How could they have missed that vital piece of information?

She searched her brain frantically, wondering what Ian would want her to be.

"I'm an art advisor," she finally said, remembering their conversation about a dealer versus an advisor and thinking how it might just work out nicely.

He nodded. "Interesting. Then I'm sure you are very aware of your ancestor's work. He was very popular for a time. At least until he fell out of critical favor. He was also rumored to have had a child with one of his models, though he never claimed it. Some say he was gay. Many contradictions, but back then, a man's private life could make or break him."

"How do you know so much about him?"

"I studied art history. I've also been to the museum dedicated to him in London. I'm sure you know of it. It was his home before it was donated."

"Yes, of course."

"What is your favorite piece there?" Jorge asked.

Lucy felt the perspiration start to show on her upper lip. "I can't have a favorite. That would be like picking a favorite child."

He grinned slowly, as though she'd won a silent sparring match. "I would've picked *Flaming June* as your favorite," he said.

"Oh? Why?"

"A woman draped in layers of crimson earth tones, curled up onto a chaise on a terrace during a hot day. She looks serene yet exhausted by the heat, her face rosy and flushed. She has a lovely, natural look about her."

"All artists want to paint the innocent maiden," she quipped.

"Well, as you know, there's more to the first glance of that piece. What with the display of oleander resting above her head. It leaves you wondering if she's asleep or poisoned. And if the latter, why. It opens a chasm of possibilities for the imagination. When you can do that with a painting, you know you've done something magical."

Lucy spied Banfield inside, hovering near the doors, waiting for a sign for him to join them. But she wasn't quite there yet. Or more precisely, she didn't have Jorge where she wanted him yet.

She bridged the distance between them, letting the side of her wrist lie against his ever so slightly. She immediately felt a shiver run through her, though the air was warm.

"Tell me about your work. What do you specialize in?"

He laughed softly. "I'm not sure how to answer that. I just go where the muse takes me. Recently, I've been attracted to the singular color of red, and I use it to embody passion and the intensity of femininity."

"Do you use models?" Lucy asked.

"Not usually. But I'd love to paint you."

Lucy laughed and kicked a foot back. When she did, her shoe fell off and clanked loudly against the terracotta. Jorge bent and picked it up then held it out for her to slip her foot into.

But first, she saw him look straight at the tissue pushed down into the toes. He camouflaged the confusion quickly and pretended not to notice, bringing his eyes up to hers as he slipped the shoe onto her foot.

Lucy's face was blazing. She could feel the crimson creeping across her skin. Probably exactly like the portrait of *Flaming June*. What was he thinking? That she couldn't afford her own shoes? Or worse?

He gave away nothing, and a gentle smile stretched across his face. "I've retrieved your slipper and put it on. Does this make me your prince?"

"That depends," she said, pouring her words out slowly and flirtatiously. "I have a favor to ask of you."

CHAPTER 6

*a*dele Wilkins wasn't thrilled that her long-lost granddaughter had used her connections in law enforcement to get an address and had shown up on her doorstep without notice. Taylor knew this because it took fifteen minutes for the old woman to even come to the door, five minutes to open it after Taylor told her she was a sheriff's deputy, and another ten to accept the fact that yes, her own flesh and blood had come calling before she stood back and said, "Well, what do you want?"

It took a bit of persuading before Adele let Taylor come in.

A fat, small-statured white dog danced around, yapping at them. It was in bad need of a grooming. And a diet.

"I wondered when one of you would find me," Adele said. "It sure took you long enough to come looking."

Taylor didn't know what to say to that, but the woman didn't wait for a response.

"I can offer you coffee or Snapple. That's all I've got."

She led Taylor out onto the back porch, where a moldy set of white rattan furniture that didn't look sturdy enough to hold them was the only option for sitting.

"Go ahead, sit down. It's been there for fifteen years and hasn't let me down yet," Adele urged. "Just don't go hopping up and down like a jackrabbit on crack, and you'll be fine."

Taylor lowered herself into a chair. Just water, please.

Adele disappeared into the house.

The backyard looked as if it had once been a beautiful place to relax, but now, it needed to be weeded, and shrubs needed trimming. Leaves had piled up in the flower beds and above Taylor in the overflowing gutters. A struggling palm tree begged for pruning.

Beneath her feet, some of the boards of the porch had buckled, and they all needed a new coat of stain, maybe some water repellent.

It all made Taylor feel better about the shape of her own place. Maybe it didn't look so bad after all. At least she knew her way around a weed eater.

Adele returned with a glass of water in one hand, a bottle of peach Snapple tucked under that arm, and a small bowl of water in the other hand. She set Taylor's water on the table then lowered the bowl to the porch floor.

"Prancer gets parched when we sit out here. She's got a bad thyroid. Well, we both do, but that's neither here nor there." She breathed heavily and sat down then struggled to uncap the bottle.

"Here, let me help," Taylor offered, reaching out.

Adele slapped her hand away. "I can get it. I'm not helpless."

Hmm... she is a stubborn one.

While Adele worked at it, Taylor scrutinized her, wondering if she or any of her sisters took after the woman.

It was too hard to tell.

She was thin, and Taylor remembered her mom as being that way. She was tall, too, especially for an old woman. From first observation, Adele's face looked hardened, as though her whole life had been one of sadness.

The dog jumped up and landed squarely on Taylor's lap. She put her hand through its hair and got stopped at a big tangle.

Adele noticed. "I know, she needs a bath and a haircut. I try to do it, but my arthritis is acting up, and I can't work the scissors like I want."

"What about taking her to a professional?"

Adele gave her a scornful look. "I told you. I don't get out much. And that takes a lot of money that I don't have."

"They do have electric dog trimmers, you know. I just picked up a pair a week ago so I could do my dog." Taylor's dad had mentioned that his in-laws used to be wealthy. Obviously, judging by the shape of the woman's home and yard, the money was gone.

"Where's your dog?"

"I left him with my friend Cecil. I didn't know if you liked animals."

"Animals are better than people in my book."

"So, speaking of money you don't have, you used it all up on attorney fees for Cate?" Taylor asked, deciding to just jump in and get it out there so she could get home.

Adele looked up. "Looks like you got something from my side of the family, didn't you? All niceties aside and no beating around the bush. What else do you want to know?"

"Is she guilty?"

"Are you asking from a legal standpoint or a family one?"

"First, from the standpoint of a daughter who needs to know. Later, we'll get to the legal aspect."

Adele stared at her, a look of steely resolve in her eyes. "First of all, it's disrespectful to call your mother by her first name, but if you can live with that, that's on you. But Cate is innocent from both a legal and a personal angle. Look, your mother is no angel, and she put me through hell, running off with that sorry excuse for a man you call your father and ruining her future, but she's no killer."

Taylor calmly took a drink of her water then set it down. "You're her mother. Of course you think she's not guilty. No mother can imagine their child being a murderer. Ask Jeffery Dahmer's mom. I'm sure she'll agree."

Adele gave a hoarse chuckle. "Not really a fair comparison, but you have a point. Still, Cate didn't do it. If I thought for one moment that she did, I'd have washed my hands of her forever."

"What makes you so sure?"

Adele took a long sip of her Snapple before she spoke. "Because I know my daughter. It may not seem like it to your dad, because he thinks I abandoned her after she ran off and married him, but I didn't. I knew exactly where they were, and I kept tabs. Cate was a good mother despite the hand she'd been dealt with your dad. She kept you all clean and fed, with a roof over your heads. Sometimes a leaky one—but she made sure you kids never suffered for anything. Your grandfather once called and offered to adopt the two youngest, before Robert was born. He told her she'd have an easier time with only two girls instead of four. Your mother told him she'd sooner chew off her own arm than hand over one of her children. To anyone—not just him. I'm telling you now, she could not have set that fire knowing that Robert could be hurt or killed."

"Did she suffer from depression or mental illness when she was younger?" Taylor asked. "I've read that it can come out later in dangerous ways when someone is under pressure, and I'd say that trying to raise five kids and keep your husband from losing his temper would be a lot of pressure."

Adele shook her head. "Never. Sometimes, I thought she was lonely being an only child, but that answered why she wanted so many children. She never gave me reason to believe she had a mental illness. Nothing you can tell me or ask me or lead me to think will ever make me say it's even a possibility that your mom is guilty."

"She couldn't have been convicted without compelling evidence."

Adele rolled her eyes to the sky. "Now Miss High and Mighty Law Enforcement is going to tell me that the justice system works, and they don't ever get it wrong? Here's some news, missy. Between two and ten percent of those convicted in the United States are innocent. And more than thirty murder cases have been overturned in Florida alone."

"But she's not in Florida."

Adele sighed heavily. "That's what's unfortunate. Montana only has four. It's the hardest state to get a new trial."

"Yeah, I heard about the rule for entering new evidence."

She nodded. "I didn't even know about what happened until year four. But I tried. I hired three different attorneys, and we appealed. Then we appealed again. Finally, Cate told me to stop trying. By that time, I didn't have any more money anyway. They all bled me dry and left us out to hang."

Taylor doubted that was true. More likely, they had done all they could and had had no recourse left.

"I'm sorry to hear you gave it all."

Adele waved her hand in the air. "Doesn't matter. It wasn't new to me to be poor. I came from nothing and married into money. Your mother married for love. In the end, both of us lost. One more than the other."

"Well, you lost a daughter," Taylor said.

"I lost her a long time before the fire."

"Do you still stay in contact?"

"We talk on the phone every other week, but I stopped visiting a few years ago. Too expensive to fly out there, and I can't drive long-distance. I write her a letter here and there. I used to write every week, but I ran out of things to tell her that I didn't say in the phone calls. My life is boring. Same shit every day. Who wants to hear that?"

"And you never thought to talk her into letting her daughters know she wasn't dead?" Taylor tried to keep the anger from her voice.

"I sure did. I told her it wasn't right. I pleaded with her. Even threatened to find you and tell you all myself, but she said if I did, she'd kill herself that very day."

"That was what she told my dad."

"I know," Adele said. "He and I talked a few times before it was all buttoned up and done. Back then, he was desperate enough to free your mom that he was willing to make a deal with the devil. He considered me that devil. I try not to hold it against him, but I still feel like if he'd been a better man in the beginning, maybe Cate's—and Robert's—fate would've been different."

"We'll never know."

"True. But has he changed? Or is he still sitting around feeling sorry for himself?"

"The latter," Taylor said. "He wouldn't even eat or shower if I didn't threaten him a few times a week."

"Let him suffer alone, Taylor. You can only live your own life. If he wants to waste his, that's on him."

"Thanks for the advice, *Grandma*."

"What's that supposed to mean?" She didn't look mad. She looked amused.

That really infuriated Taylor.

"You could've come to us, you know. Maybe stepped in when we needed a mother. Made sure we didn't bounce back and forth in the system."

"The system?" she looked confused.

She didn't know about their foster-care roller coaster. Telling her now would solve nothing, and to be honest, Taylor was beginning to feel sorry for her.

"Never mind. Forget I said anything. But can I ask a favor of you?"

"You can always ask. Don't mean I'll give it."

"Do you have any photos of my mom when she was growing up?"

Adele looked away, but a small smile played on her face. She stood and scooped up Prancer then beckoned for Taylor to follow.

"Now that's one favor I can grant."

"YOUR MOTHER WAS A STORYTELLER," Adele said, smiling at an old, tattered notebook she held in her hands. "This was one of many notebooks that Cate filled with short stories, poems, and just anything that popped into her head. They don't even read like they were done by a child. I always thought she'd be a famous writer, because the written word flowed so effortlessly from her hands to paper."

Her grandmother's statement jogged a memory for Taylor that she'd not realized she had. She recalled herself and her sisters flanking their mom in bed while she told them a bedtime story *from her head*, as they liked to call it. Her mom would make them up on the spot, sometimes even continuing the same storyline for many nights, adding new characters and magical details to keep them asking for more.

Taylor remembered one. Something about a fairy in the woods and all the fairy sisters who tried to create a world without yucky boys. Funny how she'd never thought of it, and now, it popped up in her mind suddenly.

"Cate would disappear outside for hours, content with her notebook and colorful pens. Sometimes, I'd have to go hunting for her, because she'd be so engrossed in what she was writing that she'd forget the time and be late for dinner," Adele said, smiling as though she were back in time, proudly standing over her daughter as she wrote. She picked up another notebook, and a few sheets of paper fell out onto the floor. She grabbed them and read the first one then handed them to Taylor.

"This is the essay she wrote when she was a junior in high school. It got her in line to win the Coolidge full-ride scholarship for tuition, room, and board for four years at any American university. We didn't really need the financial help, but it meant a lot to Cate to show she could earn it herself."

"What's the essay about?" Taylor glanced down and saw words in flawlessly blocked letters, all justified perfectly to the left.

"Empowering others. When she wrote it, she was determined that she was going to be an independent woman and be successful on her own, without a husband. It wasn't six months later that she met your dad, and all that went out the window."

"But did she win the big one?"

"The scholarship? Well, technically, she pulled out before the winners were chosen. But between you, me, and the fencepost, my friend on the board told me that they'd already chosen Cate as one of the recipients before she took off with your father."

"You know you've yet to say his name, right?" Taylor asked.

"Jackson," Adele said. "Jackson Lowlife Johnson Gray." She looked as if she'd swallowed a turd. "Now, are you happy?"

Taylor laughed. "I really don't care. It's just that it's a long time to hold a grudge. I promise you, karma got him. He's miserable. You can quit hating him now."

Adele shrugged. "I don't hate him, but I can't say I feel sorry for him. First, he took my daughter, then, he took my grandchildren."

"Technically, he didn't. He wasn't there when the fire happened and wasn't responsible for the fallout after."

She shook her head vehemently. "Jackson could've let me know where he was going with you girls. Sent me letters. Photos. Even ask me to come visit occasionally. But he didn't want me near you.

Told me that Cate said she wanted you girls to have a fresh start and no ties to her. He could've just kept it from her and let me know you and your sisters. He's a selfish bastard, if you ask me."

"Tell me how you really feel, Adele," Taylor said softly. Her grandmother had grit. She couldn't help but admire it too.

"Here, open and see what's in it." She tossed a box over.

Taylor barely caught it. She lifted the lid to find several photo albums stacked inside. The first one began when her mom was in kindergarten, so Taylor put that one aside and dug down for an earlier one. She wanted to start at the beginning.

"Was Cate a difficult baby?" she asked, giving her grand-mother the first of many questions to come in the hope of discovering something that could point at Cate going off the deep end and killing her only son.

"Nope. She was as mild-mannered as a little lamb. Next? I know what you're doing, and I approve. By the time you leave here, I'll convince you, too, that your mother is not a killer."

By the time they'd gotten through the last photo album and the hundreds of questions Taylor pelted Adele with, the after-noon had disappeared.

Taylor was getting hungry, but she feared that if she asked for something, with her grandmother's supposedly low budget, she might get fed cat food.

"Do you ever leave the house?" Taylor asked, easing into an invitation.

"Not much. Nothing to leave for. I get my groceries delivered, my medication comes by mail, and anything else I need is one click online."

"So, you have internet?"

Adele laughed. "Yes, I have internet. I do manage to squeeze enough out of what's left every month to be able to join the rest of the world in the deep dark web. Otherwise, I might go a bit senile, don't you think?"

"Are you on a social network?"

"I have it, just to look."

"So you've seen Anna and all the pictures of her perfect family that she stages?" As soon as she said it, she wished she could push the words back into her mouth.

"What? Isn't she happy?" Adele looked concerned.

Taylor shrugged. "I guess so. Maybe not as happy as she likes to pretend but well enough. She always hated being poor. Now she's got the status she wants."

"And Jo?"

"She's good. She and Levi sort of move from place to place, always looking for something she can't seem to find."

"Sounds like your mother," Adele said. "What about Lucy? I don't ever see any mention of her on Anna's pages."

"Anna doesn't approve of Lucy. She's the real free spirit of the mix." Taylor wasn't about to tell her anything else about her little sister. Adele might be related, but she wasn't family. Taylor was tired and not up to defending Lucy's antics to anyone.

"Well, I do what I can to try to keep up online without interfering. It can get lonely, but what do you do but keep keeping on."

"Well, you shut the computer down and get out of the house, for one. Don't you miss physically seeing things and people? In real life and not on a screen?"

She shook her head. "Not really. I drove down to Plant City a few years ago. Wanted to see that Florida Strawberry Festival they're always whoopin' and hollering about on television. Too much noise and ruckus for me. I was there for two hours then hightailed it home and haven't gone anywhere since. My adventuring days are over."

That was sad. Winter Haven was fifty miles east of Tampa and was famous for its many lakes—at least fifty inside the city limits—but her grandmother didn't live near a single one and obviously had no desire to visit them.

Taylor always did her research, and she knew the last population count for the town had been well over seventy thousand people, but judging from the drive into Adele's neighborhood, it looked to have a nice hometown feel despite the influx of new residents it harbored.

"I really should be going," Taylor said as she stood and stretched to get the kinks out of her back.

"Going? You driving back tonight? Why?"

"Well, I have a dog, and I left him with a friend, and I—well—I don't know."

Adele stood, too, putting her hands on her hips. "Poppycock. You don't need to be driving tonight. That's too much, and nothing good happens after dark. This ain't the Hilton, but I have a guest room, and you can sleep there. Get up early tomorrow and head out if that's what you want to do."

Taylor considered the offer. She really was tired, probably because of the emotional journey she'd just taken with all the stories and photos, but she'd planned on getting a hotel room partway home if she got too sleepy. She hadn't expected to like Adele, and it was strange, but she really wasn't ready to leave her yet. Adele was the only one who had ever been able to fill her in on Cate—or at least the only one willing.

"Fine. I'll stay but only if you let me take you out for dinner."

Adele laughed. "Well, that's a no-brainer. I might be old, but I ain't stupid. If you're gonna pay, I'll show you the way. Just let me go do a little something to this face so people don't think you stole a body from the crypt. You go get your bag or suitcase or whatever you have, and I'll show you the guest room in a minute."

She disappeared down the hall with Taylor still smiling at her back. Adele was a spicy one—with personality for days.

Lucy.

Yes, that was who the old woman reminded her of. Lucy was a lot like her with her quick comebacks and attitude of doing what she wanted and to hell with anyone who didn't like it.

Taylor found herself wishing that all her sisters could meet

Adele and she them. What a waste of decades. Not only for her and her sisters but for Adele, who seemed to live a lonely life.

But Taylor had no plans to keep it cozy with the old woman after she left town. She didn't have time for any more responsi- bilities, but things could've been so different.

She went outside to the truck to get her bag, and when she returned, Adele was waiting. She hadn't primped much, just applied some mascara and light lipstick, but she'd changed her shirt to something with a collar, and she'd put on a pair of new-looking sandals. Her hair was combed neatly too.

"Not much to work with here, so you'll have to just excuse the way I look." She gestured down the hall. "The guest room is the second door on the right. Bathroom just beyond that. Nothing fancy, mind you, but if you need something that's not in there, give me a shout."

"You look pretty," Taylor said then pretended not to see how the compliment lit up Adele's eyes as she moved past her to the hallway.

She went into the room and put her bag on the bed. Adele had been right. It wasn't fancy. Just a bed with a quilt set on it, a chair, and a dresser with a framed photo of what appeared to be Adele and her husband, Taylor's grandfather.

Taylor picked up the picture. Her grandfather had had a kind face. He had been a big guy too. She wondered if her dad was afraid of him after the whole running-off-to-get-married adventure.

She hadn't yet asked anything about her grandfather, and Adele had offered nothing. While Taylor was a bit curious, she really didn't have the time to get into more lines of questioning. Adele might think she'd cleared things up regarding Cate's inno-cent nature, but that wasn't exactly true. Being in law enforce-ment had taught Taylor that crimes were committed by the most unlikely suspects one could imagine. Everyone had the ability to be violent, but most knew how to control it. Among the ones who did take it to that level, it hadn't always been obvious that they had it in them.

She returned to the living room. "I'm ready. You pick the place, but I'd like to go somewhere with some history. A favorite with the locals."

Adele picked up her keys and opened the front door. "I guess that would be Harry's Old Place out on Cypress Garden Road. It's been in business for over thirty years, so they must do something right. You like fresh fish?"

"I sure do."

"C'mon, then. We'll both sleep good tonight with full bellies. Just wait until I tell you about Harry in a Bag. I haven't been there for years, so I hope they still have it. It's the best thing on the menu."

Taylor was glad to see Adele so happy to go out. Perhaps her reluctance to go anywhere wasn't so much about the money as it was about not having anyone to go with. At least for a night, it would be nice to give her some companionship.

They got to the truck, and Adele was almost in when she laughed and turned to Taylor. "Dinner conversation will be you explaining why a young woman like you hasn't even mentioned the man in her life. There's no ring on your finger, so I take it you haven't married him yet. I want to know all the details. Surely, out of four granddaughters, I'm going to have more than three great-grandkids."

Taylor rolled her eyes.

That should be a short conversation and one that was sure to be a disappointment. Her grandmother didn't know it yet, but all her granddaughters had trust issues that made having healthy relationships damn near impossible.

Imagine that.

CHAPTER 7

*L*ucy was up and sitting at a laptop that Ian had given her to use by six o'clock sharp. If she were in Georgia, she'd have been hearing roosters crow all around her. Here in the city, things were starting to get noisy outside but with a different kind of activity that included horns blowing and the occasional shout from the streets.

She'd already had juice and a piece of toast and was feeling queasy but was determined to be productive anyway. In the two weeks since the cocktail party, she'd been moved into a new role at the Banfield home. No longer was she the dog nanny, though she did take them for a stroll around the park occasionally when she was feeling too closed in and needed to be out in the open air.

A new girl came three times a day to take care of Bent and Bae now. Lucy barely noticed her between all the pointing and clicking she had going on in front of her.

Banfield had hired her to be his assistant, and the pay was something she couldn't turn down, especially since she had no overhead and could bank all of it.

He'd been impressed that she'd come up with the perfect fake career as an art advisor, and he'd figured out a way that they could work together. So far, she only had one client, and that wasn't even a solid thing. They'd know in a few hours, though, when they had their meeting with Jorge Vanzo. He'd almost turned her down when she'd asked him the favor of letting her colleague talk to him about his art. Jorge claimed it wasn't yet ready—or he wasn't ready. He was protective of it and perhaps a bit doubtful of his abilities.

Lucy had been forced to negotiate with him, and after the meeting, Jorge would be taking her to dinner. That was the bargain she'd had to make with him.

"Lucia, I need you to call and confirm our reservation at the Dakota Bar," Banfield said, coming up behind her.

"They don't open until ten, and I already told you, we don't need a reservation," she replied, not bothering to turn around in her seat at the kitchen island. One of her traits that Banfield was a bit obsessed about was that she continued to act completely bored with his prestige and money. She might have been the only one in his life that didn't bow down to him, and for some reason, he found that amusing.

"I want you to make sure we get a table on the street. He'll be more comfortable there than inside. Oh, and I've picked out your outfit, and Carmen hung it in your room." He stomped around the kitchen, fixing himself a cup of coffee.

Lucy rolled her eyes at the ceiling.

That was one negotiation with Ian she hadn't won. He said he alone oversaw creating Lucia, and that included her fake background, her colleagues, and everything down to what she wore when she went out as her new fictional character. She was now a blonde, with what he claimed was an up-to-date and age-appropriate haircut. With bangs—and oh, how she'd always hated them, but she finally was getting used to the fine fringe hanging over her eyes. At least he couldn't see how many times she had to look at the ceiling to keep the sarcasm from coming out.

He'd also been giving her quite a fast education about art over dinner in the kitchen every night. At first, it had been awkward, since she'd still never seen Suki leave her room—or even met her —but now, it felt normal.

"Fine, but it better not be short and sexy," Lucy said.

He chuckled. She'd already told him she hated wearing dresses, but until the clothes he'd ordered for her came in, that was the only thing of his wife's that she could wear. Her pants were all way too long. A new selection of shoes that fit her had already arrived, and Lucy's tiny closet was starting to get full. Soon, she'd have to shove some of the dog clothes onto the top shelf so she could have more of the space.

"Suki's shortest stuff is still too long on you, or I'd already have you in something to show more of those legs. You know that."

Lucy ignored him. Sometimes he said inappropriate things, but it never felt creepy. He simply got a thrill from dressing her. He was the most fashion-friendly man she'd ever known. She didn't have any fashion sense, so it was fine with her so long as he kept his hands off her. Speaking of Suki, Lucy had asked him a few times about his wife and why she didn't come out of her room, but that was one subject he shut down immediately. His reluctance to talk about her made Lucy more curious every day.

Was the woman a leper, agoraphobic, or what?

Ian brought his coffee around and pulled up a stool next to her. He opened his own laptop and started pecking away before he paused. "If we can snag Vanzo, I'm going to teach you how to put together a portfolio. I'm sure he doesn't have one yet. In the meantime, your role is to floor him with your beauty and coyness. Keep him on the line."

Lucy laughed. "I am *not* coy."

"I know you aren't, but Lucia is. Remember, leave the art talk to me, because you don't yet have the right vocabulary. When it comes time to advise him, I'll coach you on that."

Now she was perturbed. Sometimes he made her sound like an idiot.

"You don't think I can have a decent talk about art yet?"

He shook his head. "Not unless you want to be totally found out as a fake. You listen. Take it all in. Soon, you'll know the difference between techniques, media, and what is good and what's crap. Did you read the book I gave you yesterday?"

"You wanted me to read it in one night? That would be a solid no. I'm still finishing the one you gave me a few days ago."

He'd peppered her with books on art history, thick ones she had to read, as well as with coffee table–style books with tons of illustrations. She was trying to take it all in but looking through them usually put her to sleep.

During the day, he kept her too busy to find time to read. She was proud of herself for really catching on to the technical stuff, including social networking and even updating his website. Well, at least his art blog. She couldn't do the complicated stuff, but he was happy just to have someone to hand things off to.

Carmen was slowly warming up and becoming her friend. A little. The housekeeper had not asked her about her background or family yet, but it was obvious that she knew Lucy was more used to a lifestyle like her own—totally opposite that of the Banfields.

Lucy was determined to win her over eventually.

Carmen knew all about *Lucia* and quietly disapproved. She said that Ian had an assistant who had worked for him for seven years, but she'd finally quit when she got married and claimed to have burnout. Ian had probably totally monopolized her life day and night. He wasn't the easiest person to work with, but Lucy planned to build up a nice chunk of change then disappear.

Her specialty.

When her stomach growled, she remembered the other thing, and it made panic roll through her. She only had two more weeks before it would legally be too late to do the procedure. After that, the price and the danger would go up.

So far, she'd only made it to one clinic, and after seeing what it looked like inside and dealing with a rude receptionist, she'd decided it wasn't the right place. She needed to get busy and get something on the schedule before it was too late. A baby was not in her life plan. Not now and not ever. She also wouldn't be fitting into her new clothes if she waited much longer. With all the good food Carmen was feeding her, her bump had grown surprisingly fast for the short time she'd been staying at the penthouse.

"I might need to take some time to myself tomorrow." She also needed to swing by and see Margot. She felt guilty for abandoning her friend.

Ian perked up. "You can't. I need you here. If Jorge takes the bait, we have a lot to do."

"Sorry—not negotiable." She kept her eyes on the computer in front of her.

She could feel his irritation, but something about the way she was final with him and didn't ask but told, made him back off.

"Don't be gone too long," he said grudgingly. "It'd better not be a job interview either."

&

FOUR THIRTY ON a Monday night was surprisingly busy at the Dakota Bar, and Lucy tapped her short nails against their outdoor table. She was glad Ian had wanted the street view, since she never got tired of watching the many personalities of the city.

Jorge was nearly half an hour late, and beside her, Ian was so nervous he was twitching. It was driving her mad.

Their server approached, holding a tray of food. Ian stopped her before she could set it down. "I told you not to bring it out until our third guest arrives," he scolded. "Now you'll have to make it fresh."

She blushed and backed away. "I'm so sorry. I'll take it back."

When she disappeared inside, Lucy kicked Ian under the table, making enough impact on his shin that he jumped. "Don't be an ass. She's just doing her job."

"Sue me. I'm nervous. He's doing this on purpose," Ian said, irritated. "He knows he has me by the balls."

"Nah, he doesn't think like that. Must have a valid reason."

He laughed sarcastically. "News flash: everyone in New York does this. And you've met him once and think you know how he thinks?"

"Yeah, I'm pretty sure I got a good gauge on him, and remember, he's not a New Yorker or trying to be one either."

Vanzo was from Uruguay. Lucy had looked it up, and it was in South America. They were crazy about soccer (they called it football), and interestingly, all citizens over the age of eighteen were required to vote, even if they didn't give a damn who was elected.

Lucy had never voted and didn't have a clue who was in office other than the president of the United States. Politics wasn't on her radar, though now that she was hanging out with smarter people, she wished she knew more about it.

"How did your afternoon appointment go?" Ian asked.

She shrugged. "Fine."

The truth was, she hadn't made it to the other clinic she'd planned to visit. After she'd raided the fridge and pantry for items to make up a smorgasbord of treats for Margot to share with her friends for dinner, she'd walked over and ended up enjoying herself so much that time had gotten away from her, and she'd had to hurry back to get ready.

There was a new friend there with Margot, an older woman named Armina who held on to a swaddled doll as though it were real. A few times, she sang softly to it, some sort of Italian lullaby. She even used the corner of her black-and-gold scarf to wipe its face then looked at Lucy and exclaimed, "This is real Versace, you know?"

Margot confirmed that the scarf was real then said Armina had previously been a sought after midwife in Queens. How she'd come to be in New York City and obviously homeless was not discussed.

Margot didn't mention or even act as if she realized that Lucy had abandoned her for two weeks. Instead, she'd jumped up from the bench she and Armina were resting on and hugged Lucy as if she was seeing her long-lost best friend. She'd been thankful for the treats too. Lucy had slipped in a small bar of soap and some old shampoo she'd found under the bathroom vanity. She had also added an unwrapped toothbrush and tube of toothpaste to the gift bag because she knew Carmen would set more out.

Lastly, she'd brought the pillow off her own bed. She'd noticed that Margot usually rested her head on a rolled-up sweatshirt.

"You are an angel sent from Heaven," Margot had exclaimed as she went through the bag, holding each item up and then to her heart before putting it back in. She handed a few of the treats to Armina, who smiled hugely and stuffed them into the diaper bag at her feet.

"No. Believe me, I'm as far from an angel as you can get," Lucy said, embarrassed at the flattery. It wasn't as if she'd paid for the food or the pillow herself. She'd swiped it.

"Not true. I knew the day I met you that you were going to change my life." Margot took a bite from one of Carmen's poppy seed muffins and closed her eyes in rapture.

"I wouldn't go that far unless you see a bag of food and a pillow as life changing," Lucy joked, trying to turn the conversation to one less serious. "But I'm glad I found you today. I was worried you might have moved on."

Margot had laughed, and a bit of muffin fell out of her mouth before she snatched it out of the air and stuffed it back in.

"Moved on? Where would I go?" She looked at Armina and asked it again, and they both laughed uproariously.

Lucy shrugged. "I don't know. I guess I'm used to never staying in one spot long myself and just assumed that everyone was like me."

Margot swallowed the bite and got serious. "You, Lucy, are young and beautiful. Street smart too. You can still use that to your advantage, while me—well, let's just say I've seen better days, and they are long gone. I must rely on the long-term relationships I make, and that takes time. Where could I go that I'd get a free hot dog every Monday and Wednesday afternoon from Larry at the hot dog stand on the corner? Or where I am serenaded by Mike as I stare up at the dark sky of beautiful stars? The same Mike, I might add, who always brings me some sort of gift for being his biggest fan. It took me six weeks or more to win him over. How could I leave that?"

She didn't mention the frigid winters in which she struggled to find shelter or the technique of sleeping with one ear listening to stay safe or the multitude of other problems that being homeless in New York City entailed. Margot was definitely a glass-half-full kind of woman.

Now, Ian sat across from Lucy—Lucia—proudly. She could never explain to him about her friendship with Margot. He'd think her insane for going back.

Jorge interrupted her reflection on the visit with Margot when he suddenly appeared. He was a bit sweaty and harried, but unfortunately, there was no telling Lucy's senses that, because the second she saw him, she felt a little flip in her belly.

Ian jumped up and gave him a man hug, clapping him on the back of the shoulder as he backed away. Before Lucy could stand, Jorge waved for her not to do so, and like the first night, he reached for her hand and planted a very warm and sensuous kiss on it before taking his own seat. He made the best eye contact with her, but it was unsettling, and she nervously picked up her water and took a long swig as she studied a couple getting out of a taxi at the curb.

"Couldn't find a cab?" Ian asked

"Didn't look for one," Jorge said. "But it took me a bit more than the hour that I estimated for the walk."

Impressive. As far as Lucy knew, no one in the city walked more than three blocks unless they couldn't afford to ride. She wondered if he was frugal or wanted the exercise.

Ian let it go because the server, right on time, stepped up to the table.

She smiled pleasantly at Jorge and asked what he wanted to drink.

Jorge looked around and noticed Ian's dirty martini and her water with lemon.

"Just water for me, please. No lemon."

She retreated after whispering nervously to Ian that the starters were on the way.

They started out with small talk, discussing the cocktail party and rumors of small deals that had been made there the night they'd met. Ian led the conversation, and once again, Lucy felt the shyness coming from Jorge. His accent made his words sound warm and comforting, and she could have listened to him talk for hours.

The server returned and quietly moved around them.

Shrimp cocktail, Lucy had heard of and seen, of course, but she wasn't sure of the other thing the server set down before she retreated inside.

"What is that?" she asked.

"Bruschetta," Ian said. "Pecorino cheese, basil, and, of course, a poached egg."

"Peck of what?" she asked, peering down at the strange concoction. "Looks like a piece of tomato on dried-out toast with an overdone egg slapped on top." She poked at it with her fork. It *did not* look appetizing.

When she looked up, Ian was glaring at her, and Jorge had a slight, amused smile on his face. Then he waved at the server, and she approached.

"Please bring us a basket of French fries," he said.

They locked eyes for a moment before Lucy had to look away.

Ian had every right to look mad. She was an idiot. Of course, she was supposed to know what bruschetta was. She'd lost track of herself and forgotten that she wasn't humble southern Georgia Lucy—she was world-traveled Lucia.

Fortunately, he took over. "So, Jorge. What is your preferred medium?"

Lucy thought of Faire Tinsley, Hart's Ridge's only claim to fame, a woman who had maintained she could talk to those from the other side. Wouldn't Ian just die on the spot if she interrupted with that tidbit?

"I've used many media, but my favorite is traditional oil on canvas," Jorge replied.

"Perfect," Ian said, nodding like an idiot, as though Jorge had passed the first test on his exam. "I'd love to know what your biggest artistic influences are and how you apply them to your own work."

Lucy had seen that question on a list of twenty-eight questions to ask when interviewing artists. She could've asked it. But now, her face burned from embarrassment at being a total screwup. She sampled the toast while they talked back and forth, Ian pelting their guest with questions and Jorge gently answering some of them while gracefully avoiding others.

Next, Ian asked, "What motivates you to create?" before the conversation got too far. And he asked nitty-gritty questions like whether Jorge already had an existing customer base. Yep, she was proud that she remembered the way the conversation should go. It seemed that she was getting pretty good at research and how to apply it to her fake life.

The toast tasted as bad as it looked, and she set it aside to wait for the fries.

Jorge was talking. Finally, something interesting to cancel out Ian's droning on and on.

"My mother was a self-taught art historian, and she had more knowledge in her little finger than most art school professors. She introduced me to the world of art by giving me books to read and taking me to every museum and gallery we could get to by foot, car, or train before I was eleven. I was fourteen before she'd let me touch a canvas because she said she wanted me to understand the gift of art before I tried to contribute to it."

Ian nodded, but his eyes showed he wasn't really interested.

"Is she still living?" Lucy asked.

Jorge nodded. "She sure is. After my father died, she took a small cottage in the country. She's very proud of me, though I've tried to tell her that I'm not famous."

"Yet," Lucy said, smiling.

He smiled back at her over the basket of fries the server had just set on the table. He looked humble, and she found his shyness very attractive. Something about Jorge was different than the others. She couldn't play the part she normally played with men. He didn't look as though he'd be easily manipulated that way. She'd promised to stay on after drinks and have dinner with him, and now she wondered if that had been smart or one of the dumbest moves she'd ever made

"We'll see," he said.

"On that note, I'd love to see some of your work," Ian said. "Where are you staying?"

"I have a studio I'm sharing with someone. We got it through the Safe Haven artist residency program for international artists."

Ian nodded as though he'd awarded it himself. "Great. Yes, that's a wonderful program. How long are you in it?"

"It's six months to two years, but every three months, we must show we've made some progress in pursuing an audience for our work to keep it. Right now, I'm focusing on the work itself and haven't yet delved into ways to get it seen."

"We can help you with that," Lucy said.

"Absolutely," Ian agreed. "Could we see some today?"

Jorge looked down at the French fry he held in his hand, pausing before speaking. "I—I'm not ready."

Lucy saw a look of panic flash in Ian's eyes before he erased it and put his confident face back on. He'd already told her he'd seen bits and pieces of Jorge's work and knew he had some finished pieces.

"All artists say that. I'm sure you've got something you can show me so I can get a feel for your future audience," Ian said.

Jorge shook his head. "No, really. I need a few weeks. Then I'll get back to you."

"Can we shake on that?" Ian asked.

"Why don't we toast instead?" Jorge said. "Then we can wrap this up until next time."

Ian nodded. "Please, you go ahead."

Jorge lifted his glass. "*Salud, dinero, amor, y tiempo para disfrutarlo*. My father always said this blessing when we drank wine. It translates to 'health, wealth, love, and the time to enjoy it.' And of course, to the mother-to-be."

He looked at Lucy when he said the last few words.

Lucy felt the blood drain out of her face, and when she looked at Ian, he had turned as pale as she felt, and his eyes were blazing with condemnation, aimed straight at her.

⁂

LUCY WAS ALL the way down the block when Jorge caught up with her and pulled at her sleeve.

"Lucia—wait."

The crosswalk light was red, and cars crisscrossed the street, so she couldn't get away from him. She whipped around, anger giving her more energy than she'd felt in weeks.

"I'm sorry. So sorry!"

"It's my fault. Why would you think it was even appropriate to mention something like that at a business meeting? And for that matter, how in the hell did you know?"

She should've denied it, but he had caught her so off guard that by the time she'd recovered, it had been obvious that it was true, and it was too late to declare him out of his mind. Instead of responding, she'd jumped up and fled.

She had to admit that part of her fury was embarrassment. She thought she'd been doing a fine job of hiding the small bump. At least Ian hadn't suspected a thing, and he was always scrutinizing her hair and clothing.

She reached down unconsciously and put her hand on the slight mound.

He smiled softly. "Back home, my family used to say I had the gift. I can just see a woman and know. I'm not sure how. But I never meant to offend you. Please don't go."

"We aren't having dinner, Jorge. I need to get home." She had no idea what she was going to tell Ian. He was going to be furious. Probably even kick her out. He had wanted to take a dynamite assistant under his wing, not a knocked-up wanderer. He'd know that she'd been a fake all along—not just when he decided to give her the new identity.

She'd be back on the street by nightfall.

He grabbed her hand. "I'm so sorry. Sorry. Sorry, sorry. Please —I would love to spend some time with you. We don't have to go to a restaurant. Just a walk. Whatever you want. Just forgive me."

Lucy was astonished to see a sheen of tears in his eyes. He was sincere. She'd give him that. It must have been a Latin American thing. And the damage had been done anyway. She also didn't relish going back to the penthouse until Ian had had time to absorb the announcement. If she was lucky, he'd drink himself into oblivion and pass out, and she could get one more night of good rest before she moved out in the morning.

Maybe she could salvage something. Ian really wanted him as a client. Maybe even badly enough to give her some time to fix her problem. If she could get him a little closer, that was.

"I'll stay if you take me to your studio and show me some of your work."

He still held her hand, but now a smile spread across his face.

"*Faa*—wow, you know how to drive a hard bargain. But even if you didn't, how could I say no after my inexcusable mistake? Yes, *cariña*, my sweetheart, I will show you some of my work. Better than that, I will show you my favorite piece. No one has seen it."

Now he was desperate to keep her with him. Lucy had never had someone want her company so badly. Considering the last thing she wanted to do right now was face Ian, she finally gave in.

"Fine. But you'd better keep your promise. I want to see your best."

He smiled broadly and put his arm around her, turning her in the other direction. "Absolutely. A gentleman always keeps his promise. I have a few favorites to show you. Right this way. Just a few blocks."

CHAPTER 8

*J*orge's apartment was small but surprisingly clean. It was a studio size, all in one room except for the bathroom, and other than a mattress on the floor, piled high with colorful bedding and pillows, there wasn't any furniture. Instead, there were easels and canvases.

Everywhere.

All over the room was a dance of colors and shapes, making Lucy feel as if she'd entered another world, one built in a fantasy. She couldn't stop looking as she walked from one canvas to the other, while Jorge stood at the small kitchen area, making them drinks.

He hadn't asked her what she wanted, so when he brought over a colorful ceramic gourd-like mug without handles, she took it and peered inside then sniffed it.

"It's called mate, a very popular drink in my country. Our national tea. No alcohol. Just yerba leaves and hot water."

"Mate?" Her nose wrinkled at the bitter aroma coming from the slight foaming at the top.

"It's good. I put a bit of sugar in yours, since this is your first time. I drink mine without."

She took a tiny sip then looked up at him, trying to hide her grimace.

He smiled. "What do you taste?"

"Honestly?"

"Yes. I always want you to tell me the truth."

"It's earthy."

"And?"

She cringed. But he had said to be honest. "Kind of tastes like a dirty ashtray."

He threw his head back and laughed. "I can fix you something else. It's an acquired taste. Just like smoking cigars. At first, it is unpleasant. Then you begin to enjoy the taste of tobacco. With mate, it's bitter at first, but if you keep trying it, you begin to welcome the bitterness. The earthy taste of dirt or grass becomes soothing and quite addictive."

She handed him the gourd. "I'll take your word for it."

"Thank you for trying it. I wanted to share something of my country with you. I don't have any alcohol here, but can I make you some black tea?"

"No, I'm fine. I'd like you to explain some of your art if you would."

They needed to get to business.

He took her mug and put it in the small kitchen sink then returned, looped his arm in hers, and guided her over to the first easel. It was a seascape with a sun setting over the whitest sands of a beach. Not an ordinary seascape, though. This one screamed out for attention with slashes of bold reds, golden sun rays, and the deepest blues for water. There were dots and streaks of other colors and textures peppered throughout, breaking up what would normally be a serene scene.

"What do you think?"

She felt her face flush. She wasn't supposed to get into describing the art. Ian had said she didn't have the vocabulary yet. From her studies, she knew that it was considered semiabstract in expression. But Ian was right. She didn't have the words to express what her eyes saw and her soul felt as she gazed at the piece. So she turned the question back on him. "I asked you to explain it."

"Okay, love. I cannot deny you anything. But while most artists have a scripted, long, drawn-out, and mostly pretentious artist statement ready, I have nothing. I just paint what makes me happy. I approach art just like I do life. I give it my all with every emotion I have, even my passion. Just like my words, not a stroke is wasted."

"It feels fluid," Lucy said softly, her eyes jumping among the swatches of oranges and reds, the swirls of colors that tumbled together. "Full of rhythm and movement."

"Yes, yes, you understand."

She could hear the joy in his voice, and she felt a shiver of pride that she was able to convey what she was seeing.

"I love painting landscapes with expansive skies because it gives me the excuse to use my favorite colors and the boldest strokes. I want the viewer to feel as though they are there, wherever it may be. I want them to get lost in the imagery, as though they are witnessing God's beauty in person, not through a painting."

"Why do abstract when you could do just as well with traditional landscapes?" she asked.

"By going abstract, I can get lost in creating, and when I'm finished, it's up to the viewer to use their own creativity and emotions to interpret what they see."

Intense.

That was the one word that could describe Jorge's work. That was what she would tell Ian if he gave her the chance before asking her to leave. Jorge was talented. No—he was beyond talented. She wasn't a professional or anywhere close to it, but even she knew she was viewing something that would one day be worth a lot of money.

Ian had been right. Jorge didn't know it yet, but he would be painting masterpieces. If that prediction came true, his early pieces would be worth millions.

She just had to get him to trust her and Ian.

He took her arm, leading her away from the easels and windows. "Enough of this. You've flattered me enough when we both know I have not reached a high enough level yet to work with your boss. I want to talk about you. Tell me everything, including where you are really from and how you got here to this city that never sleeps."

"I—well, there's really nothing to tell."

"Come, sit with me. I'm sure you can think of something. You must at least tell me where you got that lovely accent."

Lucy knew it would lead to the bed.

It always did.

It was really the only thing of value she had to offer anyone.

THE WARM GLOW she felt from the long evening with Jorge had faded as soon as she'd come through the door, and now, Lucy felt like a teenager facing her parents with the worst thing that could possibly happen. Except she wasn't a child, and they weren't her parents. Perhaps she should tell them that. But first, she'd see if they were going to give her some time before making her leave. Ian might not be able to fill her position yet.

It would be nice if she could collect another week's pay or two.

At least she was finally getting to see Ian's wife.

Suki was indeed tall. And very thin but pretty in a melancholy sort of way. She'd only looked up once, but it was long enough for Lucy to see her dark, sad eyes looking through her dark curtain of hair. She was young too! Maybe as young as Lucy but possibly a few years older. Not anywhere close to Ian's age. He'd found an arm piece for sure. She looked like an anorexic model, one used in tragic ads to evoke a haunting mood.

"I'd like to tell you about Jorge and his work if you want to li▪ ii "

"No. I do not want to talk about Jorge at this moment."

To be honest, Lucy didn't either. She had only thrown it out there as a last-minute reprieve. Her evening with Jorge had felt so —so magical. He was full of passion and words of love and compliments. So affectionate, especially for their first date. Hearing the way he talked to her, a stranger would've thought they had been lovers for years.

She wanted to savor it and keep it to herself.

They hadn't slept together. He had only wanted to sit close and hold her hand and tell her she was beautiful and extraordinary without wanting anything in return. She'd have liked to spend more time thinking about their evening, but Ian was pacing back and forth, throwing his hands in the air every so often.

It was distracting. And quite irritating, even if he did have a right to be agitated.

He finally stopped and faced her. "I cannot believe that you led me to think you could be my personal assistant and let me continue to hand you more and more responsibility when you knew you wouldn't be around long." His indignation made him look like a petulant child.

"I do plan to be around. I wasn't going to keep it, but time got away from me, and now, no doctor in this or the surrounding states will perform the procedure."

He considered that for a moment. "And who is the father?"

"No one."

"Oh, so now you're the Virgin Mary?"

Suki sat as far away from him as possible, curled up in the corner of their white leather couch, Bent and Bae sprawled over her legs. She didn't look attentive, and Lucy wondered why she was even there. He didn't need her by his side just to give out termination orders, and her lack of concern or even interest was intriguing.

"I really don't know who the father is," Lucy lied. It was none of his business. "Could be a few candidates."

"Figures," Ian said. "Can you narrow down the ethnicity, at least?"

"What kind of question is that?" Lucy said, suddenly outraged.

"Black? Caucasian? Asian?"

She stood up. "I'll just leave. I'm not going to listen to your racist rants."

"Wait. Sit down. I have a reason for asking. An important one. But first, if you can't get the procedure, what are you planning to do?"

Lucy sighed. "I don't know. All I know is that I'm not mother material."

He smiled slightly. "I may have a solution if you'll hear me out."

"I'm listening."

He sat down in the armchair opposite her and leaned forward, hands on his knees. "If the baby is Caucasian, we can adopt it."

She almost didn't think she'd heard him right, but the look of anticipation and hope on his face told her she had.

"Adopt?" She looked from him to Suki. She didn't meet Lucy's eyes, so she turned back to Ian.

"Why do you need to adopt?" Instantly, she regretted the question. It was much too intrusive. "And why me? You could choose anyone to carry your child, and with your money and prestige, they'd be lining up."

"Anyone except Suki. She can't carry. Why you? Because we have a problem, and you have our solution."

Lucy looked at Suki. She still didn't look up.

"But wouldn't we have to get a lawyer and all sorts of legal stuff to do that?"

"We could do that, yes," he said. "But if you are open to it, I have a different opportunity to present to you. If we don't go to an agency, ours would be a private domestic adoption. In that case, we would pay the legal fees and your medical expenses. However, according to the law, we'd only be allowed to cover expenses for a period of two months before the birth and one month following. And no other personal expenses are allowed to be paid."

She was starting to see a glimmer of hope. Why hadn't she thought of adoption herself?

"That would be fine. I could still live here and work, right? Then I wouldn't have any other expenses."

His expression turned sad. "Well, I really couldn't have my assistant going with me on appointments and job sites while she's noticeably pregnant."

Lucy didn't see why not. Women did it all the time. But knowing Ian, she wasn't surprised. He had some strange beliefs. "But I could work remotely from here like I do now. I just wouldn't be able to accompany you to meetings."

He shook his head. "I just don't think that would work."

"Then why did you bring it up?" she asked, confused.

"Because I do have another way that we could both get what we want. First, I ask, is the child's father Caucasian?"

"Yes, he is," she said through gritted teeth. She despised bigots.

"Well, then, how does fifty thousand dollars sound to you? Payable in one lump sum, the day you give birth. You walk away and use the skills I've taught you to get another job in another place other than New York, and the child will never want for anything in its life. We keep this all between the three of us."

"Between the three of us? Why?"

"Because it's imperative that no one ever know it isn't Suki's child. Our family doesn't believe in adoption, and we would tell them the child is of our own blood."

That would work just fine for her too.

"No one will ever know? You can promise that?" She thought of what her sisters would think. Her father, even. It wouldn't be good. Anna would be ashamed of her for getting knocked up. Jo would despise her for not keeping the child. And Taylor would flip her lid if she knew Lucy had engaged in illegal activity. Her father, well... that couldn't be predicted, but she knew there would be something about it that he didn't approve of.

"Never. People do this all the time, without the burden of the courts to deal with. And you mustn't feel shame. You will be giving the child a gift—a gift of a promising future."

Lucy didn't speak.

It sounded too good to be true. She was sorry that she'd screwed up and gotten herself pregnant, but if she had to give birth, at least she could benefit from it while also doing a good thing.

Ian and Suki wanted a family.

She didn't.

But she did want a future of her own.

And fifty thousand dollars would be a hell of a start.

CHAPTER 9

*T*aylor had stopped at the Den to pick up dinner for her and her dad and was back in her cruiser and on the job before her break was up. She pulled out of the parking lot, right behind a tan Honda Accord. Once they'd gone a mile or so, she got close enough to see that that car didn't have a license plate. She turned on her light.

The driver went another half a mile or so then pulled to the side of the road.

Taylor parked behind it and put her cruiser in park and got out. When she approached the back of the car, she saw that there was an expired temporary tag in place, but it was obstructed by a tinted privacy plate cover and road grime.

She sidled up almost even with the driver's window and leaned down to peek inside. Regulations said an officer should never put their whole body at the window in case someone was armed and ready to shoot.

A young woman sat inside. She already had her license and registration out and handed them out the window. Taylor smelled marijuana.

"I'm Officer Gray with the Hart County Sheriff's department.

Turn off the ignition and put both hands on the wheel," Taylor instructed.

The woman complied while Taylor examined her license. *Darynda Jones. Twenty-two years old. Hart County resident.*

Taylor didn't know her, but there were so many new families moving to their town to get away from big-city life that she no longer knew everyone.

"It's illegal to obstruct or hinder the clear display and legibility of a license plate in the state of Georgia."

"I didn't know. I'm sorry," Miss Jones replied.

"Also, your paper tag is expired. Sit tight. I'll be right back."

She returned to her cruiser. When she ran the license, she saw that Jones had been arrested back in July for shoplifting. She climbed out and went back to the car.

"Miss Jones, I smell marijuana. Are there drugs in this car?"

There was a long pause, then Jones answered, "I just smoked a roach."

"Miss Jones, are there any more drugs in this car?"

"No, I swear."

They always swore. It meant nothing.

"Would you mind if I took a peek inside?"

Jones looked at her sideways, her attitude suddenly defiant. "Yes, I would mind. I'm late for work."

"Miss Jones, please step out of your vehicle."

"Why?"

Taylor remained as cool as a cucumber. "Because I asked you to. You've admitted to drug use, and I smell marijuana, and that gives me probable cause to search your car."

Jones slammed her hand on the steering wheel. "Damn it. I swear, you guys have it out for me. I'm trying to be good. I have a job now. I pay my bills. I just use to help take the edge off. It's not like I'm out here selling the stuff."

She was angry, but she complied and stepped out.

Taylor led her to the front of the car and spoke softly and

respectfully. "Put your hands flat on the hood and spread your legs. Don't move while I pat you down."

She quickly reassured herself that the woman wasn't carrying anything.

"Stay right there," she ordered. Then she went to the driver's side of the car.

It wasn't even a hard search. She opened the middle console to find a small makeup bag. When she unzipped it, she saw a small baggie holding a dozen or so white pills, a quarter bag of pot, and a digital scale. She got an evidence bag from her car and secured the items then returned to Jones.

"Turn around and put your hands behind your back. You're under arrest for drug abuse and drug paraphernalia. I could also cite you for expired plates, but we'll let that slide."

"Oh my God. No. Please—I've got kids at home. Please don't arrest me. It's just a little pot and Xanax."

"That's like saying you're just a little pregnant. You should've thought about your kids before you broke the law. Again." She pulled on one wrist, and Jones turned then gave her the other. Taylor put the handcuffs on. "You have the right to remain silent," she began then finished reading her rights.

She put her in the cruiser, and by then, Jones was crying and begging to use her phone.

"You get a call at the station if you cooperate and stop crying. I don't want to hear so much as a sniffle from the back seat." She really hated it when her perps ranted or cried all the way to be booked. Jones was already going to cost her at least an hour in paperwork, so the last thing she needed was to hear her whine for the next ten miles.

FOUR HOURS LATER, Taylor sat at her dad's kitchen table, picking at the pork chop on her plate, her thoughts on Adele and the nice meal they'd had in Winter Haven the week before. She hadn't dared tell her dad that she'd gone to see her. Not only did she not have the energy for arguing, but she was also still gathering all the information she could about Cate and the fire and didn't need his histrionics throwing her off course. She'd spent the last five days with her nose in court case notes, newspaper articles, and every little clue she could find online, and she was tired.

"Where's the ketchup?" he muttered.

She shrugged. Normally, she would have jumped up to get it for him, but there was nothing wrong with his legs. Adele was right: she had to stop babying him so much, or he'd never act like a responsible adult.

When he simply stared at her, she sighed and rose, went to the fridge, and brought back the ketchup. He didn't bother with a thank-you. Not for getting the ketchup or for cooking him a hot meal or even for the last two hours she'd worked to clean his bathroom, vacuum the living room, and catch up his laundry.

"You're welcome," Taylor said.

He grunted in reply.

Adele had been very grateful for Taylor buying her dinner as well as for the two peach mojitos she'd drunk, the alcohol softening her rough edges. When Taylor had stopped off at the Save-ALot discount store, her grandmother hadn't even resisted the shopping spree. Together, with the help of Sadie, a super-nice employee with a sense of humor that had had the three of them laughing through the aisles, they'd packed the buggy with fresh fruits and veggies and enough meat to fill the empty freezer on Adele's porch. And when Taylor got home, she got online and sent Adele a nice dog trimmer.

"Why didn't you let Cate's mother be a grandmother to us?"

There. She had not planned on bringing the woman up, but somehow, the question had exploded from between her traitorous lips.

He calmly set his fork down and looked at Taylor. "Where is this coming from? Have you talked to her?"

"Don't turn this around, Dad. You aren't going to deflect the question. Now that I know Cate didn't die, I want to know why we couldn't have had our grandmother in our lives to help when we were kids. The girls needed an adult mother figure, and she could've been there." She left out the part she'd really wanted to say: to keep them from being jerked around by social services.

"Well, I don't know, Taylor. Maybe because she was a horrible mother to Cate and would have been a worse grandmother to all of you? Or maybe because right after everything happened, she told me she wished I'd died in that fire instead of Robert? Or could it be that even if there was no fire and Robert was still alive, with your mother right here beside us, Battle Ax Adele would not be in your lives anyway, because she's a pretentious old hag and hated my guts from the very beginning? I suppose you can pick your own answer from all the above."

"I really doubt you ever gave her a true chance." Taylor picked up her full plate and dumped it into the trash. She'd lost her appetite. From under the table, Diesel watched her. He knew she was in a mood, and he wasn't getting involved.

Jackson slammed his fist on the countertop, and the dishes rattled in the drainer. "I've already told you. Your mother insisted that I was to take you girls and make a clean break from all friends and family. Start over. No attachments. I did exactly what she asked." He looked thunderous and enunciated every word of his last sentence carefully.

Taylor wasn't the least bit intimidated. She wasn't her mother. "Yep, you sure did. You did what Cate asked instead of doing the right thing."

Now he stood and faced her. "I wish you'd never gone through my mail, Taylor. Life was just fine, and now look what you've done. We can't even sit down and have a quiet meal together. You've ruined everything."

Taylor felt the anger hit her. She'd never really been mad at her dad before. She'd only pitied him and wanted to help him, thinking he was still distraught over the loss of his only son and his wife. A wife that he'd treated terribly and shouldn't even be pretending was his long-lost love. All of it rushed through her, and if she didn't say it now, she would explode.

"*I'VE* RUINED EVERYTHING?"

They stood face to face, both trembling with anger. Diesel came out from under the table and got between them, whining.

She had to get it out. It was burning a hole through her.

"Dad, you put all of us through hell with your drinking when we were kids. Your passing out drunk for days, letting us go hungry. Making us get jerked out of our home, put back in, jerked out again. Anna and Jo and even Lucy got the hell out as soon as they could, so they didn't have to deal with you anymore. But look who stayed."

He turned away, staring out the window.

"DAD! LOOK AT ME!"

When he faced her again, she felt the tears rolling down her face, and when she spoke this time, it was barely above a whisper. She was so tired of his ungratefulness.

"I've taken care of you my whole life, and the only thing I get in return is you constantly asking about Lucy, your *favorite* daughter. The daughter that's a runaway and a total screw-up. But since she's the baby, she's the only one you care about. Did you know she stole money from me the last time she was here?"

He looked as if he was about to slap her, and Taylor wished he would so that she could lay him out for once. He'd finally see exactly what the police academy had taught her.

"That's a damn lie," he said through gritted teeth. "Lucy might be a thief, but she ain't gonna steal from family. Why would you even say something like that?"

"Dad, she did. But speaking of money, you couldn't care less that I barely have money to pay my own bills, but I'm still trying to keep your electricity going or make sure you can still watch your stupid races while you lie back and continue to abuse your body and drink yourself to death. I still come over here and make sure you bathe. That you have clothes to wear, food to eat. I've busted my ass to keep you alive, Dad. When is it enough? When?"

She was mortified about losing control, but she couldn't stop now.

He looked taken aback now, astonished at the words rolling out of her mouth. "Stop this right now, Taylor. I'm not going to take this kind of talk from you. I'm still your father."

Taylor almost laughed at the absurdity of his reply. "Well, I'll tell you what, *Father*. When you are ready to start acting like it, give me a call. I'd love to finally have a parent in my life."

Then she walked out the door.

Her exit wasn't as dramatic as she'd have liked it to be because she forgot Diesel. Luckily, when she opened the door again, he was right there and scooted quietly out to join her.

With her heart pounding and her hands still shaking, Taylor opened her truck door and waited for him to jump in. Then she got in and shut the door. She leaned her head back and let out the breath she had been holding. Then she looked at Diesel. "Well, can you believe that just happened?"

His expression was one of disappointment.

"Yeah, I know. I lost my shit in there. Not good."

She started the truck and backed out of the driveway. She wasn't sure where to go. She was too upset to go to the Den, and she couldn't just pop in on Anna unannounced without Pete having a conniption fit.

She really didn't want to go home and be alone either.

So, she drove and let the tears fall where they wanted.

Guilt flooded through her. Everything she had said to her dad was true, but it still didn't make her feel good to know she had hurt another human being. She wasn't like a few of her sisters, who kept a hard shell tucked inside for when they needed to pull it out and use it. An ironic thing, considering her profession. Being a deputy was different, though. When she was in uniform, she was representing the law. It wasn't about her and her family, her struggles, her grievances. She was like a character in a play, with a script of laws that she enforced and a protocol for dealing with those who chose not to obey them. There wasn't any emotion to it. Or at least there wasn't supposed to be.

Without the uniform, she felt vulnerable. Naked, even. She didn't like the gutted feeling that letting her emotions out at her dad was making her feel now. She felt nauseated. And worried about him. What if she'd pushed him so hard, he did something crazy? Something irreversible.

"I am not giving in first." She turned to Diesel, who looked straight ahead out the front windshield and pretended not to hear. "I mean it. He's a grown man, and he's going to have to call and say he's sorry. He needs to learn he can't keep treating me so bad. I'm sick of it."

All her feelings had been exposed and raw since she'd visited Adele and learned about what kind of person Cate was. To hear her grandmother talk, Cate was some kind of damn saint. Or martyr.

Taylor knew that probably wasn't true, but the little girl inside her was hurt worse with the possibility that she'd lost more than she'd even thought by not having *that* mother in her life. Adele had dangled her in front of Taylor like a shiny new Christmas ornament. Something perfect and just out of reach for someone like her.

And Adele. Just spending one afternoon and an evening with her had showed Taylor that the woman could've been the positive influence and mother figure they'd needed so desperately when they were kids trying to heal from their own mother's death.

Her fake death.

It was a bit surreal that this was her life and that these things were even true.

She imagined herself telling Sheriff Dawkins any of it. He'd been a father figure to her, too, just like Chad, but this stuff was so out there that she couldn't possibly relay it to him. He'd think the whole family was stark raving mad. She'd never be promoted.

She eased off the gas when she realized she was speeding. It would have been just her luck to get caught by Kuno, and she was pretty sure he was on patrol. He'd give her a ticket, and that would be the cherry on top of the evening's full bowl of crap she'd been served.

"Not only did I insult my father, Diesel, but I threw Lucy under the bus," she muttered. Yes, Lucy was a runaway. She had run from every problem she'd ever had. That was her way of dealing. And she was also technically a screw-up. But that didn't give Taylor the right to trash her name, and she felt terrible for it. Lucy was a lost soul. Always had been, and it wasn't her fault. She was collateral damage from the crazy shit their parents had let happen.

Taylor drove by Rose Cottage and saw Rose through the window, sitting in front of the fire. She must not have any guests for the night, or she wouldn't be sitting around, relaxing. The woman was known for having the best accommodations in town.

Passing Rose Cottage made her think of Jessica and then Molly, because Jessica and her mother had stayed there until Rose had had to ask them to leave because of Sheila's inability to act like a grown-up. Taylor wondered how Molly was doing. It still made her feel sick when she thought of Joni's twisted body lying under the bridge and poor Molly living without the mother who had been so devoted to her. That was a case she'd never forget.

Taylor hoped that Joni's sister Jessica had found a way to keep Sheila, her toxic mother and Molly's grandmother, out of their lives so they could rebuild. According to the last conversation she'd had with Della Ray, that was exactly what Jessica was working toward.

Why is it that bad mothers have all the good luck, and then those like Cate end up dead or in prison for something they didn't do?

"What the hell?" Taylor realized what she'd just thought, and she pulled over, her hands shaking. She turned to Diesel. "We can't do this, boy. I'm letting my emotions overrule my logic. Just because I want Cate to be innocent doesn't make it so."

He stared back at her, concerned.

"You know what this means, right?"

No response.

"You're going to have to go stay with Cecil again, buddy. I'm going out west. And this time, I'll be gone more than a day or two."

CHAPTER 10

*I*t was already dark outside when her favorite doorman, Edward, held the door open, and Lucy stepped outside to find Jorge standing on the sidewalk, grinning from ear to ear. This time, he was dressed in a white ruffled shirt and tight black chinos, his hair slicked back in a sexy wave.

Behind him was a white horse-drawn carriage, the driver wearing a top hat and a deep-purple bow tie to match the interior of the carriage and the feathery plume his horse wore. He spread his arms in a grand flourish, stepping aside for her to get a good look at their transportation.

"What are you doing?" she asked.

"I told you our next date would be memorable. You said your boss had you too busy for an early date, so a night carriage ride around Central Park it is."

"Have you lost your mind? I'm not getting on that thing." She crossed her arms over her chest.

Jorge's mouth fell open, and he looked crestfallen. "Why not?"

"Young lady, might you reconsider?" Edward whispered from behind her. "The young man has obviously spent a pretty penny to impress you."

She whirled around. "Don't encourage him, Edward. I'm not riding."

Edward approached and looked down at her. "Oh, I see. You are afraid of horses. I can understand that. For they are very big and strong animals. However, I can promise you that those here in the city are the tamest you'll ever find. Take Lucky there. He's been doing this job now for many years and hasn't bolted, not once."

Lucy turned back to Jorge. "Couldn't we have had a normal date?"

"Not for you, *cariña*. You are special, so you deserve special."

That was not true, and Lucy knew it. She was Lucy Gray, a poor girl from Georgia. A thief. A runaway. And much more. But not the well-bred *Lucia Leighton* that came from a long line of artists that he thought she was.

To put it bluntly, she was a fraud. For once, she felt a bit guilty about it too.

"Please—for me," Jorge pleaded, giving her a puppy-eyed expression.

She looked back at Edward once more, and he nodded encouragingly.

"Fine, but if this horse so much as farts the wrong way," she mumbled, causing the driver to look away and pretend he'd heard nothing.

Jorge laughed loudly. "That's a sport. You will love it, I swear."

When she approached, the driver hopped down and took her hand then guided her up the step and into the carriage.

"Right over there, ma'am," he said, pointing at the seat facing frontward.

When Jorge climbed in behind her and kissed her cheek, the driver took out a soft purple blanket and urged them to scoot closer then spread it over their laps.

"I'm really not one to listen to tour guides," she said softly so the driver wouldn't hear.

"Good. That was why I told him we didn't need his assistance. He's staying up there to drive. I wanted you all to myself."

He got a bit closer until his thigh ran along the side of hers. She felt a shiver run from her toes to her nose. He'd done that to her before, too, and Lucy didn't like feeling so vulnerable. No other man had ever made her feel that way. Other than high school boyfriends, the men she'd been close to were of a different breed. Streetwise and tough, not worldly and creative.

Or was the difference simply that with Jorge, she was pretending to be someone she wasn't but had always wanted to be?

Nothing in her love life ever lasted long, so Lucy decided she was just going to enjoy it for the next few weeks then shut it down. She sure didn't need to leave any loose ends behind once the baby was born and she was more than a thousand miles away.

"We are starting in Central Park," the driver called out as he gave the horse the signal to go. "If you've any questions, just ask away. I'll point some things out as we go."

"Thank you, Mario," Jorge said.

Lucy raised her eyebrows. "Mario?"

"Yes," Jorge laughed. "And his horse is Lucky."

"There's a story to that if you all get bored with each other's conversation," Mario called out, and they all laughed.

The park was well lit, and Lucky moved along at a steady pace as she and Jorge talked, dipping in and out of normal second-date conversation like favorite music, favorite movies, and stuff they did in their spare time. Mario pointed out places where movies or television shows had been filmed. He was very friendly and funny, too, and Lucy couldn't believe how much she was enjoying herself. She barely paid any attention to the horse and now felt silly for having been so frightened of it. Her sister Jo, the horse fanatic in the family, would have been proud of her.

They stopped to take in the beauty of Rockefeller Center all lit up, and Jorge pulled out a cooler with wine and fluted glasses.

"I'm not drinking," Lucy began to say, but Jorge held the bottle up to proclaim it was a non-alcoholic kind.

She smiled at how thoughtful he was, and like a magician pulling a rabbit from a hat, he presented her with a small box of decadent chocolate brownies from a nearby bakery.

They dug into them like two children, squabbling over the very last crumbs and laughing when Mario feigned being insulted that they'd forgotten to save one for him.

"You can stretch your legs here, and I'll take a photo," he said, pulling up to the fountain at Cherry Hill. He offered to take photos using both Jorge's phone and hers, but Lucy declined to hand hers over.

"Jorge can send them to me." She climbed back in to get under the blanket in the sudden coolness of the night.

"We have to return in the spring when the cherry trees are blooming," Jorge said, joining her on the seat. "I've heard it's truly a sight to behold."

They moved along, and when he began to ask her about her family, Lucy turned the conversation back to him, asking him about his favorite foods.

"Well, in Uruguay, our national sandwich is the *chivito*."

"What is that?"

"It's so good. They are as popular as the Big Mac is here."

Lucy wrinkled her nose. "Sorry to ruin your analogy, but I don't like McDonald's."

"Well, you know what I mean. Our chivito is the go-to popular lunch item in Uruguay. You take a bun and slather it thickly with mayonnaise. Then you layer thin slices of tenderly cooked beefsteak, mozzarella, ham, tomatoes, and olives. I like bacon and sliced hard-boiled eggs on mine too. And we eat it with French-fried potatoes, like they do Big Macs."

"French fries," Lucy said, smiling back at him not because of his words but because of the accent in which he said them. It was beyond endearing.

"Yes. That's what I said!"

"Well, it sounds like our Subway sandwich."

"Sandwich in the subway?"

Lucy laughed. "Never mind. Your charader sounds delicious."

Later, Mario urged them to get out again at the tunnel under the park and took a video of them climbing the steps when Jorge took her hand.

"This is the famous Bow Bridge," Jorge said as the carriage began to roll across a long, Victorian-style bridge.

"Yes, built in 1862," Mario called out. "It spans sixty feet and is said to be the most romantic spot in the park. Many women have been proposed to on this bridge. Let me know if I need to stop and let you two out for a few moments."

Jorge squeezed Lucy's hand under the blanket, but she didn't squeeze back. The talk of proposals made her uncomfortable. While most women her age would already be deciding on what cut of diamond they wanted and planning a wedding in their heads, she wasn't. Jorge was genuinely a good person. And he didn't deserve to be deceived.

She withdrew her hand from his and rested it atop the blanket. "It's getting toasty under there."

"Oh, I'm sorry."

"Jorge, I really need to get back. I have a conference call shortly and need to get set up."

"I thought we'd stop off somewhere after the ride and get a late bite to eat," he said.

"No, I can't. We need to turn back now."

Jorge was quiet for a moment. Then he instructed Mario to get them back to the Dakota.

"I'm sorry I didn't ask you what time you needed to be back," Jorge said once they were underway. "So very rude of me not to consider your time is valuable. As well as you may not be feeling your best."

"Feeling my best?"

"With your—well, you know," he stammered, looking down at where her stomach was covered by the blanket.

She suddenly felt sick. How could she have forgotten even for a moment? "Oh. No, I'm fine."

"*Cariña,* I hope this is not too forward, but I wanted to ask, is the father still in the picture?"

He obviously meant the baby's father, but the question made her freeze with anxiety. That was another thing she wanted to forget. Anything and everything that had to do with the man who'd planted his seed in her.

"He is not," she finally said.

"Is there a reason you are so uncomfortable talking about your condition?" Jorge asked. "I would like to be sensitive to your needs, but I want to understand."

"I'm not going to be a mother. I'll be terminating the pregnancy next week."

Better to go ahead and rip the Band-Aid off now so he'd stop asking.

He looked shocked. More shocked than she'd even thought he would.

"But why? Giving birth is a gift—all children are a gift. Or at least in my country, they are. What am I missing?"

She felt the coldness run through her.

"You are missing nothing, Jorge. Except the fact that here in the United States, an unwed mother is subject to contempt and ridicule and a fight for survival in the awkward status that is the total opposite of the American dream. Two parents and a six-figure income to pay for a big house surrounded by a white picket fence is the goal, and I'm not meeting it."

He looked confused. "But I thought America was so understanding and modern."

"Depends on who you are. And for the record, I never want to talk about my pregnancy again." She turned her body toward the other direction, away from him.

They didn't talk for the rest of the ride back to the Dakota.

CHAPTER 11

The Montana morning sky was beyond beautiful with streaks of gold and crimson, the rays of sunlight bursting through to warm the mountain peaks. Taylor was awestruck by the scenery outside her rental car window as she drove. She could see trails in the far-away distance, winding along the rimrocks of sandstone cliffs, and thought of Diesel and how he'd have loved to explore them. He hadn't acted too badly put off when she'd handed him over in the Den's parking lot the day before. He probably loved the long walks that Cecil took him on as part of his own daily regimen. Taylor hadn't had him out too much lately because she'd gone back to work, and when she was home, she was busy looking through more of the trial documents from Cate's conviction.

However, he had been an excellent snuggle partner at night when she couldn't take reading any more about the case.

It had taken six weeks to finally be approved to visit Cate. Taylor had completed an application and sent it in with her proof of residency in Georgia, along with a copy of her driver's license, then waited to be tentatively approved. It was supposed to take another few weeks for final confirmation, but Adele had built something of a relationship with the warden over the years and had made a call. Once her criminal background check was approved, they'd made their appointment. She could've done a video call with Cate, but Taylor wanted to see her eyes in person when she asked her the questions she'd planned.

The sheriff hadn't been thrilled with her request for time off after just returning to work, but she told him it was a very serious family matter, and knowing she rarely ever asked for time off or used family excuses to get it, he'd granted it.

Taylor still hadn't spoken to Shane since the whole situation, and the few times they'd passed in the hallway or stood within spitting distance for morning briefing, it had been awkward. She felt betrayed, but she could tell from the way he tried to pretend her silence didn't bother him that he didn't think it was as serious as it was. The worst part about it was that she missed the camaraderie they'd built up.

Why was it when she finally let her guard down, a man always had to screw it up?

Taylor and Adele had flown in from Atlanta the day before, with a layover in Denver, then into Billings International, where they got a car and went straight to the hotel, both too tired to stop somewhere for dinner. They'd camped out on the beds with bottles of Snapple and tubes of Ritz crackers they bought downstairs in the small hotel store. They were asleep by nine—or at least Adele was.

It took Taylor a bit longer to try to ignore the snoring from the next bed.

Adele had hung in there without complaint, though, and had turned into a decent travel partner. Taylor had put their flights on her own credit card, and it made her nervous that she was accumulating debt, but it couldn't be helped. She could've gone alone, but having Adele with her felt like the right thing to do, and it was worth the extra cost.

She and Adele had sat next to each other on both legs of the trip, but luckily, they were both lost in thought, so conversation was limited. Adele obviously respected that this was an excruciatingly hard endeavor for Taylor, and she seemed dedicated to doing what she could to help make it less so.

"Have you told your sisters yet?" Adele asked.

"No. Not until I make my own decision about Cate's guilt. After I talk to her and the lawyer, I'll feel more comfortable in knowing when the right time is. They'll all ask me if I think she's guilty before allowing her into their lives, and I don't know yet."

"They should ask me," Adele said under her breath.

So far, they knew nothing about her either. Adele was leaving it up to Taylor to decide if and when to connect them.

There was a lot to do before that was even a possibility.

Adele had made them an appointment with Cate's final attorney, and Taylor hoped he had some useful information that she couldn't find online.

"But by keeping it from your sisters about your mom, aren't you doing the same thing to them that your father did to you?"

"I don't want to talk about it."

So much for her grandmother making things easier.

Taylor's dad was on the opposite side of the fence. He thought things should remain like they were for Cate's sake. Taylor was barely speaking to him, but she had dropped off some groceries before she left town. She didn't want him to starve. He hadn't apologized after their argument, and she had just let it go. She didn't need any more drama on her plate. She assumed he was thankful that she hadn't yet told her sisters anything about the Cate discovery, because they were in something of a silent truce.

"Fine. So does the landscape look familiar?" Adele asked.

"No. Feels like I'm seeing Montana for the first time." She supposed most of her memories of their home state were locked away because of the related trauma.

Cooke City, the town they'd lived in and where the fire had burned their home down, was only about eighty miles to the southwest, but she doubted she'd want to go there. It was best to keep those snapshots out of her head as much as possible.

"I'm not even going to ask you if you're nervous," Adele said. "I remember the first time I came here and saw Clair dressed in the prison uniform and looking pale and afraid. I was so nervous, and all I wanted to do was grab her and run out of there. But I know this: you'll be okay. You are stronger than I ever was."

"I doubt that."

"Oh yes, you are. You're more like your mother than you want to admit. She knows she's innocent, but she does her time with integrity and grace. It takes courage not to roll up into a ball and give up on life from behind those walls. She's making the most of what's been handed to her, just like you've done with your own life."

"I work the jail a lot back home. I'm used to dealing with prisoners."

"This prison isn't like jail, Taylor. I'm sure it's also a lot harder when you see a family member behind bars than when you are dealing with a stranger."

Taylor didn't answer. Her mouth felt dry, and she was starting to get a headache. She flipped on the radio and turned it to the news, hoping it would occupy her mind. She knew the rules for prison visits. Visitors and inmates could not visit the vending machines together. No physical contact other than one front-to-front embrace at the beginning and end of the visit, which she wouldn't be partaking in.

"Did I tell you she had a job?" Adele asked.

"No. I looked it up, though, and I see they can work with textiles. Designing, embroidery, and printing—something like that."

"She doesn't do any of that stuff. She earned her master gardener certification a few years ago and oversaw a prison greenhouse for a long time. But now, she's in the dog program."

"Dog program?"

"Yes, she helps train dogs. Keeps them a month at a time then turns them over to be adopted. Or in the case of those coming from a family already, same thing. Four weeks of training to help with behavior and then back to their home. Prison Paws or something like that."

"That's a good way to stay busy, but I'm sure it's not easy."

Taylor thought about Diesel and how hard it would be if she had to give him up. She couldn't imagine doing it dog after dog after coming to feel something for every one of them.

"Cate has earned a lot of respect in there from both her fellow inmates and the staff. I think a lot of them know she's innocent."

"And I think you see what you want to see, Adele."

They rode the rest of the way in silence, and when they pulled into the prison parking lot, Taylor did everything she could to hide the shaking of her hands as she put the car in park and turned it off. She'd bought a small clear pouch purse for the visit, and she grabbed it, took a deep breath, and climbed out.

She felt as if she were going to a funeral as they walked toward the building.

It took them an hour to get through the checkpoints. People were already lined up and waiting when they got to the door, eager to get in every minute of the two-hour visiting time with their loved ones. One young woman was turned away as a guard did a preliminary walk down the line.

"Do you think you're a gymnast or what?" she asked the woman. "You've been here enough to know that leggings aren't allowed."

"These aren't leggings," the woman stated. "They're just pants, and I'm covered."

The officer stood back and addressed everyone in a bored voice. "No yoga pants, no leggings, no sleeveless tops, no open toes, and no underwire bras, people. This isn't a democracy, and if you didn't check the guidelines before coming, that's on you.

Leave and go to Walmart, come back in approved attire, or return next week."

Three people dropped out and headed back to their cars, including the woman in yoga pants. Adele had already given Taylor the lowdown before the trip, and she didn't wear leggings or yoga pants anyway. She preferred people didn't see the complete outline and every inch of her back end. She was more comfortable in her deputy's uniform than in anything she could buy, and for a second, she thought about how Cate would react if she showed up in it.

Jeans and a long-sleeved shirt were what she chose. She'd almost dabbed on a bit of makeup that morning, a small part of wanting Cate to think she was pretty, but she decided that was juvenile and didn't even do the usual mascara. Adele, on the other hand, was looking brighter and healthier than she had in Florida when Taylor had met her. She'd taken the time to apply a light layer of makeup, complete with lipstick and mascara. She wore a simple pale-blue pantsuit and sensible white canvas sneakers, looking every part the doting grandmother she had never gotten to be.

They were let in and soon went through a walk-through screening. A few people, including Adele, were picked out for a pat-down search. Her grandmother was unfazed and kept her words polite to the guard, as did most of them because they were afraid to lose their visiting time.

"Is this more than fifteen dollars?" the guard going through Adele's purse asked, holding up a baggie of quarters.

"Nope. Fifteen on the mark," she answered.

The guard nodded and dropped it back into the purse, shuffled through the rest of it, then handed it back to Adele. It only took a minute to do Taylor's. All she carried was her identification in her wallet and some lip balm.

After their hands were stamped with UV ink and Adele put her purse in a locker, they were led into the visitation room and told to take a seat at one of the flimsy plastic tables. Taylor had expected to visit through glass, but that wasn't the case. It was a small room with a line of windows overlooking a grassy area that held a few picnic tables. Inside the room, it was dingy, with a dozen or so tables and an alcove in which a few vending machines sat. One of the snack machines was completely empty. The deputy part of her felt no pity for the convicted felons who wouldn't be getting as many snacks as they'd like, but a part of her hoped that Adele got to the other machine before it was wiped out too.

The other people filed in around them and quickly claimed tables, first near the window and then fanning out all over the room. Once their table was secured and Taylor sat down, Adele went to the vending machine and started loading it with quarters and pushing buttons. She gathered the food up in the tail of her shirt after each snack hit the drawer then went to the drink machine and bought four Cokes.

"Four?" Taylor asked when she set them down.

"Two are for Cate. All the snacks are for her." The food was a variety of potato chips, candy bars, and one honey bun.

"That's a lot of sugar." Taylor raised her eyebrows as she mentally calculated the grams.

"She probably hasn't had any of this stuff in over a year at least."

When a buzzer went off and a door on the farthest wall opened, there was a rush of noise, and the room filled with emotion at a level so high it felt deafening. Inmates rushed in and found familiar faces.

Taylor leaned forward, resting on her forearms so she could feel the cool plastic beneath them. She felt frozen in place. She didn't even know what Cate looked like anymore.

Adele reached over and put her hand on Taylor's arm and squeezed. "It'll be fine," she whispered.

A few more guards mingled among the inmates, and one greeted Adele. She waved back but kept her eyes on the door.

She shouldn't have worried, because as soon as Taylor saw a woman who had her exact eyes and mouth, she knew it was Cate. The face brought a kaleidoscope of memories flying into Taylor's head. Memories she'd fought long and hard to repress. Memories that told her that the woman who stood there in the prison uniform of a maroon shirt and khaki pants was indeed Cate.

It was surreal. For so many years, she had grieved her late mom, and now, here she was, back from the dead.

Adele let go of Taylor's arm, stood, and went to Cate. They held each other for a long minute, and Adele kissed her cheek before letting her go.

Taylor remained seated. She didn't trust herself to even move. Cate must not see how affected she was by this visit. By knowing she was not dead. Taylor felt many emotions, but the one on top was anger.

Anger because of the loss she had felt back then and the confusion she was feeling now. Anger because of the loss her little sisters had dealt with, leaving Taylor to mother them in any way she, a child herself, could figure out.

When the guard put a hand between them, they separated, and Cate followed Adele to the table. She had known Taylor was coming—she'd had to approve her to be on the visitors' list.

Cate was tall, like her mother. Taller than Taylor imagined her being from her childhood memories. Her hair was long, straight, and gray, pulled into a ponytail that rested down the middle of her back. She appeared to be wearing a bit of makeup on her eyes and cheeks. It was common for prisoners to create makeup using food, greeting cards, and even newspaper, but for some reason, she couldn't see Cate going to that trouble. But how often did one meet her adult daughter for the first time since she was a child?

"Hello, Taylor," Cate said softly, settling into the chair opposite her.

"Hello." *Hello, Cate? Hello, Mother? Mom?*

It all felt weird. Simply "hello" would have to be enough.

"I'm so glad you two could come together," Adele said, closing the long pause after Taylor's words.

"Too bad it wasn't twenty-some-odd years ago," Taylor said.

Cate visibly flinched. "I know you're angry about my decision not to be in your lives, but I felt it was the best way to give you a normal childhood."

"Well, that didn't work out," Taylor said. "I'm guessing that Dad didn't tell you much."

"I didn't want him to write. It was hard for me, too, Taylor."

They stared at each other for a moment. Taylor noticed the burn scars on her mother's forearms and her right hand. There were some on her neck too.

"You look great," Cate said. "I'm proud of you for being in law enforcement. That's a huge goal to reach, and you did it. So, do you have someone special in your life? I know you're not married, but is anything on the radar? Someone to help you get through the hard parts of life?"

"No. There's no one. I'm not looking for a hero. I saved myself a long time ago."

Cate acted as if she didn't know what to say to that. "Okay—well, I'd love to hear about how Bronwyn and Teague are doing."

Hearing Cate say the names of the grandchildren she'd never met felt strange and wrong. That was Taylor's life, not hers.

"I told her what I saw on Facebook," Adele said. "I know that's only the highlights of their life and not the nitty-gritty. I made her a few photos to keep."

Taylor imagined Cate's cell wall with snapshots pasted to it. She wondered if her own face was there, but she'd never ask. "They're good kids. I don't see them much because of my hours.

My schedule gets changed a lot, since we have such a small pool of officers."

"I haven't seen her in her uniform yet," Adele said. "I'm sure she looks smart."

"Not really. Our uniforms could use an upgrade. I'm sure we're wearing what Barney Fife wore in the fifties."

Adele chuckled.

"I'm really not surprised you ended up in law enforcement," Cate said.

"Oh? Why?" Taylor asked.

She smiled. "You were always the most inquisitive one out of you girls. When I'd try to find out which one of you had gotten into trouble, you were first with the questioning and gathering evidence. I was pretty sure this day would come, and you'd finally realize I was here."

"Let's get to that, then. Why did you set that fire?" Taylor said.

Cate's expression was resolute, and her eye contact didn't waver when she answered. "I didn't set that fire, Taylor. I didn't set the fire, and I didn't kill Robert."

Taylor waited.

"I didn't," Cate said again.

"I guess we'll see. We have a meeting with your attorney after this."

Cate leaned back in her chair and crossed her arms. "Why? It's fruitless because there's nothing more that can be done. I'm here for life. I can't go through the rejections again, and I don't want Mom suffering through it either."

"Oh, no, I'm not talking to him about your freedom. That's over and done with. I want to know everything he knows so I can make my own determination of your guilt or innocence."

"Taylor," Adele warned softly. "Take it easy."

Cate nodded slowly. "That's fair. Perception is reality, and unfortunately, the truth is you're guilty until proven innocent. Even then, people will believe what they want. You can ask me anything you want about evidence. But I won't repeat the sequence of that day. I won't relive it again after doing so over and over in court and the eyes of public opinion. I don't have to ever put myself through that again, and I won't."

"The state arson investigator concluded that a liquid accelerant was used to start the fire in two separate locations."

"Yes, I know what he testified to," Cate said. "The supposed accelerant was from a kerosene heater. Your dad often brought in a container and filled it in the house. He could've dripped it along the floor at one time or another, but there was no accelerant in the hall at the bedroom door. I promise you that."

"So he committed perjury? Planted evidence? Why? Why would he want to frame you that way? He took floor samples from both areas."

"I don't know. You'd have to ask him."

"His testimony was corroborated by a forensic analyst with ATF."

Cate nodded. "I know. That was a big problem. But my team hired an independent arson investigator, and he testified that there was a probability the fire was accidental. But with those two against him, his expertise wasn't considered as strong as theirs together."

"Two years in, we took it to the Montana Supreme Court, and they affirmed the conviction based on the heavy petroleum distillate being in two different areas," Adele said.

"The supreme court takes their cases very seriously," Taylor said. "In my opinion, they rarely make the wrong decision."

"You're in law enforcement, so I'd expect you to think nothing less," Adele said. She reached across the table and took Cate's hand and squeezed. "But she's innocent. I don't give a damn what they decided."

"They did at least vacate the arson on grounds of double jeopardy," Taylor said. "You have that."

Cate shrugged. "I didn't consider it a win. A win would be if they acknowledged that it was an accident and that I didn't cause Robert's death."

Taylor looked around the room, taking in the many scenes of family and friends connecting with their imprisoned loved ones. There were a lot of tears on faces, and feelings were on display. Joy, shame, anger—they were all there, making the air thick with emotion and a sense of desperation. People were trying to squeeze an impossible amount of catching up into two short hours.

A lot of the inmates were in their twenties or thirties, with what appeared to be their mothers and a few fathers visiting. There were very few other inmates in Cate's age bracket or older, and they were much less animated, visiting with one another quietly or making no conversation at all. As though their zest and hope for life were gone.

"I'd wager that everyone in here thinks their loved one is innocent, Adele," Taylor said. "The prison is full of so-called innocent inmates. I doubt many of them are owning up to their guilt."

Adele frowned at her, making furrows in her brow that showed her disappointment, and that cut a bit, but Taylor wasn't there to proclaim Cate was innocent and should be free. She was there for the truth. She had no plans on letting a murderer back into her life or those of her sisters. They'd been through enough for one lifetime.

Today was simply a test to see if she'd walk away from Cate forever and go back to considering her dead or if there might be more to explore.

"Tell me about Robert," she said, taking a different tack.

A small smile crept slowly onto Cate's face, and she glanced at Adele, who nodded encouragingly back.

"It took a long time after the fire before I could say his name. Robert was my baby," Cate said. "I'm sure this isn't a new revelation to you, but your dad was always most enamored with Lucy. I thought that a son would take her place as favorite, but that didn't happen. I mean, your dad loved him, but Robert was a mama's boy from the very beginning."

"So he was sensitive?" Taylor didn't remember much at all about her brother and had always been curious.

"Yes, I guess you could say that. But he still loved all the things little boys did. He liked to play in the woods around the house, and he loved his superhero figures. He could entertain himself for hours, concocting imaginary battles between them, and he was so good at making his own sound effects that sometimes, I thought a cartoon was playing in his room. He had a very vivid imagination."

A small light flickered in her eyes when she spoke about Robert. Taylor could see the longing and the sadness. She wanted so badly to ask about that day. What the sequence of events had been. Why Cate and Robert hadn't been together if he was sick and how hard Cate had tried to save him.

She'd planned to ask all of that and more, but now, she could see that it would be cruel. Those details were in the court documents that she could get later if she really needed them.

"I think that's enough case talk for today," Adele said. "Cate, tell us about this dog program you're in."

Taylor wanted to defy her grandmother and ask more, but if she'd learned anything in the police academy and during her time as a rookie, it was respect for authority and elders. She couldn't bring herself to be disrespectful to Adele.

Cate talked about earning her grooming license after six hundred hours of training and how she switched off between training the dogs and grooming in different months just to help keep the monotony at bay.

"My last dog was named Nibblets, and ironically, he got the name before he turned out to have a problem with mouthing."

"What's mouthing?" Adele said.

"It's one of the behaviors we work to correct in some dogs.

They want to play bite, which people encourage because they think it's cute when they're puppies. Then as they get older and their teeth get bigger, it's not so adorable any longer. Then it's harder to get them to stop. Other behaviors we train out of them are barking, jumping up for attention, and being reactive to other dogs. Or we have the simple basic manners class of just stuff like 'sit,' 'down,' 'stay,' and those easy commands, usually for puppies brought in."

"I wish I could bring Prancer for some training. She could sure use it," Adele said, laughing.

"You could if you lived closer," Cate said. "We offer leash training and a few other things too."

"Oh, we're both too old for new tricks. And you know I wish I could afford to move closer. That and if my bones could stand the cold Montana winters."

"You get used to it," Cate said.

It didn't feel as if it was her mother sitting there talking. It could've been anyone. A stranger. Taylor thought it strange how one could outgrow what they'd once thought they could never live without. Once upon a time, she'd been desperate to have her mother back, and now, it didn't feel real. Or necessary.

"Don't you get attached?" Taylor said, finally breaking into the conversation. She looked at the clock and was surprised to see they'd already used up more than half their visiting time. She wanted Cate to keep talking. It made it easier to get a feel for who she was.

Cate seemed taken off guard but pleased that Taylor was interested. "Well, the program is only four weeks, and unlike other prisons' dog-training programs, these pups already have a family. So it's different. I think for most of us, it's a chance to feel like we are getting to do something we might just do on the outside, so it's worth any discomfort we might feel when they graduate. The work helps us feel a bit normal for a few hours a day."

"I read about it in the research I did on the prison before we came," Taylor said. "I also saw they had good programs here for mothers trying to maintain a relationship with their children on the outside."

Adele narrowed her eyes at Taylor, knowing where she was going with the conversation.

"Yes, that's true," Cate said. She looked defeated. "The warden here now is probably the best they've ever had in terms of providing for the women's needs. We have a big American Indian population, and she has helped them to keep connections to their tribes by allowing them to continue their traditions of drum groups and sweat lodges. Some are even approved to receive medicine bags with cultural items."

"Let's go back to the programs for children," Taylor said. "I read that once a month, the mothers get to spend time with their children in a home-like environment set up with toys and furniture, things to make the visit feel more normal and less scary."

Cate stared at her.

Taylor stared back.

"I wish you'd come out and say what's on your mind before our time is cut short," Cate finally said. "Out of all of you, I would think you'd not beat around the bush."

"Okay. Maybe that's a good idea to stop playing nicety nice. Here's what I'm really thinking, *Cate*. It doesn't look very good for your plea of innocence that you lost one child in a fire then basically threw away the other four when you didn't have to."

Adele gasped then put her hand over her mouth.

"Oh, Taylor," she said. "Why did you have to—?"

Cate held her hand up, stopping her mother in mid-sentence. "No, Mom. It's fine. I'm okay, but I think this visit has run its course." She stood and didn't wait for Adele's goodbye embrace but simply walked back to the door leading into the prison.

She said something to the guard, and he opened the door.

Without a backward glance, she was gone.

CHAPTER 12

*L*ucy shut the computer and stared at Ian across the kitchen island. He was easily the most irritating human being in the entire world, and if she could have, she would have taken the bagel sitting untouched in front of her and stuffed it into his mouth to shut him up.

"You said you had a favorite piece," he said. "If you can't get him to let me see it, I want you to offer him fifteen hundred dollars for it. It's a small price to pay if he's as talented as I think, and that's a nice price for first works for sale. You can tell he's broke, so he should jump on the offer."

"Just because he's not as rich as you doesn't mean he's broke. Stop being a jerk."

Even if Lucy had had the ability to thwart Jorge's advances—which she did not because he was just too insistent and very convincing—it wouldn't have been possible to keep him out of her life. On their last date, she'd planned not to see him again, but Ian was insistent that she needed to reel Jorge in as a client, and he wasn't taking no for an answer.

"Don't you have other new artists you can swoop in on and

button down?" she asked. "He doesn't seem to want to work with you."

"That's ludicrous. Have you told him about some of my other clients? Some of the prices I've negotiated?"

She nodded emphatically. "I sure have. And he already knew about each and every one. He's done his own research, Ian. I don't know why he's not interested."

Ian narrowed his eyes at her. "Have you said something bad about me? Did you ruin my chances with him, Lucia?"

She sighed and looked at the ceiling. "No, Ian. I've only tried to sell you to him. He simply says he's not ready yet, and I think you need to respect that, or you are going to push him away forever."

"But if I don't get him signed before you go away, he may never sign," Ian said.

She shrugged. "I don't know what to tell you. But I do know that your latest dog nanny quit, and I need to go take Bae and Bent for a walk."

"Don't call them that. Suki doesn't like nicknames," he said, crossing his arms, a thunderous expression on his face. "When do you see Jorge next?"

"I'm not really sure," Lucy lied. "Maybe the weekend. He's been busy."

Truth was, they were meeting again that evening, but she didn't want an inquisition from Ian when she returned home. Their last date, only days before, had been a fun whirlwind during which they'd wandered up to the Metropolitan Museum and admired art then popped in and out of all sorts of small stores, trying on everything from silly hats to six-figure jewelry, helped along by her mention of working for Ian Banfield. It hadn't hurt that she'd chosen a Suki-inspired linen outfit, paired with expensive shoes and just the right touch of makeup. She'd looked as if she could afford to look. They'd ended the evening at his apartment again, and though Lucy had been feeling frisky and would've let him, he had done nothing but kiss her. She'd come home sexually frustrated and self-conscious that her small, rounded belly made her unattractive.

"Set up a date and let me know when it is. I'm serious about the offer. Fifteen hundred for the piece you told me about. Sight unseen. Make it in person and not on the phone.

"When you get back from walking the dogs, I need you to set up a flight for me to Montreal. Dates are on my desk pad. I have a customer there I'm going to show a piece to." He stomped out of the room, and as soon as his back was turned, Lucy gave him the finger.

Carmen saw it as she walked in and chuckled. "You can lose your job over that."

"I doubt that."

Carmen wouldn't tell. Lucy had slowly won her over, and though they never said it aloud, neither of them could stand Ian. So far, Carmen didn't know about her deal with the Banfields, and it was supposed to stay that way. Lucy felt a bit guilty that she was going to simply disappear, and Carmen would never know what happened to her, but it had to be this way.

As for Ian, he thought he could dictate her personal life as well as her work life, and that just wasn't going to happen. Lucy was already dreaming of the day that she could pocket her money and leave the Banfields in the dust. His pretentiousness was nauseating. She hoped he was going to spend more than a few days in Montreal.

Carmen crossed through and left her alone, and Lucy picked up her phone and began swiping through the photos again. Jorge had sent her all the ones taken on their first date, along with a barrage of text messages to get her to start talking to him again. She hadn't really been tough at all, because she'd had to admit that his affection was flattering. She never remembered someone treating her as though she were so special.

The only thing that kept bugging her about it was that it was really Lucia getting the attention, not Lucy. He wasn't courting the homeless girl from the South. The girl who'd been in jail and had couch-surfed for most of her adult life. No, he thought she was an impressive young woman with an impressive background. One day soon, it would be over, but until then, she was enjoying the parts that involved Jorge.

"C'mon, little minions," she said to the dogs at her feet as she slid off the barstool. She took them to their room and put their harnesses on over their couture shirts, which looked bedazzled with rhinestones, then grabbed the leashes and went out the door. They used the service stairs and were outside and crossing the street within three minutes.

She was glad to have the chance to walk the dogs, a simple task that required nothing but safeguarding Suki's most treasured little beings. The park was teeming with activities and people, spilling good vibes all around her as they enjoyed nature and freedom from the other parts of their lives for just a slice of the day.

Ian was expecting her to get right back, but Lucy was feeling rebellious. The dogs needed more than just a few minutes of activity—or at least that was what she'd tell him when she got back. Today, she wanted to feel free, and she dreaded returning and being tied to her laptop and Ian's constant demands for the rest of the day.

Bent and Bae were thrilled when she didn't turn them around in their usual place. She could see their chubby bodies quivering with excitement as they continued. She missed the dogs, and though she was making good money now with her new job, being a dog walker suited her better. Since the day she'd met them, the two had gone through at least four or five new nannies. It wasn't their fault, she was fairly sure.

When they got to Sheep Meadow, Lucy found a shade tree to sit under, and the two settled around her, happy for a break to catch their breath. They were both panting and looked ready to flop over and give their last grunts.

"You're both too lazy, Lucy said. She crossed her legs, and Bae crawled onto her lap. Together, they people-watched the kids that ran wild, kicking soccer balls, while others threw Frisbees to one another. Around her, couples and friends were spread out on blankets or picnic cloths, all smiles and laughter. Others lay back and read books or stared at the sky.

Over her head, the shadow of New York's tallest buildings loomed, and Lucy smiled in appreciation. If nothing else, she'd achieved her dream of visiting the most famous city in the United States and especially the Dakota building. Who would've thought that she'd be living in it? She had a moment of longing for her family and the chance to tell them all about her life right now.

She reached down and laid a tentative hand on her stomach.

No, that wouldn't do. Not at all.

They must never know about her time in the Big Apple or her connection to the Banfields. Not if she and her employers were going to pull this off the way they wanted, with no one ever the wiser that the child wasn't theirs.

A commotion over to her left snagged Lucy's attention. An older woman was arguing with a younger man, who held the hand of a child. He was yelling back, and people had started to gather.

The woman wore a black-and-gold scarf and looked a bit worse for wear. The man and girl were obviously from a different tax bracket.

"Oh, shit. That's Armina," Lucy said. She jumped up and, dragging the dogs along, went to the small circle of onlookers.

"She found that doll on the bench, you crazy old woman," the man screamed.

"It's not a doll. It's my baby," Armina cried. "I laid her there so

I could look through the bin where I think I lost my watch." She tried to pull the doll out of the girl's arms.

"Daddy, isn't it finders keepers?" the little girl asked. She clutched the doll tightly.

Lucy could bet the trash bin didn't have a watch, and neither did Armina. She'd been looking for scraps. Clumsily, clutching the leashes and dragging Bae and Bent along with her, she elbowed her way through the people to get to Armina.

"No, it's not finders keepers, and I bet you have a hundred dolls at home," Lucy said. She yanked the doll out of the girl's arms and handed it to Armina, who immediately held it to her chest and sobbed with relief.

The man's expression turned from irritated to enraged. "Who the hell are you?" he demanded.

"I'm her social worker. Sorry, but that really is her doll, and, sir, you can see that she's very attached. Please, just let this go," Lucy said, keeping one eye on Armina, who had started to walk away.

"Bunch of crazy kooks," the man said. Then he turned his daughter around. "Honey, let's go buy you a new doll. You can choose one with strawberry hair like yours."

Someone else from the crowd commented that the city needed to clean up the park and ship the homeless crazies off to Hawaii, but a woman shut him down, telling him to have a little compassion. The crowd began to break up, and Lucy hurried to catch up with Armina, yanking the dogs along faster than they liked.

"Armina, wait!"

She turned around, and Lucy closed the distance between them.

"Are you okay?"

Armina sniffled and held the baby closer. She looked at Lucy suspiciously and didn't reply.

"I'm Lucy, Margot's friend. Remember me?" The woman looked so upset and confused that Lucy was worried about her.

"I I guess."

"Do you want me to walk with you back to Margot's tent? I'll make sure no one bothers your baby," Lucy said. "You can help me with these silly dogs too."

Armina smiled slightly at the dogs then nodded.

Lucy took her arm and guided her around the right way and started her down the path. Though getting there was like taking on an obstacle course with all the people, especially towing two dogs on leashes, they finally made it.

She didn't see Margot, so she peeked into the tent.

Margot wasn't inside, either, but when Lucy came out and stood, she heard someone call her name from the pedestrian path in the distance.

"Lucia!"

She turned, and when she saw who it was, her heart fell.

Jorge looked completely confused. In all fairness, he had every right to wonder why she was hanging out near the homeless encampment with a confused old woman. It didn't help that she'd looked panicked and guilty, as though she'd done something wrong.

It was turning out that she wasn't too good at charades.

CHAPTER 13

*T*aylor parked the cruiser and got out then opened the back car door and helped her perp out of the car. He was handcuffed and had been grumbling and complaining for the entire ride. Her easy patrol day was turning out to be less mundane than expected.

She'd remained silent, not feeding his rant with any response.

"Why'd you come out there, anyway?" he asked as she guided him toward the back door of the station.

"Your mother called and requested a wellness check."

"Damn. I've told her to leave me alone."

"Don't blame her for caring about you. Blame yourself. She's giving you a place to live over her garage, so the least you can do is open the door or answer your phone. She thought you were dead."

"She won't give me my privacy. I'm sick of it."

Taylor opened the door and gestured for him to go through. "I fully sympathize with you. So, here's an idea. Get a job and get your own place. You're thirty-five years old and living off your mother. Oh, and stop doing drugs. Then you won't worry about

someone knocking on your door and taking you in for possession. Now, I'm tired of this conversation, so stop talking."

Surprisingly, he obeyed, and they went down the hall.

"I appreciate you treating me with respect," he said when they
reached the door. "Sorry about all the bitching. You were great. I
was living in Riverside, California, for a spell. Those cops disrespect every inmate as soon as they get in there. Not just me. I've
seen firsthand them breaking arms and legs of others, no matter
what color they are. Those pricks are the most abusive cops I've
ever been around."

"You don't have to worry about that here. Wouldn't have to
worry about it anywhere if you'd stay out of custody." She turned
him over for intake, glad to have him out of her hands. She didn't
believe in the abuse of power, but she still had no sympathy for
able-bodied citizens who refused to act like adults and, instead,
lived off the hard work of other people, especially their elderly
parents.

She took the long way back through the building so that she
didn't have to pass Shane's office.

In the bullpen, Penner was at his desk and looked up to wave.

"Hi, Penner." She pulled her chair out, sat down, and hit the
switch for her computer to power up.

"I saw you pull in. Whatcha got?"

"A wellness check turned minor drug possession. Deadbeat
mama's boy."

"He give you any trouble?"

"Nothing but mouth," Taylor said. "He'd just smoked one and
was too mellow to put up a fight."

"What did Mama say?"

"She was sorry she called us. Didn't want me to take her baby
boy in, but them's the breaks."

Penner laughed. "My day has been less exciting. A jaywalking
report called in from Doris at the flower shop and a theft from a

car in the Woodside Way apartment complex. They took fifty bucks, her credit cards, and her driver's license."

"She left her wallet in her car?"

"Yep." Penner tapped his pen against his desktop.

"Then she deserves the trouble it's going to be to deal with all that." Taylor couldn't believe how many people still left valuables in their vehicles.

"Agreed."

"Not to mention the two hours she took you away from possible real crimes to tend to her mistake." Taylor mentally checked herself. She wasn't usually this grumpy. She had a lot on her mind, though, starting and pretty much ending with her obsession with Cate's case. She'd even dreamed about the fire the night before.

Her father wasn't the only one who wished she'd never found that envelope in his mailbox. It would have been nice to walk away and let things go back to the way they had been before, but she couldn't. The genie was out of the bottle, and there was no stuffing it back in until she felt satisfied with her own investigation.

After taking a quick look around to make sure no one was looking, Taylor logged onto Facebook and went to her own profile. Her inbox showed two unread messages.

The first one was from Jessica, and as soon as Taylor opened it, a photo of Molly and Jessica filled the screen. They were giving silly grins in the selfie, and the happiness was contagious. Taylor felt her own smile spreading as she read the message.

> Hi, Deputy Gray. Just wanted to send you this photo and tell you some good news. I was approved to keep Molly with me temporarily until ꜱ̶ᴏ̶ᴍ̶ᴇ̶ᴛ̶ʜ̶ɪ̶ɴ̶ɢ̶ ̶ᴍ̶ᴏ̶ʀ̶ᴇ̶ ̶ᴘ̶ᴇ̶ʀ̶ᴍ̶ᴀ̶ɴ̶ᴇ̶ɴ̶ᴛ̶ ̶ᴄ̶ᴏ̶ᴜ̶ʟ̶ᴅ̶ ̶ʙ̶ᴇ̶ ̶ᴡ̶ᴏ̶ʀ̶ᴋ̶ᴇ̶ᴅ̶ ̶ᴏ̶ᴜ̶ᴛ̶ The judge said I was the oldest almost-twenty-one-year-old he'd ever met, and with my job history and good grades as proof that I was responsible, he gave me a chance. I have an appointment with a lawyer. I'm fighting for custody! Say a prayer! Love, Jessica.

Taylor sat back in her chair and studied the photo again. Molly looked happy with Jessica. No doubt she had a long way to go to deal with the loss of her mother, but what a miracle that she wouldn't be in foster care. Taylor prayed it worked out, because she agreed with the judge—Jessica might just have what it would take to be a good mom to Molly.

She clicked on the second message to find that the elderly Samuel Stone had written her back.

> Yes! That's my son's dog. He's been looking for him all over North Carolina. Call him.

He had left a phone number too.

Taylor read it again.

Then one more time for good measure.

She realized she was holding her breath. Now she'd gone and done it. She was going to have to call Sam Stone. And she might end up losing Diesel.

Sometimes, she truly hated that she always had to do the right thing. The most she could hope for now was that Sam could fill her in on Diesel and what would make him happy but wouldn't really want his dog back. The way her life was going lately, that was probably a long shot.

"Find anything useful?"

Taylor just about jumped out of her chair. She'd been so deep into the message from Sam Sr. and thoughts about Diesel that she hadn't heard Shane walk up behind her.

"Not really. Just doing a bit of investigation." Technically, it was true. It just wasn't an official police investigation. Not that it was any of his business. He wasn't her boss.

They actually did use Facebook and even Twitter for investigations at times. It was amazing what people would post publicly, and they'd found many a suspect by tracing their tracks across social media.

"Can I talk to you in my office for a few minutes?"

She'd only turned quickly to see it was him and then back to her screen, so she couldn't see his face, but his tone told her he wouldn't take no for an answer.

"What about?" she asked. They hadn't spoken since she'd returned to work, and that had been just fine with her.

"I'd like to wait until we get into my office."

"When do you want to meet?"

"Now."

"I'll be in there when I finish this." She still hadn't turned to face him and was already dreading standing in his office, where she'd have no choice but to look.

"Then I'll just pull up a chair and wait right here," he said, dragging over a chair from an unoccupied desk.

Taylor gritted her teeth in frustration and clicked out of Facebook.

"Fine, I'm done. Let's go." She stood and left him trailing her. She wasn't going to follow him like some sort of servant.

His office was open, and she quickly took a chair, ready to get it over with. He came in and shut the door then sat down behind the desk. He looked tired.

With his hands clasped in front of him, he sighed long and loud. "Taylor," he began.

"Deputy Gray is fine."

"Come on, be serious. I'm sorry, okay?" He looked earnest. It reminded her of the time in high school when he had been supposed to pick her up from her job at the grocery store and hadn't shown up. He had fallen asleep, he said. She'd walked home, alone and tired, at midnight.

"Sorry for what? Throwing me under the bus or for taking the position you know I've been wanting for years?"

"Both. Hear me out. I didn't throw you under the bus as much as you think. Everything that happened that day was going to come out anyway. Meyer's wife was brought in for her statement."

"She didn't know what was said in that house. You filled it in."

"No, I didn't. She must've come to the kitchen door and heard you yelling at him."

Taylor didn't believe that for a minute, but what was done was done. "And you taking the detective position here? The one you know I've been working toward?"

"Sheriff wasn't going to give it to you, Taylor. Not right now. Next best thing for you is for me to have it. How would you like it if some jerk who acts like McElroy came in? You'd be stuck working with them."

"Who's to say they would be a jerk? Or a man? There are good detectives, both male and female, that might've applied." She argued, but he had a point. The sheriff wasn't ready to move her up in the ranks yet, and there really could be worse out there than Shane Weaver.

He ran his fingers through his hair then rubbed at his eyes before stopping and looking at her again. "Between you and me, I'm not going to be here in Hart's Ridge forever. When I get ready to go, I'm going to give my highest recommendation for you to get my job. We both know that you solved Joni Stott's case. Not me. When the time comes, I'm going to set the record straight and make sure you get promoted. Let's let the sheriff simmer down first. Until then, can we please go back to being friends?"

Taylor studied him. It was true that she could have really used a friend right then. Shane Weaver had a way of making her feel as if he knew her better than anyone else at the station, for he knew the awkward and lonely kid she used to be. That they both had been. Together, they'd overcome their high school woes about not being popular, about being poor kids without big crowds of friends or much family support. He'd comforted her when no one else had been there to do it, not as a boyfriend but as a very close friend.

They had an unusual bond.

And Taylor needed someone besides Cecil to help her navigate the current mess that was her life. She also missed riding together, discussing old times, and being on the inside of whatever detective tidbits he was getting and sharing.

"Fine. I'm going to give you another chance, Weaver. Don't blow it."

His body relaxed dramatically with relief. "Oh my God, thank you. Can we hug it out?"

She stood. "Don't get ahead of yourself. It's going to take me a minute to shake off all the bad vibes, and we are at work. No hugging. Let's go on patrol tomorrow, because you aren't going to believe what's going on in my life. I have a lot to tell you."

He was going to be shocked when he heard about the status of her dead mother.

"It's a date," he said, smiling from ear to ear.

She stopped in her tracks inside the doorway and turned back. "No, it's not a date. Let's make that clear. We're back to the way we were before, nothing more."

He saluted her and nodded. "Yes, sir. I mean, ma'am. Patrol buddies it is."

She kept the smile hidden until she was out of his office. It was nice to have a friend back. For now. Who knew? Maybe— and it was a very slim maybe—it could lead to more.

Instead of going back to her desk, she went the other way to step outside.

In the parking lot, she went to her cruiser and leaned against the hood while she opened her phone and brought up the number that Sam Stone Sr. had sent her.

It was answered on the second ring.

"Sam Stone," a deep voice said.

She nearly hung up but knew she'd only have to dial it again. Her conscience wasn't going to let it go that easily. "Um—hi. My name is Taylor Gray, and I'm calling about a dog named Diesel."

He didn't let even a second pass before he blurted out his next words.

"Oh, thank God. When can I come get him?"

CHAPTER 14

*T*he closest thing to a dog park in Hart's Ridge was the old, abandoned ball field on State Park Road, and that was where Taylor paced back and forth while Diesel ran within the remnants of the chain-link fencing, sniffing where other dogs before him had been.

Getting through the rest of her shift had been tedious, knowing that Sam Stone was on the road, headed their way. He'd dropped everything to come and see if her Diesel was his Diesel.

Now, he was twenty minutes late, and she hoped with all she had that he was a no-show, and she could forget about doing the right thing in this one circumstance. He was the one who'd insisted on driving to meet her that very day, not even giving Taylor any time to get used to the idea.

She'd give him ten more minutes, and then they were out of there. She hadn't shared where she lived, and he only had her phone number.

That could be changed.

On the way into the enclosure, Taylor had seen a few old syringes and a pair of torn panties under the ancient wooden bleachers. The old park was still getting some love, obviously.

Though it was the wrong kind of love. She made a note to add it to her list of places to patrol after dark.

The rusty backdrop still stood, though it was bent and weathered and looked as if a slight wind could blow it over. Inside, where the dirt portion of the infield had been, it was overgrown with grass and weeds that tangled upon each other, doing their best to choke out the long-lost memories made there.

It was surprising that the old field was even still there, left just as it once was. From what Taylor knew, it had been built in the seventies. That was a long time for a piece of land to go untouched, especially in Hart County, where real estate was at a premium these days.

Diesel was happy about it. Obviously, other dog owners had had the same thought that it made a good dog park, because he was nearly frantic with all the smells and was making his way around to mark over every single one of them before his tank ran out.

It felt kind of sad that it was so rundown and forgotten except for the dogs.

Hart's Ridge had put in a new baseball field for the school district a few decades before. A nice, grand one that the county taxpayers had provided, whether they wanted to or not. Taylor had gone to see a few games back in the day. If she remembered right, it had been with Anna, who had had a boyfriend on the school baseball team. Either that, or it had been Jo. Taylor had always been strict about them not going around town alone, and sometimes, she was their only choice as a tagalong.

She turned when she heard a motor and saw a vintage army-green Jeep truck turn in and slow down as it came through the gravel parking lot.

"Shit—he made it."

Now what did she do? Walk toward him? Call Diesel and lead him over there? Pretend she didn't see him?

He parked next to her truck and cut the motor then quickly

climbed out and headed her way without hesitation. He was tall and lanky. Well-built but not overly so. He wore a baseball cap, so she couldn't get a great look at his face, but she could see from the angle of his head that he was watching Diesel in the distance as the dog scampered along the far fence line.

She held out hope that it wasn't his Diesel. Just a big, fat coincidence.

He got to the gate, and she held out a trembling hand. "Taylor Gray. Thanks for coming."

Sam took it and gave her a solid but not painful shake. "Sam Stone. Thanks for reaching out. Seriously. I can't thank you enough. I've been looking for him."

"I wasn't sure if you were the right Sam Stone. There were so many on Facebook. And—well, you might not be the right one. We don't know yet, do we?" Wow. That sounded lame as hell. Why didn't she just keep stammering on like an idiot? Make it even more awkward?

"Yeah, lucky me that good ol' Dad decided to stay in touch with relatives on that thing. I don't know nothing about it, myself." He was looking past her, still watching Diesel. "How long have you had him?"

"A few months. How long have you been looking for your dog?"

"Since the week I got home. Biggest mistake I ever made."

Ouch. That hit her in the soft spot. "Well, I guess I should call him on over. See if he knows you."

"Wait—let me give it a try." He put two fingers into his mouth and let out a shrill whistle that stopped Diesel in his tracks. He turned his head, and when he looked their way, Sam did it again.

Diesel turned and practically jumped into the air to head back to them.

It was like watching a movie—Diesel galloping as fast as his legs could go, much faster than she'd ever seen him run, and Sam bending down to catch him in midair as Diesel flung himself into his arms. His impact was so hard that Sam fell back and landed on his butt in the dirt as he hugged and buried his face in his dog's neck. They wrestled back and forth like a boy and his dog might do.

Diesel's tail wagged so hard she thought it might fly off.

"Well, damn. I guess I was right. He's your dog," she said glumly, her stomach sinking at the confirmation.

Sam's hat had fallen off in all the chaos, and now, she could see that he was handsome. Not in a movie-star sort of way but wholesome and manly. He looked older than her, maybe in his mid- or late thirties, but he was the kind of guy that aged well. His sandy hair and crow's feet at his eyes and around his mouth told her he was used to being out in the sun.

He didn't dress fancy. He wore a long-sleeved shirt and filled out a rugged pair of Wranglers in such a way that she just knew he could fix her flat tire or her leaky faucet and then pick her up and throw her on the bed.

Jeez, Taylor. Get a grip. She stopped her line of thinking.

If the tables had been turned and he'd thought she looked like the kind of girl who could make a mean fried chicken and rub his feet, she'd have been pissed.

Anyway, she could change a tire faster than anyone else she knew, and she could also fix her own damned faucet.

Sam struggled to his feet then ran his hands up and down Diesel's flanks, causing him to tremble with ecstasy, though he sure didn't do that when Taylor made the same move. She could already see him in the back of Sam's truck, his tongue out and his face in the wind as he was carried away from her. It made her sadder than she thought she'd be.

"So now what?"

He stood and, with a huge smile still pasted to his face, he shrugged. "I don't know. I mean—do I owe you some money? Did you pay for him?"

"No, I didn't pay for him. I adopted him from the shelter, and they took an adoption fee."

Sam held his hands up. "Oh, sorry. No disrespect intended. I just meant I want to give you something for keeping him and taking care of his needs and all that. I really appreciate it, you know."

"I didn't say he was going with you."

The smile disappeared. "What do you mean? You can see he's my dog."

Taylor bent and hooked the leash to Diesel. "Maybe so. I mean —it's apparent he knows you, but I can't just let a stranger walk off with my dog without verifying ownership."

Sam looked crestfallen. "I don't have anything. I sent it all with the foundation when I dropped him off."

She thought of the packet of papers on her desk and knew she was being dishonest, but she wasn't ready. She just wasn't.

"Okay, well, how do I know that you're ready now to be a responsible dog owner? That you have a safe place for him and can provide for his needs? Do you even have a fenced-in yard? Diesel likes to roam."

"I know he does. I raised him," Sam said evenly. Then he took a nicer tone. "Look, let's go sit down over there and talk. This doesn't have to be so rushed. I'm sorry—I should've thought about your feelings. I'm sure you've gotten attached to him. He's pretty much perfect."

She felt a bit vindicated but not enough to turn over the leash. "Maybe not exactly perfect. He does have a few issues."

"Don't tell me: he's been stealing your toilet paper?"

If she'd had any real doubts at all, his statement settled it. Diesel was his.

"Well, yeah. But it's not a big deal," she lied.

They walked over to the bleachers, and Taylor pulled a flask of water and a small bowl out of her backpack then poured some and put it at Diesel's feet.

He was tired from all the excitement and dropped to the ground, his head over the bowl as he lapped up a good-sized drink.

"I see he's still a lazy drinker," Sam said, laughing.

Taylor laughed too. "Yeah, and he makes a mess all over my kitchen floor."

"Dribbles it in a beeline back to the couch, huh?"

"The chair. The one by the window where he can sit and gaze out all day. He keeps acting like he's waiting for someone. Looks all sad and mopey. That was what got me nosing around."

Sam thumped a fist over his heart. "Ouch."

"Sorry. Not trying to make you feel bad. Just letting you know that I don't go around adopting dogs and then searching for their first owners. There was a reason behind this."

"I call it fate. The gods know that I made a mistake, and they've been trying to reunite me and Diesel. It's like he's a part of me. I can't believe I ever thought it was better for me to let him go permanently rather than get him back when I came home."

"Oh, that's right. You were deployed. Where'd you go?"

"Here and there." He looked off into the distance.

She raised her eyebrows at him when he met her gaze again. "Hmm...can't say? Are you Special Ops?"

He shrugged.

"No worries. I understand. I'm in law enforcement."

"You are?" He looked surprised.

"Yes. Just a deputy. Sheriff's department here in this county."

He reached down and stroked Diesel. "Hey—don't say that. There's no *just a deputy*. You serve and protect. It's a hard job, and I respect that. Thought about doing it myself when I got out."

"But you didn't?"

"Nah. I decided to give it some time before I figured out a long-term commitment. For now, I work for my dad in his body shop. He's getting older and is having a hard time with the heavy stuff, so he likes me to be there. At least until I decide what I want to do next."

Taylor thought about the tire scenario. Her fantasy interlude hadn't been far off.

"I like your Jeep." She looked out toward the parking lot. "It's a beauty."

"Thanks. Dad gave it to me when I came home. It's a—"

"—1982 Jeep J10, four-wheel drive."

He smiled big again, and she noticed his perfectly imperfect teeth. "Hey—how did you know that?"

"My dad."

"Oh, okay. Did he give you that truck?"

She laughed. "No. He's never given me anything but a hard time. I got the truck after I read your letter about Diesel. Dad wasn't too pleased when I came driving up to his home in an old Silverado. He's a Ford man all the way. But I had no idea how expensive trucks were until I went looking. I was lucky to get that one for what I sold my car for. The bull bar will come in handy if I hit another deer, though."

"Hey—it's a decent truck. It could be fixed up nice. Black buffs out well. Is your dad a mechanic?"

"Not as a profession, but he always knew his way around a car and liked to call out the make and model when he'd see them out and about. He thought it made long road trips more fun. It didn't, but it did teach me to know my cars."

Sam laughed. "That's awesome. I'll have to remember that one day when I'm a dad."

"Yeah, I'm sure my future kids will think it's pretty cool too." If she ever had any. Unlike other women her age, she hadn't yet felt her biological clock tick or tock. She'd thought many times that she probably wouldn't have children. She'd already practically raised her sisters.

"I hope Diesel is still around when I have kids," Sam said.

Taylor remembered how good he had been with Molly.

"Yes, he's great with kids. Where did you get him, anyway?"

"I found him. He and a few other pups were in a box down by where I liked to fish. They were nearly dead. I think back to how everything had to work out for me to be there that day. I was supposed to work, but I woke up from a dream about fishing, and it was so strong and vivid, I thought it was a sign telling me that I needed to go right then and would be getting a trophy fish. Instead, I got something better. I found him."

"What about the others?"

"My two brothers took them, but I got the best one." He looked proudly at Diesel lying at their feet. "He's so smart."

"So you did all the training? I discovered he knew some commands in German."

"Yeah, that was an ode to my grandfather. He was German and taught us all a smattering of the language. I thought he'd get a kick out of it."

"And did he?"

"He sure did. He died last year, but he loved Diesel. He would've taken him while I was deployed, too, if he could've."

"Why didn't your dad or one of your brothers?"

"They could've, but they all have their own dogs, and Diesel is the kind of dog who needs a best friend and wouldn't like being second fiddle. I wanted him to be someone's everything, like he was mine. I thought I was doing the best thing for him. The foundation I picked told me their matches were always perfect. I had no idea he'd get bounced around."

He sounded sad, but for all she knew, he was putting on a show.

Diesel saved her from having to answer. He stood and quivered all over, looking out at the field.

"Squirrel," she and Sam said at the same time.

Taylor rose and took Diesel to the gate, let him back in, and stood back and watched his fruitless chase.

"I love that you decided to meet at this old field," Sam said. "I used to play baseball and went to college on a scholarship. These old fields always make me melancholy. When I was a kid, my brothers and I played in one just like it. Even the slope is the same. We had to bring along a ton of baseballs because we lost a lot of foul balls over the fence."

"Yeah, I bet they chased a lot of them here too."

"Our field sloped so bad out in left field that if the ball was hit over our heads, it rolled and rolled, half the time landing back in the creek before we could chase it down. We had some good times out there. Those are some of the best memories I have with my little brothers and me."

"Sounds like it," Taylor replied. She didn't say what she was thinking, which was that she wished she had some great memories like that with her sisters. "How many brothers do you have?"

"Two. And you know what? A lot of great baseball players came from fields just like this. Just small-town boys with big dreams."

Taylor was getting a great vibe from Sam. He was so friendly that she didn't want to make things harder for him, yet she still wasn't ready to turn Diesel loose. Just the thought of saying goodbye to him made her stomach queasy.

"Hey—I was going to put together a pot of chili tonight. Do you want to join me? You could see where Diesel's been living."

He turned to her and smiled. "I'll follow you. And Diesel, of course. I'm assuming you aren't going to let him ride with me."

She paused. He could take off with Diesel right there, and she'd never see either of them again.

"I don't know. Can I trust you?"

He held two fingers up and smiled. "Scout's honor."

CHAPTER 15

The ride up to Ian and Suki's summer home in Hudson Valley was just over a hundred miles but took them twice as long as it should've because of the traffic getting out of the city. Lucy sat in the back seat with the dogs competing for her lap, listening to Ian talk—*or lecture was more like it*—to Suki about the alarm systems, cameras, and all the things she needed to remember before going to bed each night.

Suki barely answered. She stayed huddled against the window in the front, her eyes closed for most of the ride.

Lucy had hoped this would be an opportunity to get to know her and finally see what she was like. Now she felt embarrassed that she'd hoped to maybe have a friend during her banishment.

It was going to be a long, lonely few months.

Jorge was on her mind. As well as the look on his face when she'd acted like an idiot at the park and had basically frozen when he'd asked what she was doing. She'd made herself look guilty. Of what, she didn't know, but it had been so awkward that she'd ended up telling him she had to go and then hurrying away as if her butt was on fire. Then she'd ghosted him, refusing his calls and ignoring his texts. If Ian thought for a second that Jorge might doubt the façade of Lucia, he would be livid. And if he was livid, it might hurt the deal they'd made.

Fifty thousand dollars was worth more than a few great dates. She had to move on and leave Jorge behind. She'd been the one to talk Ian into going to the summer house earlier than planned. No reason to stay cooped up in the penthouse when at least in the valley, she didn't have to worry about running into Jorge.

Once they got out of the city, the scenery was spectacular. They passed lush orchards and sprawling farms and vineyards, but the experience was marred by Ian's incessant monologue and the nausea that had begun to plague Lucy whenever she got into a car.

The arrival was worth the misery, though, because as Ian showed her around the home, it felt like a dream that she would be spending the next few months there, being catered to as her body cooked up a baby for the two of them to raise.

"This exterior is solid cedar and pine finish, and inside, the floors are black walnut. We spared no expense to make this place my sanctuary."

His sanctuary.

No mention of it being for his wife too.

And as usual, while Lucy was being awestruck by the sprawling landscape and picturesque view of Hudson Valley behind the house, Suki had taken Bent and Bae and disappeared into her own room as soon as they arrived.

She was a strange one. Gorgeous and ethereal but weird.

They passed a closed door on the first floor, and he barely paused.

"That's my office, and it's out of bounds," he said. "No one goes in but me."

She shrugged and gave him an *I don't care* look.

"This is the gym." He led her into a small room that held a few pieces of equipment. "I have installed a Peloton, and it's programmed with maternity workouts."

"I have no idea how to use that and no urge to learn."

"It's not an option, Lucia. I'll show you before I leave. Suki will sign off on your schedule every day and report back to me, and that will include what time you wake up, how many laps you swim, your meals, and your Peloton time."

Lucy bit her tongue against the retort that threatened to spill back at him. She wasn't used to someone telling her what to do, but for fifty thousand dollars, it wasn't as if she was going to argue. Ever since she'd signed the contract, she'd been daydreaming about how to spend the money and had come up with lots of ideas, but the night before, she had awakened from a dream in which she was living on a boat.

That's it.

She was going to buy a houseboat.

Then she'd never be homeless again.

It would be a cozy boat. Colorful rag rugs on the floor and a patchwork quilt on the bed. She would even teach herself to make the curtains. In high school sewing class, she'd made an apron, so how much harder could it be to do a curtain?

He led her through the living room. "It's a wood-burning fireplace, and there are bundles outside. Do you know how to start a fire?"

"Of course, I do. I grew up in the—"

She stopped. That was one of the negotiations she had won. She would not tell him her real last name or where she came from. Her argument was that if he never wanted the baby to know that Suki wasn't its mother, she was allowed some anonymity too.

He raised his eyebrows, challenging her with his expression.

"You almost slipped up there." He laughed then pointed at the hearth. "Anyway, the slate was shipped in from Vermont, and all the cabinetry is handmade."

Lucy really didn't care about the details or whether the slate was a twenty-thousand-dollar expense from Vermont or something she could easily get for a few hundred bucks anywhere near Hart's Ridge in Georgia.

Yep, a simple houseboat would work just fine for her.

Sure, it wouldn't be a multimillion-dollar house in Hudson Valley, but she didn't need to live like that. Finally having some money to work with would be amazing, but she'd never allow herself to change into the type of woman who depended on labels and status to make her feel relevant. With fifty grand, she could buy her boat and live off the rest of the money until she found some way to earn an income. Something that didn't require hustling ever again.

She couldn't wait to show her sisters that she had her life together. In her own home, she would be respectable. She wouldn't ever have to depend on handouts from anyone again. She'd never have to hustle up a way to get by.

The only thing she hadn't figured out yet was where to tell them the money had come from.

"All of your needs will be taken care of. You won't have to work, cook, or even do your own laundry. Just enjoy this time because I'm sure it will go by fast." He stopped and turned to face her. "I've also hired a midwife, and she'll be coming weekly for now and then more often in the last month. Like we discussed, you'll have our baby here, in this house, with her overseeing the delivery."

Lucy nodded, swallowing back the anxiety his statement brought on. It wasn't the term "our baby"... She was fine with that. She wanted no part of being a mother. Lucy already wasn't thrilled that there was a little human growing inside of her, but she was terrified of labor. It would be fine with her if they knocked her out completely and just took the baby. Lucy didn't know much about childbirth, but she was pretty sure that wouldn't be an option unless she was in a hospital.

I'm tough. I've been through worse. I can do this. Fifty thousand dollars.

The reminders helped keep her from running out the door screaming.

"No one must know you're here," he said. "We have all the privacy we need on these seven acres. All groceries and supplies will be ordered online and dropped at the gate. I've hired a very trustworthy housekeeper, and she's signed a nondisclosure. On Mondays, she'll come in on the Amtrak, as it's only a few minutes away. She'll go back on Fridays. She'll oversee your diet as well."

Diet. She already knew she was going to be forced to eat a bunch of healthy stuff that probably tasted like gruel. Or cardboard.

Fifty thousand dollars.

"I'm tired, Ian. Can you show me to my room?"

He stared her down for a minute, daring her to argue about nutrition, then turned and led her up the stairs.

Lucy couldn't help the smile that spread over her face when he opened the door and let her go in. It wasn't too fancy— nothing like the rooms in the New York penthouse—but the coziness and simplicity were perfect. It would be the nicest bedroom she had ever had.

The queen-sized bed centered on the faded gray floors was covered in a simple but fluffy-looking gray-and-white comforter. It faced a long bookshelf that ran along the opposite wall, and Lucy went to it and ran her fingers down some of the spines.

She would have plenty to read to take up her time.

There was also a small desk with a laptop. She thought of Taylor and, for a moment, considered putting an email in their group draft account. Her sister worried about all of them to the point of ridiculousness, and just a few words letting her know she was still alive would mean the world to her. It must have been the hormones making her feel guilty, but she'd been considering reaching out.

Ian walked over and shut the laptop, unplugged it, and tucked it under his arm.

"Remember, no internet. No communication with your family or friends. Not even scrolling through Facebook, Snapchat, or whatever is the latest thing, because you might slip up."

"I'm not going to slip up, Ian." She sat on the end of the bed and slipped her shoes off. Her feet were killing her. "Remember, I don't want anyone to ever know anything about this deal either."

"You mean the baby."

"You said you'd stop using that word. Remember, you don't want me to attach." Lucy knew there was no chance of an emotional connection, but she also knew how to use things to keep him in line, like he was using them to keep her in line. Even though she didn't want a child, she really didn't want to call it a baby either. She'd rather think of it as leverage for this once-in-a-lifetime deal.

Ian left her, and she got up and closed the door then went to the window.

The lush and rolling landscape continued beyond the trees, with an outline of distant mountains as a backdrop. It reminded her of her first home, and she thought of her dad. She wondered if he ever missed Montana or if it brought him too much pain to think about it. None of them ever talked about it.

The fire.

And losing her mom and little brother.

They all thought she had been too young to remember, but she wasn't. Lucy had memories. Something as simple as seeing a mother stroke the hair of her child would rekindle them. Or a certain smell of perfume that she could never quite name.

She remembered that her mother had been soft. And kind. She had never yelled the way their father had. Why couldn't he have been the one to leave them?

Lucy turned from the window, feeling sick with guilt. She went to the bed and sat down then leaned back and covered her face with a pillow. That was a horrible thing to think. She loved her dad. They all did. But it wasn't as if he'd given them any sort of childhood after their mother had died.

All he had to do was stop drinking and quit feeling sorry for himself.

It was his fault she was so screwed up—that they all were—but he'd never own it.

That was why she could never be a mother. She never wanted to mess up her kid because of her own problems. Parents were supposed to compartmentalize their own shit for the well-being of their own children. Put it away and, even if they had to pretend, act like normal human beings. At least attempt to give the kids some semblance of a life. Not let them go hungry and be bounced back and forth to foster care while they worried if their father was going to die too.

The anger welled up inside her like a dragon unfurling from a cave, its breath spitting daggers of fire, the heat burning her chest like it always did when she let herself go there.

Lucy wouldn't pass down all her problems. It stopped with her. She turned over and closed her eyes, willing herself to sleep.

And to forget.

CHAPTER 16

*T*hree weeks after her last visit to Montana, Taylor was back there and sitting in the basement office of Don Hayes's home. He was the independent arson investigator who had testified for the defense in Cate's case. She was grateful that he'd agreed to see her and was surprised he was still working and not yet retired.

"Don will be right with you," said the young woman who'd ushered her in and led her downstairs. "Can I get you some coffee?"

"No, thank you. I'm fine."

She disappeared, and Taylor heard her walk upstairs and speak in a hushed voice.

Earlier that morning, she'd met with attorneys at the office of those who had worked on Cate's case during the last appeal. It had been a waste of time. The original attorneys were now retired and no longer even consulting. No one currently practicing there wanted to touch it.

The meeting was supposed to have happened when she'd last been in town, but Adele had been so upset that Taylor had run Cate out of the visiting room that she'd refused to do anything but go back to the hotel and call for an earlier flight back to Florida.

It had gutted Taylor that Adele was disappointed in her, and she'd thought of trying to smooth things over to save the rest of the trip. But then she'd decided that it would be easier to do it without her grandmother, who was much too emotional about the case.

Taylor knew how to compartmentalize, and that was what she planned to do. Get in. Get the facts. Walk away.

Or if, by some miracle, the facts made her think a little harder, she'd cross that bridge when she came to it.

Letting Shane back into her friend zone was already paying off, because after she'd gotten him up to date with everything about Cate, he'd gone to bat for her with the sheriff to get her more time off without her having to beg for it.

"You'll never be at peace until you figure this shit out, Taylor," he'd said. "Do what it takes."

He was right. It was all driving her mad.

Speaking of the friend zone, Diesel was with Sam but only for the long weekend. After he'd come out to her place and had dinner, they'd sat out on the porch and talked for two hours. Then he'd shown Taylor the full range of commands he'd taught Diesel, which were many more than she'd known he could follow and impressive as hell.

By the end of the night, Sam had determined that it wasn't fair to just jerk Diesel out of her life abruptly, and for a while, they would share him. Taylor would have him most of the time, and Sam would get him two weekends a month. He lived in South Carolina now and not in North Carolina, where he'd been originally. It was still a long drive, but he said he didn't mind it at all.

He had sent her a good-morning text and photo from Diesel just that morning: the two of them snuggled together against pillows, a selfie of two boys with morning mussed-up hair. She'd tried not to notice the glimpse of Sam's bare muscles in the selfie.

She couldn't have lucked out with any nicer an owner to deal with, and she hoped that in time, she'd be okay with letting Diesel go back to Sam permanently.

Don Hayes shuffled in along with a strong whiff of cigar. He was old or at least older than Taylor's dad. He sat down at his desk and moved aside several tall stacks of papers before giving Taylor his attention.

"How can I help you?"

Here goes nothing. "I'm Catherine Gray's daughter."

She'd thought he might take a minute or need more details, but no, he knew immediately who she was talking about.

"Oh, Cate? How's she doing? That was a sad case. Travesty, really."

"Yes, we lost our brother, and he was barely more than a baby."

He shook his head. "That wasn't what I meant, but sorry for your loss. I'm talking about what they did to your mother. She shouldn't be serving time. She's innocent."

Taylor felt relief wash over her. She'd been afraid he might not remember the case. But he remembered. And he appeared sharp as a tack.

"Can we talk about it? I'd love to hear your thoughts on the evidence and the outcome."

"Sure." He fumbled with the drawer in front of his lap. "Mind if I smoke?"

She did, but she'd suffer through it. "Not if it helps you remember."

He smiled then reached in for an ashtray that held the remains of a cigar. He lit up, took a few puffs, and closed his eyes in what appeared to be relief.

"I used to hide down here and smoke these to get away from

my wife. Bless her soul, she's been gone now for a few years. She's probably up there watching me and shaking her head."

"Sorry to hear that." She wished he'd get on with it. She had to make it to the prison by visiting hours, and it was a hundred miles in the other direction.

Hayes leaned forward, his elbows on his desk. "Cate's in prison because of Boswell Fisher and his buddy, Bill Kinley."

"Go on." She knew the names from the court documents.

"Fisher was the Montana state fire marshal, and he wanted to pin it on your mother from the first minute he was at the scene. Kinley was the forensic analyst with ATF, and he took floor samples from both the front room and the bedroom where the victim died. He testified that both samples were found to have a heavy petroleum distillate."

"But they didn't?"

"Not according to my investigation."

"Then why were they out to get her? She'd never met them in her life."

He shrugged. "It happens. Not every official is good. Some are corrupt to the core. Fisher saw a case he wanted his name on, and a simple accidental fire wasn't going to get him any mileage. He wanted murder by arson, and Cate was an easy target because she was young and poor. She was there alone with the boy. No one else for miles around. Your father had you and your sisters as an alibi. So they ran with what they had and manipulated and fabricated their way to a guilty verdict. Your mother didn't have a chance against their so-called experts."

Taylor felt her body tense. "I looked into it, and the only credential that Fisher had at the time was that he'd graduated a forty-hour correspondence course to be able to call himself an arson investigator. That's the same number of hours it takes to become a manicurist. Yet he gets to play with people's lives. It doesn't make sense." Taylor rubbed at the back of her neck where it was starting to ache.

"That's right. Fisher didn't know a fraction of what he should about fire investigation. He claimed he'd discovered a V-pattern pointing down from the wall and that it showed the point of origin, where a liquid accelerant was used. That's old-school thought. I testified that fire burned down not because of a liquid accelerant but because it was seeking oxygen. It's science, not supposition. His evidence of the burn pattern should've been disproved, but a judge wouldn't allow it in the appeal. He said it was the same evidence packaged differently."

"That's insane," Taylor said.

"Agreed. As you probably know, I testified that the cause of the fire should've been classified as undetermined because I found there was a probability it was accidental. There was no evidence whatsoever pointing toward arson."

Hayes went into more detail about the evidence, and Taylor listened intently. When he was through, she only had five words.

"Now what can I do?"

Two HOURS LATER, Taylor was in the prison visitation room, waiting for Cate. She'd sped all the way there, praying she wouldn't get stopped. Local law enforcement didn't appreciate it when out-of-state LE came to their town and broke laws.

She got there with four minutes to spare.

While Taylor waited for Cate to come to the room, she checked out the people around her. One guy looked familiar. She did a second take and figured out who he reminded her of.

Brandon Little.

Unfortunately, his name fit his physique. He had been a tiny guy when they were in seventh grade together. A loner, too, rarely interacting with anyone. He had eaten his lunch alone, staring into space, and she had never once, through the years they were in school together, seen him smile.

In gym, no one chose him for sports. They laughed at him, calling him faggot and homo just because of his size. Taylor had tried to befriend him, feeling sorry for how lonely he looked, but ʇʰǝ ᴡɐs ɐ ɭoɴǝɾ iɴ ʰǝɾ oᴡɴ ɾiɢʰʇ, ɐɴd ǝʋǝɴ ʇʰouɢʰ ɕʰǝ'd ʇɾiǝd, he'd brushed her off.

She remembered one time when he had been absent from school for a week. She'd thought he'd moved away, but the rumor was that he'd tried to kill himself. But when he returned and they all showed up for gym class, everyone in there went silent when they saw him standing there, dressed out, his head down in shame. It was so bad that Taylor had never forgotten the black-and-blue welts all over his arms and legs. She'd only been able to imagine what it looked like under his clothes. For the rest of the class, everyone had left him alone, giving him a wide berth as he moved around the gym stiffly under the close eye of the coach.

Della Ray, her foster mom, had eventually told her that Brandon's stepfather had a long history of beating the kids under his roof, and that specific encounter had put the boy in the hospital for three days. The mom had protected her husband for a long time, and it was only when Brandon came to gym class and showed signs of the abuse that the school had gotten social services involved, and both parents went to jail.

Taylor remembered thinking that she and her sisters were lucky—their dad hadn't ever laid a hand on them. He'd only neglected them. A therapist would have told her to never think like that, but truth was truth. Some had had it so much harder than she had.

A few weeks after the incident, Brandon was gone, and she never saw him again. Most likely another kid sent spiraling through the foster-care system from county to county.

She stole another peek just to make sure, but no, it wasn't him suddenly showing up in a prison visitors' room in Montana, though that would've been quite the coincidence. She'd always wondered what had become of him.

The noise around her rose as the door opened, prisoners started filing in, and family members rushed to greet them. Taylor remained sitting at the table.

She saw Cate, her expression unsure as she looked around the room for a familiar face. When she spotted Taylor, her face relaxed. She hurried over and sat down. "I'm so glad to see you, Taylor."

"Yes, thanks for meeting with me."

"I'd meet with the Son of Sam himself if it meant two hours on this side of that locked door. Oh, thanks," she said as she saw the soft drinks and snacks waiting. She picked up the honey bun and tore it open. "I was afraid you'd change your mind and not come. I haven't eaten all day."

"I met with Don Hayes this morning." Taylor decided the only way to broach the subject was to be blunt.

Cate dropped the bun. "You did? Why?"

"I wanted to talk to someone who knew the case inside out. Pick his brain. I tried the attorney's office first, but it's all new, young blood, and they didn't seem too interested in digging into twenty-year-old case files."

"I see. Well, I can't blame them."

Taylor could see that Cate was trying not to show too much emotion or even interest.

"Well, how was Don doing? He's such a good guy. Did you meet his wife, Angela?"

"No, I didn't. Unfortunately, she's deceased."

Cate looked crestfallen.

"You aren't asking the right questions," Taylor said.

"Oh? And what are they?"

"How are we going to try one more time to get a new trial?"

Cate sighed. "I really don't think you know what you're up against, Taylor. We've tried. And tried again. I just don't think I have it in me to be rejected again. I'm too old. Too tired."

"Don't say that. You're strong, or you wouldn't be sitting here talking to me. Don had an idea. Since you got in here, there's been a lot of attention on a new group called the Innocence Project. They work to free people who have been wrongfully convicted. He's going to help me put together a package to send to them and hope we get a meeting or at least a phone call. That's the first step."

She could see that Cate's eyes were getting misty. She used her sleeve to wipe at them before answering. "It's enough for me to know that you believe I'm innocent. That means more to me than my freedom."

Taylor held her hand up. "Wait. I'm not totally decided yet, Cate. I want to go through all the evidence from both sides. If that foundation helps us, they'll evaluate everything, and if they think you're innocent, that will help me figure out where I stand. If they decline, then I'm out. All I'm saying is that I'm willing to do the work to get it to them."

"Thank you," she said so softly that Taylor could barely hear her.

"Don't thank me yet. If something in the case files screams 'guilt' at me, you won't hear from me again. I'm doing this for Lucy. For Anna and Jo. They deserve to know the truth. Now, let's talk about other things. Adele said you were also into horti-culture."

Cate nodded. "I am, or at least I was. I've taken a break from it to do the dog training, but for years, I supervised one of our greenhouses. Thanks for pretending interest, but I know you really want to know about the day that Robert died, and I'm ready to tell you."

"Why now? You said you never wanted to tell that story again."

"Because if you really want to fight for me, I want you to understand what you are fighting for. I don't want to go over it twice, so please listen carefully."

"Okay." Taylor sat back in the chair, determined not to ask

questions, just to let her talk.

"The night before was just a regular Saturday evening. Because you didn't have school the next day, we were all up late, watching a movie. We ate popcorn. At nine o'clock, Jackson promised we'd all get up and go fishing the next morning, so everyone went to bed."

So far, her story matched up with what Taylor already knew.

"You girls loved to go out on the boat. We never had much money, but one year, we used our tax refund and bought an old, broken-down Bayliner outboard. Jackson fixed it up, and it was a cheap way to have a family day. Ironically, I was always very worried about having all of you on the boat. It was small for all of us, and my nerves were always on edge. That morning, we were all supposed to go, but Robert had been sick through the night. He was in the bed with me, and Jackson was on the couch. He got up around six in the morning, ready to get going."

"Dad said you wanted him to cancel that day on the lake."

Cate sighed. "Let's just say that ultimately, I decided to let you all go on ahead, and I'd stay home with Robert."

"Go on." Taylor had to admire that she didn't throw the blame.

"I got everyone into their swimsuits and shorts and packed sandwiches and juice boxes, and you all left. Robert's fever had finally broken, and he was resting good, so I left him in my bed and moved out to the couch to rest for a bit before tackling laundry. I was exhausted from the night before and didn't mean to fall asleep, but I did."

She paused and drew in a long breath.

"The next thing I knew, a noise woke me. I sat up and saw a small fire on the living room floor. I was disoriented, but I tried to put it out with a throw pillow. When that didn't work, I tried the blanket. Then I searched for the fire extinguisher and couldn't find it. I was running around, panicking, and then I saw that the small fire was now a wall of flames separating me from the hall that led to my bedroom." Her chest rose and fell erratically while she told the story, and she looked off toward the wall of windows, her words rushing out faster.

"I didn't know what to do, so I ran out of the house, screaming for help. I realized there wasn't time for anyone to come to our rescue, so I went around and tried to break the window in my bedroom. I threw a big rock, and it only cracked it. Then I threw Robert's little bike into it, and when I looked around for something to climb on and pull myself in, the fire department was flying up our long driveway. I still tried to go in, but they pulled me down and held me back. I don't remember what exactly happened next, but someone told me that Robert had already perished. That was the word they used: *perished*. Like a wisp of smoke or something. Not like a real flesh-and-blood little boy who, just a few hours before, lay snuggled in my arms."

She closed her eyes in a pained expression.

"I'm so sorry," Taylor said softly. For the first time, she realized that the trauma of losing her brother didn't hold a candle compared to that of a mother losing her little boy. Cate spoke of him as if it had been only yesterday that she'd held him.

Cate opened her eyes. "At the hospital, I was in bad shape. They kept me completely medicated for the first few weeks to let the burns begin to heal. When I began staying awake for longer periods, the investigators came in and told me that they believed the fire was arson. I was shocked. I didn't know what had started the fire, but arson? It didn't seem plausible that someone came in while I was sleeping right there and set a fire and got out before I woke."

"They didn't accuse you right away?"

She shook her head. "No. They asked me who would want to hurt me or Robert. They asked if Jackson could've snuck back and done it. He had all of you with him, so that was impossible. They had no one to blame, so they eventually pointed the finger at me."

"What would have been your motive?"

Cate shrugged. "I have no idea. We didn't have life insurance, and Jackson had let the homeowner's insurance lapse months before. There was no monetary gain, and I had no reason to want Robert gone. We loved that boy. Just like we love all of you."

Taylor cringed inwardly. She was giving Cate some grace, but she wasn't yet ready to forgive her for letting them believe she was dead all these years. To her, that wasn't love. That was cowardice.

"The prosecutor began and told the jury that motive was not an element of this crime, and he didn't have to prove motive. He said people commit horrific crimes for no rhyme or reason all the time."

"I've seen that opening before," Taylor said. "They don't have to prove why you did it, only *that* you did it."

"Right." Cate looked pale, as though telling the story had drained every bit of energy from her body.

"That's enough for today," Taylor said, feeling guilty. "I think I should probably go."

She started to stand, and Cate reached out and grabbed her wrist across the table. The guard called out and scolded her, and she let go as though she'd touched something hot.

"Wait. Before you go, can we talk about something else? We still have an hour, and I don't want to go back in there with this so deeply on my mind."

Taylor sat back down. "Of course. What do you want to talk about?"

"Well, we could talk about Jo and Levi. Or Anna and her family. But I'd love to hear something about you, Taylor. I know you don't do social media and you are private about your life, but is there anything at all you can share?"

"Hmmm...well, has Adele told you about the dog in my life? Diesel?"

Cate lit up. "No, she hasn't. But I want to hear all about him."

CHAPTER 17

*H*ensley Bowers was the epitome of a young but hungry attorney that a crusty old veteran lawyer would probably not want to face in a courtroom, and Taylor knew she could be the perfect fresh advocate for them to see where they could take the case. Hensley was tall, thin, and blond, looking more like a fashion model than a legal professional. But at the first word out of her mouth, Taylor could tell she was whip-smart.

Don had introduced Taylor as an up-and-coming detective—which was a bit of a stretch—and had run through the case history all in the span of twenty minutes. No grandstanding or embellishments. Straight to the facts.

It had been impressive.

The lawyer had sat back in her chair, her fingers laced together on her lap, and hadn't taken a single note.

That had been discouraging.

"I'm telling you, Hensley," Don Hayes said, "she's innocent. I would've staked my career on it back then, and I'd do the same now."

Hensley chuckled from behind the huge mahogany desk.

"Didn't you tell me you were retiring for real next summer and going on an extended fishing trip in Alaska? I don't think you have much more career to lose."

He shook a finger at her. Taylor could see they had a good camaraderie, and she hoped that would be enough to push Bowers into saying yes.

"But I have a reputation. A legacy. And you know I wouldn't be here if I had any doubts. They've done this woman wrong."

"What do you think?" Hensley asked, looking at Taylor. "Innocent?"

That was a hard question. Her answer could sway the lawyer one way or the other.

"I don't know." She sighed. "I want to investigate more."

Hensley raised her eyebrows. "Impressive. It's your mother. I would think you'd scream her innocence to the world, even if you didn't believe it."

"It's complicated." Taylor sighed again. She hoped she didn't have to get into the family dynamics. At least not yet. "And I don't ever compromise my values. If she's guilty, she's guilty. Simple as that."

"Hensley, I have ten more boxes of files in the car," Don said. "If you've got more time, I can show you the good stuff. All we want is for you to use your connections to get someone over at the Center for Unjust Convictions to hear us out. Please."

"I do not have time to go through any case files. One box or ten." She gazed at her phone and scrolled through it for a minute before she looked up at them.

Taylor had hoped she'd at least look through the file box they'd brought in and maybe a few more, especially considering the time it had taken to dig them out of the rows of shelving in Hayes's dusty storage room then drag it all upstairs and out to the car. Good thing she'd worn her cargo pants and hiking boots.

Hensley looked up. "I don't know how you do this, Don, but I'm having dinner tonight with Jan Randolph."

Don sat forward in his chair, and his eyes lit up. "It's fate."

Hensley rolled her eyes at the ceiling. "More like someone told you my schedule. Probably Trina at the front desk. You've spoiled her with those donuts you keep bringing."

"Who is Jan Randolph?" Taylor asked.

"Only the actual staff attorney for the center," Don said. "We couldn't get into a meeting with her on our own if we waited months. She and Hensley are good buddies."

"Close colleagues. Not buddies. We've gotten to know each other working on another case and have become friends. Our husbands are connected, too, so sometimes, it works out to do dinner," Hensley said.

That *was* big.

But Taylor wouldn't beg. It would either happen or it wouldn't.

She tried to stop bouncing her leg up and down, but it suddenly had a mind of its own.

Hensley was watching her, sizing her up.

She turned her attention to Don. "I'll tell you what, Don. You've been good to me. Helped me out a time or two, especially when I didn't know my butt from a hole in the ground. And you never tried to take credit for anything you walked me through. If you want to accompany me tonight as my plus one, I'll tell Danny he can stay home and watch that game he's been whining about. He hates this kind of stuff. You can go and pitch this case to Jan, and if she bites, then great. If she passes, we keep it cozy for the rest of the meal, and I've done all I can do. Deal?"

Taylor felt the tension drain from her body, and her leg stopped jumping.

He smiled. "Almost. You know that game Danny wants to watch? I really can't miss it either. What about if Taylor goes with you? She's been studying this case, and she can spout the facts and details better than I can. You know my brain gets a little foggy after six o'clock or so."

Taylor had a feeling he didn't care anything about a ballgame on TV, and his brain was sharp until it hit the pillow. He did care for Cate, though. And possibly the fact that Taylor was her long-lost daughter that she might have a chance to reconcile with.

Hensley nodded. "We can do that. I'll text her and tell her I'm bringing my new friend Taylor. You go home and smoke one of those stinky cigars and drink a beer. I'll tell Danny you suggested he do the same. Then he'll owe you one."

"Perfect," Don said. "He and I need to get together and wet a line soon anyway. You two girls have a great dinner, and I'll say a little prayer that you can work your magic, Hensley."

"No magic here. Just brains and tenacity," Hensley said. "And we aren't girls. But speaking of that, do you have anything fancier to wear, Taylor?"

※

THE ONLY THING that Taylor hated worse than shopping was shopping malls. Despite that, she emerged from Rimrock Mall at half past five with a racing pulse and a sheen of sweat across her brow, wearing a new outfit that wouldn't embarrass Hensley Bowers.

She'd bypassed all sorts of Montana-like styles of patterned dresses and blouses and gone with her usual understated black slacks and crisp white blouse. She probably should've gotten a pair of shiny pumps, but she didn't want to walk in and break her neck in front of everyone, so she picked out a pair of half boots with a side zipper. The young salesclerk had fun putting it all together. Against Taylor's style and better judgment—and her crying credit card—the girl had added a deep-turquoise scarf as a pop of color.

Taylor had firmly rejected the idea of new matching earrings. Her simple faux diamond studs worked just fine. She planned to return everything before she went home, anyway.

In the car, she punched in Hensley's address and then headed there, her time of arrival showing she'd be six minutes late.

Shit.

It would've been nice to be able to stop at the hotel and shower, even touch up her makeup, but there wasn't time for that.

Despite her reluctance to break traffic laws, Taylor edged the needle up just a few digits and then slid through a yellow stoplight, her eyes on her rearview mirror in the hopes she wouldn't be caught.

When she pulled up to the curb in front of Hensley's towering house, she was only a minute overdue, but it still made her palms sweaty. She despised being late.

Hensley came out the door before Taylor could even decide if she should get out of the car. Hensley had changed from her work suit and was wearing a long skirt and boots. The flowered blouse that looked fantastic on her would've made Taylor look as if she were wearing a muumuu. She was thankful she'd stuck to something basic and low-key.

"You look nice," Hensley said as she opened the door and plumped down in the seat. "Hope you don't mind driving. I can check some emails."

"No problem. Where do we go?"

"Walkers on First Avenue." She already had her phone open and was tapping at the screen.

"And that is where?" Taylor felt like an idiot. "If you have the address, I'll put it in my GPS."

Hensley looked up. "Oh, sorry. I forgot you weren't from here. Take a right at the stop sign, and I'll direct you. It's just a few minutes from here. Jan already has our table."

Between tapping out texts or emails, whatever she was doing, Hensley directed Taylor the rest of the way, and they pulled into the parking lot. Taylor's stomach felt cold and empty, but she didn't think it was from not having anything to eat. There was a lot riding on this meeting.

Basically, the rest of Cate's natural life.

"Listen." Hensley put her hand on Taylor's arm. "Before we get out, I need to warn you that Jan is a no-nonsense kind of attorney. You're here because I have a bit of a bleeding heart. That's not going to be the case with Jan, and I just want you to be prepared if she shoots you down before you feel like she's heard you out. This is a long shot, and Don knew it. But I'm doing it for him."

"I understand, and I appreciate this chance, slim as it may be."

"Okay, then. You follow my lead. I'll feel her out and see what kind of mood she's in before we bring it up. Remember, this is supposed to be a fun dinner out."

Taylor hoped it didn't show that she was rusty with having fun dinners out, especially with female friends. Somehow, she didn't think it would feel the same as her cozy suppers with Cecil.

She followed Hensley to the door, wishing suddenly that Cecil was beside her. He knew her. Understood her. She didn't have to play a part.

Hensley saw her friend wave, and they bypassed the hostess and went straight to the table.

"This is my friend Taylor Gray. She's visiting from Georgia."

"Nice to meet you," Taylor said, sticking her hand out across the table and giving Jan one of the firmest and best handshakes she'd ever given before taking a seat.

Jan was older than Hensley by probably eight to ten years. She looked like a more stoic personality. Less frilly, too, with her jeans and simple yellow blouse. Her jewelry was the main attraction of her outfit, a thick gold chain around her neck and diamond earrings that looked like they were worth a fortune.

"Where's Alan?" Hensley asked.

"He heard Danny wasn't coming and copped out. He and the

dog are going to enjoy spreading out on the whole couch, and I'm sure they're binging on cooking shows. Alan thinks he's going to be the next Gordon Ramsey, yet he can only cook on a grill.

They laughed.

Taylor thought of Diesel and wondered what he was doing. Probably stretched out over Sam's legs in front of the TV too. She pushed down a twinge of jealousy. She missed Diesel more than she had thought she would.

"What are you drinking?" Hensley asked. "Your regular?"

"Yep. No one makes an old-fashioned like Walkers."

On cue, their server appeared. She was a petite, smiling girl with eyes that twinkled behind her glasses.

"Hi, Jessica," Hensley greeted her. "How are you?"

"Fine. It's great to see you, Hensley!"

"Got any gigs coming up?" She turned to Taylor. "Jessica is the vocalist for the Rimrock Hot Club. They play gypsy jazz, but she can sing anything."

Taylor had no idea what gypsy jazz was, but she nodded encouragingly.

"Sunday night, as usual. Come on out. Bring Danny," Jessica said. "But let's get you something to drink. What's your poison?"

"I think I'll have a ginger vodka with chili flakes."

"You got it. And you?" She looked at Taylor.

"Just sweet tea."

"Oh, I love your accent," the girl said. "But sorry, we don't have sweet tea. Only unsweetened iced tea. I can give you sugar packets."

Now she felt like an idiot. Hensley and Jan watched sympathetically, probably thinking she was a poor country bumpkin who didn't know how to drink alcohol and was bumbling at just trying to give her drink order.

"Just water with lemon is fine." No quantity of sugar packets could make unsweetened tea palatable.

"Got it. Be back in a minute," Jessica said. She whirled around and headed for the bar.

"Before I forget," Hensley said, looking at Taylor, "their Korean BBQ bowl is to die for. You should really get it."

"Oh. Okay." Taylor had never eaten Korean cuisine before.

"That's what I'm having too," Jan said. "So, Taylor, was it? What brings you to Billings?"

Taylor glanced at Hensley.

"She's a friend of Don Hayes," Hensley said.

Jan looked curious. "Oh. A friend? Or a client?"

"You're too smart for your own good," Hensley said to her, laughing. "Her mother was a client a long time ago."

Jessica returned with a tray and set down their drinks and a small plate.

"Sweet—you ordered the deviled eggs," Hensley said to Jan.

"Always."

"You have to try these," Hensley said to Taylor. "It's a favorite. Blue cheese, candied bacon jam—all sorts of good layers."

Jessica left, and both Jan and Hensley slid an egg onto their small saucers.

"I think I'll wait for my entrée," Taylor said. She wasn't a fan of deviled eggs in general and didn't know how to eat one without looking messy.

"Don's a great guy," Jan said. "Did he do okay with your mother's case?"

"Jan works with the Center for Unjust Convictions," Hensley said, directing her statement at Taylor as if she didn't already know that. "Her love language is case files."

Jan laughed. "That's probably true. I can't get away from it, even on a night out, can I?"

"Well, to be honest, Taylor here works in law enforcement and was a child when her mom was convicted. She's in town doing some investigative work about the case, trying to see if there's any hope of a new trial."

"Oh, so your mother is still incarcerated?" Jan put down her fork.

"She is. Nearly twenty years now."

Jan looked from Taylor to Hensley and smiled slightly. "If I didn't know any better, I'd think this was a setup. But since this night out was at my invitation, I'm going to disregard that thought, Hensley."

"You know me better than that," Hensley said, winking conspiratorially at Jan. "But if you really want to hear about it, it's interesting."

Jan shrugged. "Hit me."

Hensley began relaying the facts of the case, Don's suspicions, and the appeals that had been filed and denied. She'd obviously done some reading in the hours since Taylor had left her office and picked her up at her home, because she had covered most everything by the time she paused to take a drink.

"Nobody saw her set the fire or even prepare to set a fire. No one ever heard her talking about setting a fire before or after. The trailer wasn't insured, and we lost everything, including my little brother, who was the most cherished of the family. It doesn't add up," Taylor said.

"And she never tried to make a deal?" Jan asked.

"No. She's never wavered about her innocence."

"It sounds like abuse of power to me," Hensley said.

"That's nothing new, and it's why, as a nation, we have more than twenty-five hundred confirmed exonerations since 1990."

"How can the legal system get away with it?" Taylor asked.

"Many of those convictions were based on officials and/or experts lying or falsifying reports. They keep doing it because they rarely suffer consequences when they're discovered."

Taylor felt tightness in her chest and knew it was a bundle of anger at the justice system that she fought so hard to uphold.

"Take Richard Raugust. He got life without parole for the shooting death of his best friend at a campground when he wasn't even there. He spent eighteen years behind bars before he was exonerated," Jan said.

Taylor listened as they discussed more exonerations and trials, and her hope for Cate built a bit more as each case was dissected.

"But it's hard to get that exoneration," Jan said to Taylor. "Extremely difficult. Nearly impossible when you consider how many people behind bars claim their innocence compared to how many ever see the light of day again."

Taylor's hopes deflated instantly, along with the conversation. They all stared at their drinks.

Finally, Hensley made the pitch.

"I've got the transcripts for Taylor's mother in the car if you want to read over them, Jan. See what you think. Maybe give us some idea as to if there's any use looking at it further or if Taylor should go home and leave it alone."

Jan didn't answer right away, and just as she was getting ready to, Taylor's phone rang.

"I'm so sorry. I thought I turned it off," she said, fishing for it in her bag, which hung on the back of her chair. When her fingers found it, she pulled it up and saw it was Adele.

Her grandmother never called her.

"I need to just see if she's okay." She held the phone to one ear and covered the other as she turned away from the table. "Hello? Adele? What's going on?"

"It's your mother, Taylor. The warden just called me and said she's in the hospital, and it's bad."

CHAPTER 18

*T*here are moments that mark a person's life. In one breath, they realize that things will never be the same. There will be a *before this happened* and an *after this happened*.

Taylor stood beside Cate's hospital bed, listening to the steady beep of the monitor that proved that despite how she looked, she was still alive.

"I just don't understand why they would do this to her."

"Knowing Gray, she ain't gonna tell you she got her ass whooped because of you," the guard replied.

Cate was handcuffed to the railing of the bed, with a prison guard in the room to keep her from making a miraculous run for freedom.

"What are you talking about?"

The guard scratched at her armpit then yawned. She took her eyes off the *Family Feud* episode on the TV that hung in the corner. "Seems you came to the visiting room with her mother, and someone on Cate's block overheard the talk about how smart you looked in your deputy uniform. A couple cop haters caught her in the back of the greenhouse."

Taylor's breath caught in her throat, and she felt lightheaded.

She still didn't know if Cate was innocent or guilty of the fire that had taken her brother's life, but she did know that she didn't deserve the beating she had received simply because her daughter had chosen to make her career in law enforcement.

"I want their names," she said softly.

"Not gonna happen. The warden is taking care of it."

A nurse came into the door and to the bedside. She checked the IV and pressed a few buttons then carefully examined Cate's handcuffed wrist.

"You might have to take these off if they start to inhibit keeping her blood pressure leveled out."

"Not unless the warden tells me to," the guard replied.

The nurse shook her head and let out a heavy sigh.

"Hi. I'm Taylor Gray, Cate's daughter. Can you give me a full assessment of her injuries?"

The nurse went to the computer next to the wall and started pressing keys.

"She must've been hit with something heavy, because she's got a heck of a contusion on her head and a concussion. A few cracked ribs. Hematomas on and around both breasts, and in addition to lacerations around her left eye and ear, she has an acute bilateral fractured mandible."

"They broke her jaw," the guard said. "Could've been worse. At least they didn't have a shank. Just a broken mop handle and a sock with a bar of soap in it."

Taylor felt sick.

The nurse gave her a sympathetic smile. "Don't worry, we're keeping her comfortable. I doubt she'll wake up tonight, but first thing in the morning, she'll see an oral surgeon, and they'll determine if they'll wire her up or if she'll need surgery. If it's real severe, it may take some metal plates."

"Liquid diet either way. Happened to my cousin," the guard said matter-of-factly.

Taylor wished she'd shut her mouth. No doubt her cousin hadn't had to recover in a state women's prison.

"How long do you think they'll keep her here?" Taylor asked.

"I really can't say," the nurse said. "But I'd guess that as soon as they've fixed up her jaw, they'll let her do the rest of her recovery in the prison infirmary."

"They won't try to keep her pain down at the prison," the guard said. "Just basic over-the-counter pain relievers from there on out."

"Listen. That's not helpful. She can probably hear you," Taylor said. "This was a conversation between her nurse and me. If you can't muster up some compassion, how about keeping your mouth shut?"

Both the guard and the nurse stared at Taylor.

She was beyond caring.

"Isn't your shift about up anyway?" she asked. "And now that I think of it, aren't you supposed to be sitting in the hallway outside the room? You're in here because of the television, aren't you?"

"I can state no visitors in here, you know," the guard said.

"And I can get the doctor to override that," the nurse retorted. "Look, let's just play nice. Okay, you two? The patient is under enough duress as it is, and God knows she doesn't need to wake up to more trauma."

They all glanced at Cate, but she hadn't moved. Her eyes were still closed. But the nurse was right. It wasn't appropriate. Making an enemy of the guard wouldn't serve Taylor well either.

"I apologize," Taylor said. "I'm just upset. There's no excuse for what they did to her."

"I agree," the guard said. "Gray is a good one. Never gives us a bit of trouble. A shame to see her so broken up."

The nurse smiled at them both. "Good. You two make nice, and I'll get another reclining chair in here for you, Ms. Gray. I'm assuming you will want to be here when she wakes up." She slipped through the door to the hall.

"No—I'm actually not going to—"

Her words trailed after the nurse, who was already gone. Taylor would stay for a while, but it would be awkward to be there when Cate woke. She was glad she'd gotten to come, though, and get a clear report on what was going on. Adele was waiting for her to call back and give her the details and was probably beside herself with worry.

For once, luck was on Taylor's side. She was glad she had stayed another night in Montana to meet Hensley Bowers and attend dinner with her and Jan. Otherwise, she'd have been in the air, on her way back to Georgia.

Cate's pallor was deathly white, and the bruises were already forming around her face. It was going to be quite a rainbow when it all set in. Taylor hoped she could sleep as long as possible before she had to face the pain.

"I'll be right back." She stepped outside and called Adele.

"Adele. Please, stop crying. They are taking care of her. I'll check back in before I leave tomorrow, but at this point, there's nothing we can do. I'm going to call the warden in the morning to talk about what they are going to do with the ones who did this."

Adele rambled on and on until Taylor finally had to cut her off. "I'm sorry, but I need to get back in there. I'll call you when I leave here."

She hung up and went back into the room. The guard was looking at her watch.

"Have you been here a long time? I can go get you something to eat from the dining hall if you want. And I didn't get your name."

"Officer Pagan. Or just Loretta. Thanks, but they'll send my relief soon."

"How did you draw the short straw to be here?" Taylor leaned against the window, suddenly exhausted.

"I volunteered. I'd much rather be here, watching an inmate sleep, than listening to five hundred of them bickering before bed."

"Is it that bad? I've only had experience with the county jail, but I figured the inmates had more to lose and behaved better than they do there."

Loretta chuckled. "Nope. It's like high school for criminals. They all form their little cliques, and one group is always mad at the other for something stupid. Or they fight over the attention of the latest male correction officer to join the ranks, hoping he'll throw them a bone."

"And Cate, is she part of a clique?" Taylor asked, lowering her voice to a whisper.

"Nah. She's an old-timer and stays mostly to herself. The girls go to her for advice. Many of the women don't have family near enough to visit, so they tend to form their own pseudo-families inside. Helps them deal with loneliness. Gray won't turn anyone away. You better believe there will be some big-time retaliation going on because of this attack. The girls in her circle aren't going to take it lightly. The warden has put two suspects in isolation, not only for punishment but for their safety. She's met with the officers on that block and set up some new security parameters to follow, too, hoping to ward off reprisal."

Listening to the guard talk about Cate being a mother figure and having a family in the prison felt surreal. It also made her curious to know more about Cate's life for the last twenty-odd years.

"I've heard about the prison-family phenomenon," Taylor said. "I guess it helps the inmates cope with the lack of contact from the outside."

Loretta nodded. "From what I've heard, Gray wasn't always that way. She was one of the angry ones for the first years. Then she mellowed out, like most lifers do. To be honest, I didn't know she had a daughter. The only visitor I ever saw before you was her mother."

That hit deep in the gut. But it wasn't as if it was their fault.

"Yes, it's a long story."

Loretta held her hands up. "No judgment from me. It's not uncommon for families to shun the inmates. Some can't handle the visits, and some are angry that their loved ones ended up there. Relationships are complicated."

That was the understatement of the year.

Taylor looked at her phone and saw it was almost ten thirty.

"I should probably get to the hotel. No sense in sitting here all night."

"Tttttt errrr."

She turned to Cate and saw that her eyes were open wide, a look of wild alarm flashing through them. She tried again to talk, but it was unintelligible.

Taylor went to the bed and took her free hand.

"Shh... don't try to talk. You're safe. You're in the hospital, and they are taking good care of you. Just rest. I'm not going anywhere."

Cate searched her eyes for a few seconds then nodded off again.

The nurse chose that moment to arrive, rolling in a big green chair with a starched white blanket folded in the seat. "Sorry, but the reclining option is broken," she said. "I brought you a blanket, though."

CHAPTER 19

*L*ucy was out walking again, wanting to squeeze in as much time outdoors as she could before the rain came. The sky was already clouding up, and the thought of being cooped up inside for the next few days was depressing.

"C'mon, you two, pick up the pace." She pulled on the leashes to give the dogs a jolt. Her stomach was huge now, and her feet had completely disappeared from view, but she was still faster than the dogs. She was thankful that the weight wasn't sticking anywhere but her belly. That would make it easier to slip back into her regular clothes and her life.

This was her third walk of the day, and it was only half past noon. They were lazy, and she'd had to force them outside. Lucy was sure they missed the park in the city and all the other dog smells, but she needed to be anywhere but within those walls, and she needed them to support her.

"I know, I know. This is boring, but at least maybe you two fat-asses will lose some weight while we're here."

The excursions around the property didn't excite them much.

Vira, the midwife, had been there earlier and had examined

Lucy, taken a bunch of notes, then given her the thumbs-up and left. Suki had waved her off when Lucy asked if she wanted to witness her morning exercises, so of course she'd cheated on the check-off sheet stuck to the fridge.

Now she was alone again. Except for her reluctant walking buddies.

The seclusion in such a nice home had been wonderfully relaxing for the first month, but now they'd been there going on three, and it was slowly driving Lucy mad. She was itching to be around people again. Noise. Crowds. Lights. *Life!* She longed for the usual chaos that made her feel alive.

Ian wouldn't even let her work remotely. She was going out of her mind.

What had once felt like an oasis now felt more like a prison. Especially since the week after they'd arrived, a crew had worked from daybreak to sundown for seven days to put up an eight-foot fence all the way around the entire parcel. She had never had this kind of privacy in her life and was finding it hard to get used to.

And Jorge.

She couldn't stop thinking of him. He was probably going out of his mind with worry. Lucy didn't feel good about the way she'd cut off contact, but it had to be done. Other than the Banfields and Margot, he was the only one who knew about the pregnancy. He had also known something weird was happening when he saw her with Armina.

She couldn't have him asking questions.

There would be other Jorges. There always were.

Still, she couldn't help but think of some of their long talks and how easy it had been to be with him. He'd told her he wanted to take her to Uruguay one day to meet his mother. That they'd visit the Casapueblo, one of the most popular tourist attractions in his country. He said a Uruguayan artist had designed the building and used it as a workshop once upon a time. It was hard to imagine, but he said it was shaped like the nest of a Uruguayan bird.

"There are no straight lines in the whole building!" he'd exclaimed, looking like an excited boy. "It's like a maze, with thirteen floors and staggered terraces where you stand and look out over the Atlantic Ocean. I promise, *cariña*, I will take you there."

He was the only man in her life other than her father who had ever used an endearment, and that didn't count. Her dad. That was another thing. She wondered how he was doing. Surely, he was wondering where she'd gone without checking in for so long. Taylor, too, who she knew would be livid about Lucy's silence.

Right now, she had to just get through this, and then she could get back.

Ian's rules were senseless, and she didn't know if she was going to be able to stand eight more weeks. Just two months and then she'd get her body back, along with her freedom. Growing a human had turned out not to be so bad, though. Once she was out of the first trimester, she hadn't had any more nausea. The worst part of the whole thing was the crap that Ian wanted her to do. He'd said a personal trainer had put together the exercise plan, but it was too much. She didn't mind the walks, but the fancy electric bike was her nemesis. She could barely work it.

Also, Ian's strict regimen of fish and vegetables, no carbs, was great for not putting on any bad weight, but Lucy was dying to have a bag of chips or a bowl of ice cream.

She had gotten angry with him on the last visit, and he'd said if she did all her exercises without prompting and ate well, on his next visit, he'd surprise her with a pint of Moose Tracks ice cream. She wanted a gallon, but she'd take what she could get.

If she'd had the code for the gate, she would have grabbed an Uber and gone into town for some secret goodies, but he was stingy with that too.

"You aren't a prisoner, Lucia," he'd said the last time he'd come to check in.

"Then why can't I have the code?"

"I change it every day for security reasons. Sometimes twice."

He always had an excuse. It was ridiculous how the place was secured as though it were Fort Knox. She assumed that somewhere in the house, he had a stash of art and was afraid she'd let some hooligan in to visit, and his precious cache would be cleaned out. That was the only thing she could think of, because from what she knew of it, Hudson Valley wasn't an epicenter of crime.

At least he'd put a television in her room after she'd nagged him during his last three visits. But now she'd binged on so many series that she didn't want to even turn it on again for a while. Always bouncing around from place to place, she'd never watched much TV, and now, she could finally have a conversation about all the top series she'd been binging on. But she had no one to talk about them with.

Bailey stopped and stuck her nose into a pile of leaves. Bentley tried to push her out of the way, and Lucy pulled them both back.

"Oh, hell no. I know what's in there. Squirrel poop. Y'all aren't getting me in trouble." It took some wrangling, but she finally got them to move on. "This is why your mama won't let you run free on the property, little poop detectives."

That made her think of Taylor, and she felt bad that she hadn't been able to pop off an email or text message before Ian had taken her phone battery. She'd also wanted to send her the cash she'd stolen now that she had some money, but she didn't want Taylor to know where she was and couldn't figure out how to get it to her without a postmark waving at her like a red flag.

"Let's go back." She turned the dogs around.

She'd spend the afternoon reading. That had been a surprise that her isolation had revealed. Lucy had never been much of a reader, but with television getting on her nerves, she'd decided to try a book from the bookshelf in her room.

She'd started reading a book by Truman Capote called *In Cold Blood*. The publication date on it was 1965, but it was interesting. It was like true crime before the term had even been invented, mixing fact and research with enough prose that it almost read like fiction. When Ian had discovered her reading one morning, he'd brought her a book on childbirth on his next visit. She'd barely opened the cover before it had scared her senseless, and she'd hid it under the bed. She'd rather be surprised at childbirth and stick to reading about things not related to squeezing a watermelon out of her vagina.

Bent let out a growl and then a bark, and Bae joined him. They pulled at the leash, trying to get to the front of the estate.

Lucy let them go to keep from straining herself too hard.

She followed and found them greeting Ian, who had pulled the car through the gate and was standing beside it now, watching to ensure the gate closed properly behind him.

"Hello. We didn't think you'd be back for a few days," she called out.

He turned and narrowed his eyes. "What did you tell Jorge about me?"

Lucy was taken aback at the venom in his tone. "What are you talking about?"

"You must've told him something. We offered him fifteen hundred dollars for that painting, and he refused, then he goes and sells it to the art witch for five hundred!"

Bent and Bae sulked back, no longer interested in getting his attention. They headed for the house.

Lucy even took a few steps back, unaccustomed to seeing Ian's wrath pointed at her. Once she was over the initial shock, she could feel the heat rise in her cheeks. Her hands flew to her hips, where she dangled the leashes. Her feet were swollen, and her stomach felt so tight it would pop. He was messing with the wrong woman.

"Look, I don't appreciate you talking to me that way, and I can assure you I know nothing about it. I haven't talked to Jorge since we left the city. Who is the art witch?"

"Jackie Schafer," he spat out. "Now she has his first piece and obviously plans to start his career for him. I could've really used him on my portfolio."

It did make Lucy curious about why Jorge would do something like that, but perhaps that was his only way to strike out at her for ghosting him. Or it could have been that he just liked Jackie better than he did Ian. It wasn't as though Ian had a fan club going. He could come across as prickly, and she'd told him that herself. She warned him he'd lose clients over it one day.

"I'm sorry that happened, but again, I had nothing to do with it. As you can see here"—she pointed at her belly—"I'm otherwise occupied. Don't forget, you told me you didn't want me even thinking about work while I was carrying your son. What was it you wanted me to do? Meditate, eat clean, exercise, and do yoga?"

He jangled his keys and pulled the sunglasses from his head down over his eyes. "Why do I feel like you are playing with me?"

She shrugged. "Sounds like paranoia to me. I'm not. I've been doing my part with all your orders. Even Vira says I'm in excellent shape. So, where's my ice cream?"

"Absolutely not. I've heard of harmful bacteria and even listeria being found in ice cream, depending on where it was manufactured. Ice cream is nothing but empty calories and will make you bloat and cramp. Not to mention I'm not bringing you anything when I still have my suspicions that you had something to do with me losing Jorge."

He was insufferable. She should've known he wouldn't keep his promise. He knew damn well that grocery store ice cream was perfectly safe. And God forbid she gain any of what he considered "detrimental" weight that would make his future child unhealthy or inhibit a productive and safe childbirth.

Pure bullshit

She turned on her heels and joined the dogs on the porch, then went inside and let the door slam behind her.

CHAPTER 20

*T*aylor was a model therapy patient, and she'd listened to and acknowledged most of the analysis of her personality traits told to her over a year of visits. One of those was her tendency to always try to fix things and to take care of people, even to the detriment of her own mental and physical health. She'd reminded herself of this fact more than once since she'd arrived home, carrying a ton of guilt that she'd left Montana as soon as Cate had been discharged back to the prison.

There is nothing you can do for her right now.

That was her mantra, but it wasn't working, because she was having trouble sleeping, and when she did doze, she fought off nightmares of Cate being cornered in the prison kitchen or the laundry room then victimized again.

And it would be her fault.

Of course, she knew it wouldn't be her fault—but the constant critic in her head wanted to argue that point nonstop.

It had been two days, and she hadn't heard from Jan at the center, and the wait was killing her nerves. At least the family gathering would give her something to divert her thoughts.

"Diesel, come get your supper." She set the bowl of boiled

ground turkey on the floor and watched him come skidding across the linoleum. Levi was right behind him, laughing as they both nearly crashed into Taylor's legs.

"Is that one of Dad's bowls?" Anna said, a grimace covering her face.

"Sure is." Taylor wasn't in the mood to put up with her sister's snark. "And top-quality turkey. He's getting a treat tonight because I missed him so much."

Anna pretended to gag. "That's gross, using real dishes."

"It will be washed in hot water, Anna. Stop being like that," Jo said.

Taylor shot her a grateful look, even though she really should've used a paper plate.

The family gathering was rare, and it felt nice. It was also rare that Anna would join them for anything, especially at their dad's trailer, which she claimed was too small and uncomfortable. But Jo visiting was a cause for celebration, and Anna had relented. Fortunately, Pete was out of town again, though he probably would've found an excuse not to come anyway.

He and their dad weren't on the friendliest terms. They were cordial, but there was underlying understanding that they were from two different worlds and would never be friends.

After a hearty meal of spaghetti, garlic bread, and salad that her sisters had prepared while Taylor tried to keep the three kids entertained, they sat around the cleared kitchen table, drinking coffee.

Their dad was back in his recliner, feet up and belly full.

Bronwyn and Teague were like fish out of water and sat in stone silence on the couch. Levi's energy made up for their lack thereof, and he played with a very happy Diesel. It was hard to believe the kids were all nearly the same age. Levi was a bit older but seemed younger because Anna's two acted like they were senior citizens.

"I've got a few balls in the back of my truck if you guys want to go outside and throw them to Diesel when he's done," Taylor offered. "He needs to run off his meal."

Bronwyn shook her head no, and Teague shrugged, not lifting his gaze from his phone.

"I'll take him, Aunt Taylor," Levi said.

"They really need to get out more and play with kids their age," Jo whispered to Anna. "Is all that screen time good for them?"

"They're fine," Anna retorted. "And they have friends."

"Yeah, they're fine," her dad agreed, his hearing suddenly top-notch, when normally, he couldn't hear anything Taylor had to say. "Leave them be."

They didn't look fine to Taylor, but she was picking her battles, and offering guidance on kids wasn't in her wheelhouse.

"Can we watch YouTube?" Bronwyn asked.

Dad tossed her the remote. "I don't know what that is, but if I have it, you can sure watch it. Just don't put it on anything dirty, or your Aunt Taylor will have a cow."

He was happy that Anna had finally come over and especially that she'd brought the kids. Of course, he'd pouted at first because they were missing Lucy, but Taylor couldn't pull off miracles, and he was lucky to have Anna.

"Dad, we're going to your room, okay?" Jo asked.

There wasn't enough sitting space in the living room, and the dining chairs were getting hard, so Taylor was glad she'd asked.

He waved an arm. "I don't care."

Luckily, Taylor had gotten to her dad's before her sisters arrived and had neatened everything up, even putting new sheets and a fresh coverlet on the bed. She'd run the toilet brush around the bowl and thrown all the dirty towels into the washing machine before tackling the kitchen, getting it cleaned up just in time to dirty it again when they all arrived.

Jo took a running leap and did a belly flop right in the middle of the bed.

"God, I missed you," Taylor said, joining her but in a more dignified manner. It felt so good to get off her feet.

She really did miss Jo. She was so different from both Anna and Lucy. She was always full of positivity, spreading that stuff everywhere and making it easy to be near her.

Anna sat gingerly on the edge, as though teetering on the rim of a volcano.

Jo sat up and grabbed Anna around the waist then flipped back with her onto the pillows.

"Loosen up, weirdo," she said, holding on to her tightly.

"Stop it!" Anna yelled and kicked but fell into giggles when Jo refused to let go.

Taylor felt her heart leap. The Anna they used to know was still in there.

"You two are crazy. And you're making the bed back up. I already did it once today."

They all settled back on the pillows, with Jo sandwiched in the middle. It reminded Taylor of the old days—minus Lucy, of course. She couldn't count the times they'd all piled up in the same bed and talked, sometimes for hours, telling everything on their minds and strategizing on how to get past it. School, boys, even the woes of figuring out life on their own with a dad who was there in body but not in spirit.

Taylor thought of Cate and suddenly wanted to spill it all and have them share in the discovery that their mother was alive and the agony of trying to figure out if she was a murderer or if she was innocent.

It all nearly tumbled out of her mouth, but the words of Jan Randolph rang in her ears.

"I'm not making any promises because this is much worse than a long shot, and I don't want you to get your hopes up that we can do anything. I'll read over the transcripts and call you when I'm done."

Hensley had followed up the conversation by telling Taylor

that she didn't think they had enough for Jan to believe in Cate's innocence, but at least they'd tried.

Taylor wasn't giving up hope until Jan called her and told her no. And she couldn't let her sisters go through the mental stress she was dealing with because of it all. If Cate wasn't innocent or didn't have a chance to get out, it was better that they never know about her.

Was that fair? No—but Taylor had been making decisions regarding their well-being for most of their lives, and she couldn't stop now. Not when she had the power to save them from more heartache.

"I think we might move back to Hart's Ridge," Jo said.

Taylor sat up. "Really?"

"Really. I'm tired of being too far from you guys, and Levi needs to know his family better. He's getting to the age that he's asking questions. I talked to Sissy at the Den, and she said Payton might be able to get me a job at the ranch now that I have experience."

That was the best news Taylor had heard in months, and she couldn't stop smiling.

"Well, I guess that's good," Anna said. "Where are you going to live?"

Jo shrugged. "I don't know yet. I'll have to figure it all out once I get here."

"You can stay with me for a while," Taylor said.

"I know. That was my plan." Jo laughed. "I'm about to go tell Dad, but I wanted you two to know first. Just in case you had any reason you thought I shouldn't come back. Any new family drama I should stay away from. I mean, besides Dad's situation. That's not going to change."

"We'll always get through the drama. You know that." Taylor hoped that if and when they found out her secret, they'd forgive her.

"Speaking of drama," Jo said, "what's this about Shane Weaver being back in town? And someone told me they saw you at the old ballpark with a tall, handsome guy that wasn't Shane. Two possibles? Sister dear, you've been holding out, and we need to know all the juicy details!

Taylor felt her face flush. That was the thing about small towns—no one could get away with much without everyone finding out their business.

"And I was starting to think you were gay," Anna said.

For a second, Taylor was offended. Then they all burst out laughing.

"First of all, I'm not seeing either of them like that. They're just friends. But how did you know about Shane?" Taylor asked. "Oh, never mind. Probably Dad. He watched the press conference."

Jo wiggled her fingers. "I have my ways of keeping up with you, Taylor. So, really, is Shane a thing? Or going to be a thing? Is he still as shy as he used to be? I saw his photo, and he grew into himself. I think you can agree."

"He's not a *thing*," she said, laughing. "And he's definitely not shy anymore."

She left out the fact that she'd considered him a *possible thing* for a few minutes. Until he had gone and stolen her detective position and thrown her under the bus. That had hurt deeply, and she wasn't over it yet.

"If he's not a thing, he needs to be, if you know what I mean," Anna said, winking at Taylor. "Better do it before Lucy comes back to town, or she might snatch him up."

Taylor's smile disappeared. That was too close to the truth, and she wasn't decided about Shane just yet.

"Aww, I miss our little Lucy," Jo said. "What do you think she's doing right now?"

"Boosting a six-pack of beer from a gas station, most likely," Anna said.

"That's not funny, Anna. Back to you, Taylor. Who was the guy at the park?"

Keeping secrets from her sisters was harder than she remembered, and Taylor hoped they didn't ferret out the big ones she was hoarding now. Best to keep them interested in the small stuff.

"His name is Sam, and he's Diesel's dad. Like I said, just a friend."

"His dad? You mean his owner?" Anna asked.

"What? I thought you got him at the shelter," Jo said. She sat up and pulled a pillow to her belly then dragged Taylor back down to the bed. "Tell us everything. You aren't leaving this room until you do. I want the real story too."

※

TAYLOR DROVE up the driveway to her house, exhausted after finally leaving her dad's trailer. She couldn't wait for a bath and then bed. Her heart felt full, though. It had been a happy visit that had done their dad good. She'd even seen a smile or two when he was joking back and forth with the kids. Anna had finally been able to relax and be herself, something they didn't see much of these days.

After their sister sharing had wrapped up and Taylor had successfully convinced them that Sam was simply a friend and not a future contender for her heart—and that Shane wasn't going to be her latest fling, either—they'd helped clean the kitchen. They had worked together like old times, each of them falling into their usual roles to wash, dry, or put away, as they'd done when they were kids.

Lucy had never helped with kitchen duty, since she was the baby, but it would've been nice to have her there, being lazy, to complete the picture.

"What about those kids, boy?" she asked Diesel. "Is Levi your new best bud?"

Diesel had had almost too much fun, and Levi had run him ragged with a game of chase. Now he stared out the truck window. His ears perked and his posture turned rigid, then his tail started thumping against the seat.

Taylor saw a Jeep parked in front of the house. As they got closer, she identified Sam sitting on the edge of the porch, his elbows on his knees as he watched them pull up.

"What is he doing here? I thought he went home."

She pulled up and cut the ignition. She had barely opened her door when Diesel pushed into her seat and squeezed past her to jump down and run to Sam and plaster his quivering body into Sam's open arms.

"Hey, Diesel," Sam said, laughing. "You sure are excited considering I just saw you a few hours ago."

"I thought you were on your way back home," Taylor said.

"Yeah, me too. I got just out of town, and my radiator started running hot. There's no way I can make it all the way back. The parts store is already closed too. I'm going to have to wait until morning to get what I need to get it back on the road."

He looked apologetic, and she was confused. Then it dawned on her.

"Oh. You want to stay here?"

"Could I? I mean—unless you aren't comfortable with that. I can find a place in town, I guess." He shoved his hands deep into his front pockets, suddenly deflated.

"No. That's fine." She climbed the steps and went to unlock the door. "Have you been sitting out here all this time? I've been gone for hours."

"Yep, but it was nice. This place is so quiet and peaceful. Now it makes sense why you live way out in the sticks. I also walked down to the lake and sat on your little pier. You've got some rotted boards."

She opened the door, and they followed her in. Diesel went to his toy box and pulled out a squeaky bone then settled on the floor between her and Sam.

"Oh, now that your dad is here, you're interested in those, huh?"

She set her keys and bag on the counter before answering Sam. The condition of the property was a sore spot for her. There wasn't enough time or money to get it into tip-top condition.

"I know. There's a lot to fix around here. Maybe in the spring."

"I can do that for you. At least the pier. It's dangerous if someone isn't paying attention to where they're walking."

She leaned back against the kitchen sink. "Thanks, but I've got a tight budget right now and nothing extra for handyman services."

"Oh, I meant I'll do the labor for free. You buy the boards and nails."

"We'll see. Thanks." She wasn't sure that she wanted Sam around that much. He was nice, but she'd found herself wishing lately that she'd never opened that can of worms. Losing Diesel back to him permanently wasn't going to be easy.

"Okay," he said, drawing the word out.

She glanced at the clock. "Wow, it's getting late."

"Yeah. Nine o'clock. Past your bedtime already?" He smiled.

"No," she laughed. "Well, sometimes. Have you had dinner?"

"Yep. Stopped into a place called the Den. Do you go there? They make a heck of a patty melt. And those homemade fries. Wow."

"Oh, the Den is the most popular dining option in town. Did you meet Mabel, the owner?"

"Sure did. She was sweet. But she sure was intent on finding out who I was. She got just about everything out of me except my Social Security number."

Taylor felt her heart fall. "Did you tell her about us? And Diesel?"

He nodded then looked concerned when he saw her expres sion. "Why? Was it a secret?

She hated people knowing her business, but she was saved from answering when her phone rang. When she pulled it out of her purse, she saw it was a Montana number.

"Make yourself comfortable, Sam. You can take the first room down the hall on the right. I need to take this call." She slipped out onto the front porch and answered.

"Hi, Taylor. This is Jan with the Center for Unjust Convictions."

Taylor felt her legs get weak, and she sank down to sit on the step. Despite the two

helpings of spaghetti and bread she'd had earlier, her stomach suddenly felt empty.

"Hi" was all she could get out.

"I've spent the last two nights reading over the transcripts."

"Okay." Taylor stood and ran her hands through her hair. It felt as if she was going to be sick.

"This morning, I met with a fire forensic expert I'd used before."

"Okay." Damn, couldn't she think of anything else to say besides "okay"? Her brain was frozen. She realized she was pacing on the porch.

"He's got some concerns about the arson testimony that was presented by Cate's prosecution team."

"Okay..." Taylor slapped her forehead, incensed at her stupidity. Jan was going to think she was an illiterate idiot.

"We're going to take the case, but I have to remind you, it would be a miracle if we were able to get her a new trial."

Tears sprouted as if from a spigot, running down Taylor's face as she silently cried, hoping that Jan couldn't hear her. It felt as though a weight had been lifted from her back. Finally, someone would help her figure it out.

"I know you're overwhelmed. Don't feel like you have to say anything. I just wanted to let you know. And I'm not looking for gratitude. Too early for that," Jan continued, all business. "On Monday, I'm going to subpoena the ATF files on the original investigation. Hensley Bowers has agreed to work with us on this, so that will help us get it on the fast track. However, I'll run lead, and she'll be a part of my discovery team."

Taylor stopped pacing and found her voice, though it was thick with tears. "When do we talk about your retainer? Can I set up monthly payments?"

She had no idea where the money would come from, but she'd figure out something.

"All costs will be covered by the center," Jan said. "That's what we do and why we only take cases that we truly believe in."

Another flood of tears. "Thank you," Taylor whispered.

"I said no thank-yous. Not yet. We need to dig in and see what's what before we get any confidence going. There's a lot to be done. I'll talk to you soon."

When Jan disconnected, Taylor stood there for a moment, taking it in. She felt a sense of accomplishment that she'd never felt before, which was silly, because it didn't mean that Cate was innocent or that she'd be freed even if she was.

But it meant something.

She wished with all her heart that she could share the good news with Anna and Jo. Maybe even Lucy. But if it all fell through, she would be responsible for bringing them more heartache. More trauma. She could talk to her dad, but he wasn't the best one to find comfort from, and it would most likely end in an argument.

Rubbing the tears off her face, she opened the door and went in.

Sam was sitting at the kitchen table, scrolling on his phone, his feet shoeless and propped on Diesel's back. He turned and looked at her with a smile that disappeared instantly. "What is it? Is everything okay?"

Taylor nodded, not trusting herself to speak.

Sam stood and approached. "No. Something is wrong. Listen, if you need someone to talk to, I'm here and a hell of a listener. I'm a pretty good secret keeper too."

She didn't answer.

"I'm also good for a simple hug if that's all you can handle." He opened his arms.

For once, Taylor decided to let her guard down, and she walked right into them.

CHAPTER 21

*S*heriff Dawkins lectured Taylor for a full five minutes before he paused to take a break. He looked as though he was going to give himself a stroke if he didn't calm down. She'd have been afraid if she hadn't known him so well and recognized when he was trying to look more upset than he really was. More than likely, he wanted anyone hanging around outside his door to think he was blowing a gasket.

Someone knocked once at the door and cracked it open. It was Shane, and when he saw the sheriff's thunderous expression, he mumbled an apology and eased the door shut.

"I wouldn't ask if it wasn't a family emergency," Taylor said evenly, taking the opportunity to speak.

"Emergency, huh? What has Lucy done this time? You must stop swooping in to save her, Taylor. You have a job and can't take off whenever your sister has a problem. We're already a man down with McElroy gone. Kuno doesn't know his ass from a hole in the ground yet and is going to need a lot more training. Why couldn't this all have been taken care of during the time I gave you off after the Joni Stott case? You had time."

"It's not Lucy, and it just came up. I'm sorry. Fine—I revoke the request for a month. Give me two weeks. Please. Thomas and Grimes would probably pick up some extra shifts. Grimes has a baby on the way, and his job at Purina doesn't pay that well. I'm sure he could use the money."

"Don't tell me how to run my shop. And I'm not even going to ask if this is about Jackson. You know how I feel about that. I'm giving you a week. No more. If you've got a family emergency that requires time off, apply for FMLA like everyone else must. Now, this meeting is over. Clear your paperwork before you leave for this fantasy emergency. I'll update the sergeant." He turned his chair away from her, toward the window, as he always did when he wanted to be done.

"Thank you. I appreciate it." Taylor stood and left the office.

"Next time, don't jump rank," he called out. "Follow the proper chain of command."

Her face flushed, but she didn't stop.

Yes, she'd used her relationship with the sheriff to get something she wanted without going through her supervisor, and it made her feel dirty. But this was too important to be shot down in one swoop, which she knew Sarge would do if she didn't share enough details.

She also wouldn't be filing for FMLA. For one thing, helping get her mother a new trial in a murder case wasn't a qualifying event. Even if it had been, everyone in the station and probably the town would then know her business.

She went to her desk, sat down, and pulled a stack of papers closer.

Penner spoke, and she gave him a distracted wave. He declined to pursue more conversation, probably because of her body language.

For years, she'd never missed any work and had rarely taken vacation. Now that she needed more time off to go back to Montana and try to help with Cate's case, she felt like a deadbeat.

Suck it up, Taylor. You can't be perfect all the time.

Didn't she know it? And why couldn't she stop trying?

She probably had a half hour or more of admin to get done. Then she could get home and talk to Sam about Diesel. He was still there, working on his truck. She'd taken him to the parts store and then dropped him back off before coming to work.

They'd had a late night. Poor Sam had happened to be in the wrong place at the right time, and Taylor was weak. Nothing sexual had happened. No kiss and tell.

Much worse.

She'd bared her soul to him.

Now someone who was basically a stranger knew all about their family secret and Taylor's quest for the truth. She'd only meant to give him a brief outline and ask him to hang on to Diesel for a bit longer, but once the gate was opened, the dam burst, and before she knew it, the whole sordid story was out there.

Sam hadn't judged. Or at least if he had, he'd kept it under wraps.

He let her cry. She'd straightened up, and they'd made popcorn and turned on a movie. Then something in the movie triggered her, and she was furious with herself because the tears began again.

"I never cry," she swore.

"Maybe it's time to let it all out, then," Sam said gently.

They turned the movie off, and she gorged herself with handfuls of popcorn while she cried. And talked. And ate.

Eating. Crying. Talking.

All at the same time.

He was so patient, even getting up at one point and going to the bathroom and returning with a wad of toilet paper for her runny nose.

Even though she was mortified at looking like a damsel in distress, he'd been helpful. He hadn't fallen to pieces at the sight of a crying woman. He'd been cool and collected, and once she was able to be more coherent, they had talked through things and come up with a plan.

She'd decided to ask the sheriff for a week off so she could go to Montana and do what she could to help speed along the process for a review of Cate's case. With her role in law enforcement, she was sure she could talk Jan into letting her conduct some interviews with the forensic experts or witnesses or even be a courier if that was what it took.

Anything to let her feel useful to a group of people who were trying to help her family for free.

She thought of her dad and what she was going to tell him about yet another trip to Montana. So far, he didn't know about her visit to Hayes or attorney Hensley Bowers and for sure not Jan at the Center for Unjust Convictions. He hadn't asked her the first question about seeing Cate. Not how it had gone, how she'd looked, or anything.

Taylor wondered if her parents were talking on the phone. If Cate was keeping him apprised, it would explain his lack of curiosity.

"You okay over there?"

She turned to Penner. "Yeah. I'm fine."

"You sure? You've been holding your pen in the air and staring straight ahead for five minutes. I thought you turned into a statue. Hard case?"

If you only knew.

"Nah. Just a bunch of paperwork to file. Property damage by Mrs. Butterman, who says a contractor from out of town splattered tar all over her residence and now won't answer her calls. And there was a fire call to Hock & Shop. Albert lost the combination to the safe, so he had Lonny down there, trying to saw through it. The smoke set off the alarm."

Penner laughed. "What kind of pawn shop owner can't open his own safe?"

Taylor chuckled too. "He was so embarrassed. He'd told

Lonny not to park the locksmith van in front, so he was blocking the alley. Alex came in with full sirens, and now the whole street knows."

Luckily, Alex hadn't started anything with her, and they'd both done their jobs professionally and gotten out of there.

"That's some major excitement for the downtown folks."

He was right. They'd all be buzzing about it for weeks, and it might even stop the endless talk about Joni Stott and the rotten cop, though she doubted it.

"Listen, Penner. I'm going to be out for a week. Just wanted you to hear it from me."

"Again? What did you do this time?" He looked crestfallen.

"Ha. Nothing. This time, it's a personal request. Keep an eye on my desk and computer, will you? You know how it is when someone is gone. Everything comes up missing, and I'll return to find a monitor from 1990 and a dial-up modem."

"10-4. I got your back."

"Thanks. Now, I gotta put my head down before the sheriff catches me talking. I'm already in the hot seat."

She turned her attention to knocking out the paperwork, and twenty-five minutes later, she was done. She turned off her computer, gathered her things, and pushed her chair under the desk.

Penner had already left to take his lunch hour. Taylor didn't want any more words with the sheriff and didn't feel like saying goodbye to Shane, so she quietly left for the parking lot, keeping her head down to avoid any conversation with anyone else she might pass.

In the truck, she texted Sam and told him she'd bring home a late lunch. Then she shot off a message to Cecil to meet her early before putting her seat belt on and hitting the road.

As she drove, she thought about what to order for Sam. If he thought Mabel's patty melt was to die for, he was in for a big surprise when it came to her country plates. She probably should've asked if he had any dietary restrictions or foods he hated, but something told her he probably ate anything set in front of him.

That thought led her to think about how strong his arms had felt in their embrace the night before and then how hard his thigh had felt as it rested against hers on the couch, and she felt a line of sweat pop out over her lip.

She looked in the mirror quickly, feeling disgusted. First the crying fest and now thinking of Sam's body. She was turning into a girl, and she didn't like it one bit.

Get your head out of the clouds, Taylor.

When she pulled into the Den's parking lot, she saw that it was packed as usual, and she hoped Cecil had grabbed them a table.

She climbed out and went in, and he waved from the corner booth.

"I'm so glad to see you," she gushed as she slid in across from him.

He had a glass of sweet tea waiting for her, and she gulped down a few drinks.

"Same back 'atcha, girl. What's been happening? Catch me up."

Taylor felt a rush of guilt that she'd spilled the beans to Sam, a stranger, when she should've been bringing Cecil up to speed first. He was her closest friend and the one she should've called last night.

"You are not going to believe this," she began then leaned in and quietly started telling him about the meetings with Hayes, Hensley, and then Jan.

When she got to the part about the assault on Cate, she had to stop and take a drink and push back tears.

Cecil reached over and took her hands. "Have you told your dad? Or Adele?"

"No, not yet. I'm going to call Adele on the way home, and I'll talk to Dad later tonight. He's going to be devastated about her attack, and I haven't found a way to tell him yet."

"Sounds like she got through it, and it wasn't your fault. Or his. She's in prison, for goodness' sake. These things happen. Go on. What else is going on with the case?"

She took a deep breath and continued. She detailed the call from Jan the night before, all about the new forensic expert and the possibility of a new trial, ending her barrage of details with a triumphant note in her voice.

He smiled broadly. "See? You just don't know how amazing you are, Taylor."

She blushed. "No, I'm not."

"Oh, you shut up. You and I both know you are the cream of the whole darn crop." He winked at her, and she felt a rush of affection.

"We sure do know it, but what'd she do this time?" Sissy asked, coming up on them quietly.

"Oh, hi, Sissy," Taylor said. "Nothing. Cecil is always trying to win me over with flattery. You know how he is."

"Yep—a real old-fashioned charmer," Sissy said, grinning at Cecil. "They don't make 'em like you anymore. If I hadn't finally wormed a ring out of Payton, I might scoop him up myself. So, y'all eating today, or you just visiting?"

Cecil gave her his order, and Taylor decided on chicken and dumplings with biscuits on the side. It was double the biscuits, one for each hip, but today, she didn't care.

"Got it," Sissy said, scribbling on her pad.

"Oh, and can you make another one just like mine but to go?"

"Sure will." She twirled and headed back to the kitchen.

"Taking dinner to Jackson?" Cecil asked.

Taylor hesitated. She'd never lied to Cecil before, but she didn't want to talk about Sam.

She sighed.

"No—it's not for Dad. Remember I told you about Diesel's

owner? Well, he's at the house, working on his Jeep. It's a long story, but before you jump to conclusions, it's nothing."

His eyes twinkled as he nodded slowly. "Didn't you say he was a young man, about your age or so? And unattached?"

"Cecil! I mean it. It's nothing." His knowing expression made her laugh. "Anyway, I'm leaving in the morning for Montana. A week this time, and he's going to keep Diesel while I'm away."

"I thought you were going to let him have his dog back. Wasn't that the point of finding the man?"

She fidgeted with the small box of pink and white sugars. "Yes, but I'm not ready. We're sharing Diesel until I'm ready to let him go. I need more time to make sure he'll be okay."

"Hmm..." Cecil said, raising his eyebrows. He sipped at his water.

Sissy saved her with a quick return to the table.

"Piping hot." She set the dumplings in front of Taylor before serving Cecil.

They dug in as soon as Sissy was gone, and Taylor nearly passed out from the ecstasy of the best dumplings on the planet hitting her tongue. One day, she wanted to weasel that recipe from Mabel.

"Eat up," Cecil said. "Sounds like you have a busy evening ahead of you."

CHAPTER 22

Sam wasn't in the house when Taylor arrived home. Diesel was also gone, but the Jeep was in the driveway, so she knew they were there somewhere. She set the bag of food down and went back out.

There was only one place they could be, and she went around the house then took the trail down to the lake. Just as she'd thought, she could see Diesel wading around in the shallow water, and Sam was on the small dock, bent over and hammering.

He didn't hear her coming, and she got within a foot before he looked up.

"Hi."

"What do you think you're doing?" she asked, though it was obvious by the small stack of rotted boards piled up next to him and the new boards in their place.

Diesel ran up and rubbed against her legs, smearing lake slime all over her pants. She pushed him off affectionately, and he ran back to the water.

"Riding a bike. What are you doing?" He winked as he stood and wiped the sweat from his forehead with his wrist.

"Funny. I told you I was going to get to this in the spring."

"I know you did. But I really appreciate that you reached out to me about Diesel. I don't like to let kindness go unreturned, so please—don't hurt my feelings." He held his hands apart, pleading, but a smile played upon his lips.

Taylor didn't like receiving kindness. It felt foreign and awkward, and she didn't know how to react or what to say.

"I brought you some of Mabel's dumplings."

Sam rubbed his hands together. "Whoa. Why didn't you say so? I'm starving."

His laid-back nature made things easy. He seemed to pick up on things that made her nervous and had a way of moving past them without making it worse.

"Come get it while it's hot."

"I'm on it. But hey—I wanted to ask you, are you a smoker?"

"No. Why do you ask?"

He reached into his pocket and pulled out a handful of cigarette butts.

"I didn't think so. These were on the dock. I mean—maybe they're from a boyfriend or something, but I thought you should know someone is being messy. You don't strike me as someone who would allow visitors to contaminate the lake with nasty toxins."

"Let me see those." She held out her hand, and he poured them into it. She held them up closer. "They look fresh, and I don't have visitors."

"You look worried. Has someone been giving you trouble?" Sam asked, suddenly serious.

"I—I—well, not really," she said, skipping over the fact that she'd felt as if someone was in her house recently. "It's probably someone sneaking in for fishing, but I don't like trespassers. I've been meaning to get some security cameras up. Just haven't had the money."

He tilted his head, not breaking eye contact. "Hmm... I'm not sure I believe you."

She laughed uncomfortably and put her hand on her holster. "Even if someone is coming around, don't forget I'm armed. Come on, let's get up to the house. And thank you for doing this work."

When she turned and headed up the dock to the bank, he followed and whistled at Diesel, who obediently fell in behind them.

"No problem. I love working with my hands. It's a great way to get lost in your thoughts. By the way, you look like a different person in your uniform. Very, um—professional."

She laughed. "Thanks, I guess. What about the Jeep? Were you able to fix it?"

"Yep—good to go. Just a clogged radiator fin."

When they got up to the house, Taylor pointed out an old towel hanging on a nail just inside the kitchen door. "That's for Diesel, if you want to give him a quick dry."

While Sam rubbed down Diesel, Taylor transferred his dumplings to a plate, propped a biscuit on the side, and poured them both a glass of sweet tea. She set it all on the table.

"Gonna sit with me?" Sam turned his head to ask while he washed his hands at the sink.

"Sure. I got a few minutes. You headed out after you eat?" She sat down.

He came to the table and joined her. "I wanted to talk to you about that."

"Okay."

"Do you know an old man named Diller? Duane, I think."

"Yes, I know Mr. Diller. Why? Did you tell him about being out here?"

"No, of course not. I ran into him at the parts store this morning. He couldn't get any help, so I answered his questions, then he asked me to repair his car. I thought I might stick around a few days to do that. Put some extra cash in my pocket. Things have been slow at my dad's shop."

"Oh nice. What's going on with Diller's car?"

"Not sure exactly, but from the way he described it, it might be a fuel pump or fuel system issue. He said he didn't drive it much, and these days, gasoline has the shelf life of a gallon of milk. I might have to drain the whole system. Unfortunately, the ethanol in the fuel attracts moisture and starts to caramelize. But we'll see once I get in there." He took a huge bite of dumplings and rolled his eyes to the ceiling with a smile. "Oh my gawd, these are so good."

"Mabel should have a patent on her recipe," Taylor said. "But hey—that sounds expensive for Mr. Diller. Did you let him know it might be costly?"

"Yeah. He said the local garage here in town was backed up for weeks. He's called the dealership in Atlanta where he bought it, but he thinks we can get it done a lot cheaper here. He's right. I won't gouge him."

"I'm sure he probably figured that out, or he wouldn't have asked you," Taylor said. "Mr. Diller can be a prickly sort, and sometimes, he thinks everyone is out to take advantage of him. Your golden-boy looks must have charmed him."

Sam laughed then put down his fork. "'Golden-boy' would not be an adjective I'd use for myself."

"Want to elaborate? I did a lot of talking last night, but I still don't know much about you except you were in the service, went overseas, and got out, and now you help your dad with his car-repair business. There's a lot of missing pieces in there, Sam. Do you have a girlfriend? Divorced? Serial killer?"

"Froot Loops, maybe. And no to the girlfriend and the ex-wife. Long story that we can get into when you get back if you're still interested." He said it like an invitation and waited for her reply.

She busied herself picking a piece of invisible lint from her sleeve. "Sure, I'd love to know more about you. I mean, after all, I'll be sending my best buddy off with you. Eventually."

Sam grinned. "Okay—yeah. You need to get all the back-story for Diesel's sake. Gotcha. I was wondering, though, if you'd mind if I stayed here with him while I fixed Diller's car. I've got most of my tools in the back of the Jeep. Otherwise, what a motel would cost me would eat up what I'd make. I mean—if you're comfortable with that, and it you're not, then—"

"It's fine, Sam," she interrupted. She thought about the cigarette butts still in her pocket. Butts that would be going into a plastic baggie for safekeeping. "Stay if you need to. Be nice for you to look out for the place while I'm away."

"Thanks, Taylor. I can knock out some other chores around here, too, if you want. What else needs fixing?"

She waved a hand at him. "Nope. You focus on taking care of Diesel and Mr. Diller. The two of them will keep you busy enough."

He swallowed another big bite and winked at her. "Fine, but if some repairs magically happen while you are gone, don't be mad at me."

"Sam, don't—"

Diesel barked and ran to the door.

"Someone's here," Taylor said, standing to peek out the window. She saw Shane's car. "I'll be right back."

Shane was already out of the car when she got out there, and he leaned against the hood and crossed his arms. She couldn't see his eyes behind his dark shades.

"You weren't going to tell me you were leaving town again?"

"I didn't know I needed to." She casually sat down on the steps.

"Who does that Jeep belong to?" He jerked his head toward it.

"A friend."

She could see a tic in his jaw as he looked from the Jeep up to the house. "Oh, a friend, huh? Does your *friend* have a name?" He kicked at a rock at his feet.

"Shane, I'm sorry I didn't talk to you before I left today, I had a lot to do. Didn't mean to hurt your feelings." She meant that. Shane was trying hard to be her friend, and she should've thought about just up and disappearing on him without explanation.

"Didn't hurt my feelings. Just wondering." He shrugged as though it didn't matter, though the stiffness in his shoulders told another tale.

"The Jeep belongs to Sam Stone, and he's Diesel's original owner. I found him and then reached out because Diesel seemed so sad. We're sharing him for now, and Sam is going to keep him while I go out of town."

He lifted his sunglasses and raised his eyebrows. "You're telling me that you've reached out to a perfect stranger and allowed him into your house? While you are out here in the boonies all alone? Sharing custody of a dog? Have you lost your mind, Taylor?"

Taylor sighed and shook her head. "Come on in, Shane. You need to meet this *scary stranger*. Be careful, though. He might try to hurt you."

He didn't look thrilled about it, but he followed Taylor onto the porch and inside.

Sam was at the sink, washing out his bowl. He turned and picked up the dishtowel and saw them.

"Oh, hi."

"Shane, this is Sam Stone. Sam, Shane works with me at the station. He's a detective."

"Nice to meet you." Sam held his hand out. Shane hesitated but then took it and shook.

"And Taylor and I are good friends. Not just work colleagues," Shane said.

Sam looked from Taylor to Shane and back to Taylor.

She felt warmth rush up her neck and into her cheeks.

"He means we go way back. We went to high school together," she added. "Shane, have a seat. Do you want something to drink?"

"No, I'm fine." He sat down at the table, and Sam took a chair opposite him.

They stared at each other, Shane in his creased slacks and dark looks and Sam with patched jeans and the forever smile in his eyes.

Total opposites.

It reminded Taylor of a Rottweiler sizing up a golden retriever in a pissing contest, and Shane had the bigger teeth.

"What are you going out of town for, Taylor?" Shane broke the silence.

"Just some family stuff."

"Hmmph. Okay. Does *he* know why you're going?" He jabbed a finger toward Sam as though Sam couldn't hear him.

Sam looked entertained.

"Shane, let's go outside," Taylor said, embarrassed all the way to her toes.

"I'll put my things away and take a shower," Sam said.

Shane stood and looked as if he was going to pounce on the younger man.

Taylor took his arm and led him to the door. "Come on."

Outside, he stomped over to his car and then turned to her. "Why is he staying here? And why the secrets suddenly?"

"He's staying here with Diesel, though it's really none of your business. And do you really have to ask why I'm not being totally forthcoming with you, Shane? After what happened with Joni's case, I think you need to earn my trust back, don't you?"

He glared back at her.

"You've known him a full five minutes. You've known me for years. So tell me which one of us you should trust more. Taylor, are you sleeping with him?"

Taylor took a step back and crossed her arms over her chest. She couldn't believe the audacity.

"Wait," Shane said, holding his hands in the air. "I'm sorry. I'm so sorry, Taylor. I'm just concerned, and I want you to be careful. People are crazy these days. You never know who you are putting your trust in." He looked suddenly contrite.

She felt bad for him. "I'm fine, but thanks for your concern. When I get back, I'll tell you everything that's going on, but right now, I just need to go sort some things out. And I'm glad Diesel will be taken care of."

"I don't like this at all."

"Sam is just a friend, Shane."

Shane's shoulders relaxed, and he let out a long breath. "I would've kept the dog for you," he said, looking hurt. "I should go back to the station. Can you leave me with a hug at least?"

Taylor looked back at the door then walked up to Shane. "I guess so. But I really need to get in there and pack. I've got to call my dad and let him know what's going on too. I'm going to try and get Anna to go check on him while I'm gone."

She leaned in and gave him a hug. When she tried to pull back, he clung to her, bringing her in closer for a second before letting her go.

"All right. Call me. Text me. Something—just keep in touch," he said. He got into the car and shut the door. He put the window down and leaned out. "Okay?"

"Yes, I will. Now, get out of here and go get some work done before the sheriff figures out you aren't being productive."

He laughed, and suddenly, they were okay.

While Taylor headed back inside, Shane began backing up the car. She turned to see him stop at the back of the Jeep and take a photo of Sam's license plate.

CHAPTER 23

A rivulet of sweat dropped into Lucy's eyes and stung like fire. She couldn't believe that women would choose to go through labor more than once. She swore she'd never have her own children. This was a one-and-done, and she planned to live her life footloose and fancy-free, with no more vaginal trauma.

The final eight weeks had passed excruciatingly slowly, and she'd been eager to get to this day, but now she wished she could rewind time back to when she hadn't been aware a woman could experience such pain and still live through it.

They'd moved to the guest bedroom on the first floor but not before she had paced just about every room in the house during contractions.

Ian had followed her through the house, getting on every nerve Lucy had ever acknowledged. Luckily, Suki didn't want to be that involved and was waiting for the grand finale.

In the kitchen and the office, Lucy noticed every cupboard and drawer was open, and all curtain ties were untied, and Vira made her stay still enough to unbraid her hair, which Lucy had worked hard on that morning.

"It will help you open faster." She ran her fingers through the plaits to unravel them.

By then, Lucy didn't care what crazy custom she wanted to follow if it would shorten the time she had to suffer.

"Childbirth is one of life's most significant passages," Ian said to her after one particularly brutal contraction.

"No, childbirth is like taking your lower lip and forcing it over your head," she'd retorted. It wasn't her quote but Carol Burnett's, but it fit the moment.

Before they entered the room set up for birthing, Vira helped Lucy step over the threshold three times. "Now, we are in this world that you will try to escape. Later, after the birth, you will be in the other world and leave the hardship behind."

"I'm ready to leave it behind now. Do you have any drugs?"

"No. This will be a clean birth. Your baby will not meet you through a drugged haze."

The baby—*their baby, not hers*—wouldn't be meeting her at all. That was the deal.

"Please turn the music up," Lucy said through gritted teeth.

"I don't like this music," Ian said.

"I DON'T GIVE A DAMN WHAT YOU LIKE!" Lucy screamed at him, and Vira ran over and turned the volume up.

Ian glared at her from his spot in the corner.

Queen's "Another One Bites the Dust" came on, and Lucy breathed in time with the beat, trying to convince herself that she was almost through the nightmare.

"Stop breathing like that," Vira chastised her. "It's not a real breath, and you will hyperventilate."

If she could only keep moving her hips, Lucy thought, she could handle the contractions, so she danced along the far side of the room, breathing how the hell she wanted to and not how she was being told. Another wave began in the small of her back and built momentum, moved up in a circular radius until it found the crescendo, and enveloped her entire body in agony.

"I—I—can't—keep—this—up," she said between pants as the wave began to creep down in severity.

"You need to get on all fours," Vira said. "And listen to me!"

"All fours?" Lucy looked at her as if she'd grown another head. "Shouldn't I lie on the bed?" The mattress had been outfitted with a sheet of plastic and adorned with towels, all ready for the grand finale.

"No. Do what I say." Vira nudged her and gestured at the floor then pulled the plastic sheeting down and smoothed it out. "All fours. Lucia, you are too small to have the baby on your back. Kneel and put your arms across the bed or on the floor."

Lucy had to find relief. She obeyed, but the bed was too high.

Vira slid a few pillows under her knees, making it more possible. "Now, this will open the birth canal and allow him to come through easier. The only reason Western doctors have you lie on your back to give birth is because it's convenient for them. So many infants have been forever damaged because of a social norm dictated by those deemed superiors in your society. This position is the way God meant for us to have our children."

At this moment, Lucy couldn't have given two flips about society or superiors. She just wanted it out. When the next wave came, she couldn't help the grunting that came from her.

"Don't fight it. Embrace it," Vira said. "Push now."

"Lucia, listen to the nurse," Ian demanded.

She wanted to scream that her name wasn't Lucia. *If only he were closer, and I had a knife...* Her arms came off the bed, and she supported herself with her hands on the floor. She pushed with all her might until it felt as if her brain was a wall of flames. She wished Taylor were here. Her sister would never have allowed her to bear this much pain. She'd have thought of something— done something.

Lucy screamed a long and feral howl, feeling like an animal. No one had ever told her giving birth felt like something inside was ripping you apart. And here she was, stuck with people who didn't give a rat's ass about her and really didn't even know her, for that matter.

No sympathy at all. If the baby survived, they'd be fine. If Lucy gave her last breath for its life. That was close to happening too. Just when she thought she'd pass out, Vira praised her and told her to take a short break and get her breath then brace herself for the next one.

"This could be your last push if you give it all you have."

She hadn't even had time to catch her breath from the last one, but if Vira thought it could be her very last contraction, then she was on board with that.

This time, with all her humanity stripped away, panting on the floor like a dog in heat, Lucy raised her head to the ceiling, her neck arched as far as it would go, and pushed harder than she'd ever thought possible.

"I see the head," Vira called out.

Ian rushed to see, but by now, Lucy didn't care.

"Push, girl! He's coming now," Vira said, her voice the most excited that Lucy had heard it thus far.

"Oh my God," Ian muttered. "There he is."

Lucy could see him unbuttoning his shirt.

The midwife caught the infant, then there was instant relief but only silence.

What was going on? Was there something wrong with it? Had she given birth to an alien? Lucy was afraid to ask.

Vira kept out of the line of sight while she worked then invited Ian over to cut the cord. A book about European art history was placed beneath it, since it was their belief that it would guide the child in the direction the father wished, which, for Ian, would be to follow his success in the art world.

The baby had still not made a sound, and after the snip of scissors, when it finally let out a loud cry, Lucy released her breath.

It was weighed and measured then quickly swaddled and

handed over to Ian, who held it to his bare chest and immediately went to the window with it, cooing unintelligible words.

"You aren't done yet." Vira turned to Lucy and coached her further. "Gotta get the rest of this business out of the way."

Lucy pushed again until everything was out, and Vira smiled. "This will be wrapped in an old shirt of the father's and buried on this property so that this is where the child will feel the most secure."

"And the baby?" she couldn't help but ask. "Is it okay?"

"He looks handsome and healthy and is a big boy. You, Lucia, are a very brave girl. You can relax now."

Lucy let out the breath she'd been holding, and the rush that flooded through her felt amazing. It was a sense of euphoria unlike anything she'd ever experienced, even with the high-powered drugs she'd occasionally sampled. Vira could have offered her pain meds right then, and she'd have refused because she didn't want the amazing feeling to be dulled. She felt relief, happiness, and a myriad of emotions she couldn't even describe. She'd given birth to a human being! If she'd had a Stanley Cup, she'd have held it over her head.

It felt surreal.

She watched Ian's back, swaying side to side before he left the room. He was most likely taking the baby to Suki, who, from this moment forward, was its mother.

Now that it was here, maybe she'd be more interested. Ian now had the son he'd always wished for: Theodore Ian Banfield III.

It was an absurd name, but she hoped it would make them both into nicer people.

CHAPTER 24

*T*aylor tapped her short nails against the metal table. This room was small, with only one table and no concessions. It felt cold and depressing.

"How did you get approval on such short notice?" she asked.

"Montana only needs a twenty-four-hour notice for attorney–client visits," Jan said.

"The warden here is also friendly if we have to call her," Hensley said. "Especially for Cate. I think she's afraid of a personal-injury lawsuit."

"Could she even do that?" Taylor asked.

"Sure. The Federal Tort Claims Act allows prisoners to sue for injuries resulting from other inmates. Hard to prove who did it or who instigated it, but it can be a real headache for state prisons to sort through. She's playing nice right now."

Taylor wanted to jump out of her skin. Jan and Hensley hadn't wanted to give her the update on the case until Cate was present, so she'd spent the morning pacing in front of her hotel until it was time to meet them at the prison. Her stomach was empty, and the butterflies were having a circus inside.

The door opened, and Cate was ushered in.

She still looked rough. Jan and Hensley had already met with her once while Taylor was back home, so they weren't surprised, but Taylor had been expecting to see her looking much better than she had in the hospital. It had been almost a month. Nearly four weeks that had moved excruciatingly slowly.

She was pale—disturbingly so. Dark circles ringed her eyes, and the bruises around her face had faded to a nasty yellow. She'd lost a lot of weight, too, which was understandable considering Taylor couldn't imagine what they were giving her from the kitchen that satisfied her liquid diet requirement.

"Hello, ladies," she said through her clenched teeth, grimacing at the effort.

The metal in her mouth showed, and Taylor felt a chill go up her spine. It looked painful, and the bolts were going to have to stay in place for a month.

The guard opened Cate's handcuffs and attached one to a metal hook on the table before he went to stand at the doorway.

"Cate, we received the original ATF files. Because of the incident, we've put you on the fast track, and they've already been scrutinized," Jan said.

Taylor cringed at the word "incident," instantly imagining Cate at the mercy of a gang of women out to kill her, but Cate only nodded solemnly.

"Fisher and Kinley, the original forensic analysts for the ATF, are as crooked as a barrel of fishhooks," Hensley added. "We found a draft report from an arson expert that said the test for heavy distillate liquid was negative, and absolutely no accelerant was found in the bedroom that Robert died in, as the prosecution claimed."

Cate lowered her head, and Taylor could see the muscles in her neck tensing as she swallowed.

"Later, that report was changed to show a positive result for distillate," Jan said.

Taylor felt instantly sick to her stomach.

"We had a meeting with the prosecuting attorney, and they claimed they knew nothing about it," Hensley said,

Cate looked up, her eyes wide.

"They falsified the report to achieve the results the local police wanted," Hensley said.

"They lied?" Taylor asked.

"Yes, they lied," Jan answered. "Fisher and Kenley had an agenda, and they lacked sufficient grounds to make the allegations stick. They had to manipulate the reports to support their thesis that the fire was arson, set by Cate, and they never turned over the original report. That is a direct violation of the U.S. Supreme Court's 1963 decision in *Brady v. Maryland*, which requires prosecutors to turn over exculpatory materials to defense lawyers prior to trial. Undisclosed documents give us a fighting chance."

Taylor's body was so tense that pain wracked her throughout. She reminded herself to breathe. "So now what?"

"Last week, we filed an application seeking post-conviction relief—what we call state habeas—arguing that Cate is entitled to a new trial because of the new developments in fire science. To support the plea, we attached affidavits from our own forensic efforts."

"In layman's terms," Hensley said, "we argued that we had new evidence that would prove your innocence and that no juror could find you guilty beyond a reasonable doubt."

"What about the one-year rule?" Taylor said. She was embarrassed at being so confused by the legal jargon.

"Yes, it's true that in Montana, you usually only have one year from conviction to bring a claim seeking post-conviction relief. However, the only caveat to that is that if a person has newly discovered evidence that can establish their innocence that wasn't presented at the trial or wasn't in the defendant's possession before or during the trial, they can still be heard."

Jan smiled. "We've saved the best part for last. Hensley, you tell them."

Taylor held her breath.

"The judge accepted the application because of the legal criteria for new evidence. He agrees that the undisclosed ATF evidence directly contradicts Kinley's trial testimony that the fire originated in two places," Hensley said.

Jan smiled at Cate. "And you were not aware of the original, undisclosed ATF report. So, Catherine Lea Gray, what this means is that combined with the acknowledgment of the evolution of fire science, twenty years after being found guilty of arson and felony murder, you are entitled to a new trial."

TAYLOR LOOKED at the menu and considered ordering a celebratory glass of wine like Jan and Hensley. Don Hayes had joined them, and he sipped a glass of whiskey. They were back at Walkers for dinner, this time one with a much different vibe than the first time they'd all met. Now Jan and Hensley felt like friends.

"Just water," she finally said to the server then closed the menu.

While Jan and Hensley were over the moon with excitement, Taylor was happy but still subdued. She tried not to let them know it, but she couldn't get Cate's face out of her mind.

When Jan had declared she was getting a new trial, Cate had looked stricken. At the end of their meeting, when Cate had been led out, she'd been hunched over as if she'd aged twenty years in the span of half an hour. Almost fearful. Was it that she was afraid to hope? Or frightened of the possibility of reentering the outside world after so many years? Or could she have been guilty after all and having second thoughts about being exposed further?

"You don't drink at all?" Hensley asked.

Taylor shook her head. "Nope. Never have. To be honest, my father is an alcoholic, and I'm afraid of the stuff. I don't know if, for him, it was a slow decline, or he was trapped from the get-go. He drank when I was young, and I suspect that Cate's conviction accelerated it. But I don't want to take any chances."

They both nodded politely, and Hayes gave her a nod of approval, but unless any of them had ever had an addict in their family to turn their lives upside down, they'd never fully understand Taylor's fear of falling victim to the disease herself.

"You know, this sort of thing happens all the time," Jan said once the server was gone. "Your mother was young and naïve. She told the police exactly what happened, and they turned everything against her. She should have immediately asked for an attorney, but she hadn't done anything wrong, so why would she think she needed one?"

"Yes, she sure couldn't have predicted the ATF withholding documents and violating her rights," Hayes said. "No one could."

"What happens next?" Taylor asked.

"It will start at the same trial court where Cate was heard, with the same judge. The prosecution will have a chance to prepare, but we should have a date soon. If we are unsuccessful at that level, we'll be allowed to appeal to the Montana State Supreme Court and possibly even the Supreme Court of the United States."

"What about the intermediate court of appeals?"

"Montana doesn't have that. Our supreme court hears direct appeals from all over the district courts," Jan said.

"Interesting."

The server returned with her water and took their dinner order. When she was gone, Taylor sat back and listened as Jan and Hensley relayed more details to Hayes about the case.

He bounced questions back and forth, and they got into complicated legalese while she thought more about Cate and how it must have felt for her to go back to her cell. It had to have been tortuous to have a tiny sliver of hope while knowing that one document or a bad day had by a judge could squash it in one afternoon.

Beyond that was the fear that if Cate did have to spend the rest of her life behind bars, she'd be attacked again because of who her daughter was. Taylor couldn't get over the guilt she felt about Cate nursing a broken jaw because of her.

"Taylor? You okay?" Hensley asked, her hand on Taylor's arm. "You sure are quiet."

"Oh, yes. I'm just tired."

"I'm sorry," Hensley said. "We forget this is your mother we're talking about. Usually, the family isn't this involved in the behind-the-scenes stuff."

"No, it's not that at all," Taylor argued. "I really appreciate you allowing me to be involved."

The server returned with their dinner and set it down then left.

"It's a lot to process," Don said. "Even for someone in law enforcement. Be kind to yourself."

She nodded, but it wasn't herself she was worried about. She picked up her fork and took a bite of the baked salmon on her plate. It held no taste.

"I think I might be coming down with something. Do you all mind if I head back to the hotel? I've got an early flight."

"I'll get them to pack up your dinner," Hensley said.

Don stood. "Want me to drive you?"

"No. I need to turn my rental in tomorrow anyway. But thank you. Thank you all so much for everything you are doing. I can't say that enough."

"Enough said," Jan said, laughing lightly. "And we'll call you as soon as we have a trial date set. I know you'll want to be here."

"Of course," she replied, though she was starting to wonder

whether she did or not. She couldn't imagine what it would feel like to witness a negative outcome now that they'd gotten this far. It was all affecting her more deeply than she had thought it would when she'd started this journey.

Maybe Taylor wasn't as tough as she'd thought she was.

CHAPTER 25

*T*hough she'd wanted to be out of Hudson Valley the very next day after giving birth, the recovery was going to be harder than Lucy had thought, and it was just over forty-eight hours later when she felt strong enough to take a shower, dress, and pack her things. She'd tried to sleep during the last two days but had only found snippets of rest, since the infant had decided that forty weeks of silence were enough and was ready to make his presence in the world known.

She couldn't get out of there fast enough. As soon as the deal was done, she'd call a taxi and be at the Greyhound station before nightfall. A long trip on a silent bus was just what she needed. Hell, she might even splurge on a plane ticket.

She found Ian in his office. He tried to wave her away as he held the phone to his ear, but she went in anyway. He quickly ended the call.

"What do you mean you don't have the money?" she said, trying to keep her tone under control when she really wanted to scratch his eyes out.

"I do have it—just not at this moment. It takes time to get that sort of cash without raising a lot of questions." He barely met her eyes before glancing out his window.

"You should have thought of that sometime in the last five months! A deal is a deal, Ian. I gave you a baby. You are supposed to give me the money. Then I leave and never see or talk to either of you again. That was the deal."

"And that will be our deal, Lucia. I promise. Just give me a week. I do not want to be flagged by the IRS when they wonder why I suddenly took out fifty thousand dollars in cash."

"Then why did you wait until now? You've had months."

He shook his head as if he was looking at a sad case. "Because it wasn't the right timing. What? Are you so desperate to leave luxury, then? If you are, I have ten thousand that I can give you today, and you can go. Tomorrow, I go back to the city, and I'll make arrangements to get the rest to you."

She felt the rage run through her. She narrowed her eyes at him. "Oh, I bet you wish I would take it and go, don't you? I don't trust you, Ian. Sorry, but I've been lied to and taken advantage of by men like you my whole life. I'll go when I have the money in my pocket, and you'll not know where I am once I leave this house. So I suggest you put a rush on it. Don't forget, keeping this all quiet is beneficial to us both."

He tapped the pen against his desk impatiently and a bit menacingly. "Are you threatening me, Lucia? Because if I were you, I'd think long and hard about that. I have people in very high places that owe me mounds of favors."

"What the hell does that mean? You going to send an assassin after me?" she quipped sarcastically.

"Don't push your luck."

Lucy stood and leaned forward and put both hands flat on his desk. "Get my money, Ian. You have one week. I have friends too. But mine are in low places, so they are much more willing to do anything to lift their status."

They glared at each other for a few seconds. Then Lucy whirled and left the room.

She went outside and screamed, her hands over her mouth to muffle it. She didn't want to stay another day in the house with Suki and the baby. It was taking an emotional toll on her, and she needed to get as far away as she could as quickly as possible.

She ignored the sudden pains as she paced along the back of the property, trying to outwalk her rage. She never should've trusted Ian, and now she was furious at herself. If she'd have been smarter, she would've gotten at least half of the money up front. Money and prestige didn't make a man nobler, and Ian had just proved that he could crawl along the ground just as low as other snakes she had known. What ever happened to a man's word, as her dad used to say?

No honor.

As her pulse slowed, she felt the stabbing needles in her abdomen and down below, and she stopped walking.

Get through the next week.

Get the money.

Go.

Yes, soon, she'd be able to put this all behind her and start a new life.

LUCY STARED at the clock on the nightstand, watching it reach midnight. She was still fuming over her conversation with Ian and the fact that she was now stuck there for another week, and the incessant wailing was icing on the cake of her sudden shit show of a life.

12:03 became 12:04, and she sat up and put her hands over her ears.

It was the third night in a row that Suki had put a bawling Theodore into his crib and shut herself into her room, refusing to come out. Between howls, he made sad little hiccup noises and ragged breaths.

Three days and three nights of crying.

There was nowhere to hide from it. Even in the sprawling house, she swore she could hear him from every corner and behind every closed door. Even when she stepped outside onto the back patio, his cries echoed in her head. She'd been outside after three in the morning the night before, refusing to come in until the baying of coyotes got closer and she feared a pack would jump out of the darkness and tear her to pieces.

She climbed out of the tangled sheets and paced between the end of her bed and the bookshelf. The cries penetrated through her fingers.

"Oh my God—please. Just *please*, go to sleep," she muttered. She was furious with Ian and his ridiculous rules. What rich mother didn't have a night nanny?

Lucy was sore—so very sore—and exhausted out of her mind. Her rage-walking the day before had really done her in, and now the cramps that came and went nearly made her buckle to her knees.

Everything hurt, and Vira thought the answer was to keep a giant ice pack on her crotch.

But what if it wasn't?

Ian wouldn't care if she was bleeding to death. He'd never let her go to a hospital because that would mean their secret might be exposed. No one could know she'd given birth. He'd said it was *imperative* for their future peace.

Lucy went to the bed and lay across it, burrowing her head under the pillow.

Suddenly, everything got quiet.

She held her breath.

One minute. Two.

Slowly, she lifted the pillow from her head.

He started again.

This time, with every breath he took to give another wail, her breasts seemed to throb in sync, as though joining in the melody. She sat up and banged the pillow with her fist over and over.

"Suki!" She was already shouting her name when she flung her own door open and stomped to the primary bedroom and banged on the door. "Go get him. Feed him. Rock him. Something!"

"Go away. I'm sleeping," Suki called out.

"I'd like to sleep too! But that little brat won't let me. You need to do something!" She tried the knob, but it was locked.

"He'll stop eventually!"

She banged again. "No, he won't! Open this door, Suki!"

"He doesn't like me. So go away."

"Damn it, Suki. He doesn't even know you yet. You haven't tried to bond with him. It takes time, and you aren't giving it a chance! Open the door!" She leaned her head against the door, closing her eyes as she tried to relax her neck muscles.

A memory came to her of her sister Jo the first week after her son Levi had been born. They had all tried to help with him, but Jo had refused to let him out of her sight. Even when they'd talked her into passing him to Lucy or Taylor or even Anna, Levi had screamed at the top of his lungs and had not shut up until he was back in his mother's arms and against her skin. Then and only then did he fall into peaceful sleep.

But this baby didn't understand that Suki was his mother. Because Suki wasn't even trying. What was it with Ukrainians? Were they all this cold, or was Suki some sort of psychopath?

Damn her.

Lucy was terribly tense. Her head hurt. Her neck ached, and her teeth vibrated from so much clenching. Her breasts were engorged, and Vira's recommendation of putting cabbage on them had done nothing to ease the pain.

She couldn't take it anymore.

Quietly, she padded across the hall and peeked into the nursery.

He was on his back, and she could see his little fists and feet in motion, flaying in a tantrum. The railing of the crib blocked his face, and for that, she was grateful.

She backed away and padded down the hall, down the stairs, and into the kitchen. In the front of the fridge, she found a nearly full bottle of breast milk. She still couldn't believe that they were having someone else's breast milk shipped in when it seemed easier to just use infant formula. She grabbed the bottle and headed for the stairs.

At the bottom, she hesitated.

Was she ready for this? If she went in there, there would be no erasing the image of his face from her mind.

Another wail exploded.

She took a deep breath and continued up the stairs, clutching the bottle so hard she thought it might shatter. She was determined to finally get a good night's sleep. She just had to stick it in his mouth, prop it up, and walk away.

Easy.

Maybe she could even do it without really looking at his face.

She got to the door, full of hope that he'd just stop crying and she could turn around and go to bed.

But he didn't.

Now she was trembling.

There were times in her life when she'd faced drug-crazed meth heads and desperate criminals, yet here she was, quaking in her slippers because of a baby.

It was ridiculous.

She walked in and went to the crib, keeping her eyes on his little stockinged feet as he pulled his legs in and out, his arms up and down, plump fists white-knuckled in his rage at being ignored.

"I get it, buddy," Lucy whispered. "She ignores me too."

Peeking through her eyelashes to blur her view, she aimed the nipple of the bottle in the general vicinity of his mouth. She didn't want to see every detail of his face. Whose nose he had or what color eyes.

When he threw his head from side to side without her being able to get the nipple into his mouth, she finally had to look. Quickly, she shoved it in. Then she bunched up the receiving blanket under it as a makeshift cradle and jumped back from the crib as though she'd been burned.

I did it!

He hungrily grabbed at it, quiet for a second or two before it fell out.

She released a sigh and stepped back up to the crib, trying again.

Same game. He had it, lost it, and wailed.

"FINE!" Lucy said a bit too loudly. She leaned over and slid one arm under his neck, the other under his butt, and lifted him out of the crib. She held him away from her, not touching her body. "I'm going to feed you this bottle. Then you sleep. Deal?"

He stopped crying and looked shocked at seeing her face.

"Yes, you don't know me, and you don't want to, believe me. Pretend I'm the housekeeper. Or the nanny. Let's get this over with."

She took him to the rocking chair in the corner and sat down, leaning him back against the small valley of her arm and side. She took the bottle and aimed directly for his mouth, ignoring the magnificent fringe of the longest lashes she'd ever seen on a baby.

He took the nipple, but he jerked his head away, refusing the milk.

"What? What is wrong with you?" She welled up with frustration. He'd already made her go against her oath that she'd never look upon his face. She'd come out of her room. Tried to get his mother. Got a bottle.

Touched him!

And this was what she got in return. He was in full banshee mode now, and she felt tears of exhaustion and frustration spring forward in her eyes.

"What do you want?"

She tried again, but this time, in his rage, he slapped the bottle and nearly flung it out of her hands. Droplets of milk sprayed across her cheek.

She was an idiot.

It was cold! She should've heated the milk!

Lucy couldn't believe her stupidity and was just about to get up and put him back in the crib so that she could go back down and heat the milk when he started rooting around against her chest with unbelievable strength. She tried to pull him away, but before she could, he found a nipple that had peeked through the opening of her gown. He latched on before she could stop him, and she was astonished at how instant the transformation was.

The screaming banshee no more, he sucked at her as if he was starving, his hands rubbing back and forth against her breast.

"No. No." She tried to pull him away, but he was determined not to lose what he'd finally found, and the sudden silence was such a relief that Lucy was too paralyzed to continue fighting him.

She'd always heard it was hard to get a baby to breastfeed, that it took several attempts and sometimes even a coach to help new mothers get it right.

Not this boy.

Lucy was flooded with shame. She shouldn't have let it happen.

But it would only be just this once. And she'd never do it again. Or tell a single soul about it. No one would have to know, and she could have at least one night of rest.

One. Night.

Sleep.

While he ate, she figured she was already in deep, so she

might as well see what he looked like. She gazed down at his face. He gazed back at her.

She gasped with the shock at how mature he looked, as if he knew exactly what he was doing and was pretty damn proud of himself.

Damn it all, he was beautiful.

More beautiful than anything she'd ever seen in her life and probably ever would again. The lyrics to John Lennon's "Beautiful Boy" flooded her mind, but she would not sing it.

"Ian Theodore III. Theodore for short, they say. What a handsome fellow you are," she whispered. When a tear fell on her bottom lip, she realized she was crying. "I am not crying over you. I am just tired. Exhausted, actually. Because *you*, little boy, are a mini-sized asshole who won't let anyone sleep."

He stared at her, his eyelids getting noticeably heavy. She used her thumb to stroke his cheek. His soft, soft cheek. It felt as if the warmth of his skin was branding her through both layers of their clothes, and the smell that wafted up from him was intoxicating.

She suddenly couldn't figure out why in the world Suki wasn't head over heels in love with this baby and spending every moment she could with him.

He was perfect.

One hundred and twenty percent perfect.

Suki was crazy.

Stupid.

Blind.

Out of her mind!

And Lucy was going to tell her exactly that in the morning. No, actually, she wasn't, because Suki could never know about this meeting, or they might refuse to pay her. Ian would say she'd broken the contract, even though it had been her own wish that she never see the baby's face.

On second thought, he'd broken the contract first! She was supposed to be able to leave after handing over the baby.

You get your fifty grand when you give birth, and then you leave.

Those were his terms. It was his fault this was even happening.

~~Still, she'd never tell.~~

He was fast asleep now, and she studied his teeny fingernails and the small dents in his fingers. She noticed his skin was a bit flaky over and around his ears, but those ears—they were shaped exactly like hers.

His hair was dark, or at least the peach fuzz was, and she wondered if it would fall out and come back in another color.

With a longing she didn't know she'd had in her, she wished that her sisters could see this baby. That they could know what an amazing thing she'd made. She thought of her dad and how maybe having another grandson would shift him out of his life-long pity party. Or would Theodore remind him of her little brother, the only son he'd ever had and then lost?

She wondered suddenly if her own mother had held her like this, looking down in awe at what she'd created. Had Lucy looked up at her the same way Theodore had looked up, blind trust and milk-drunk love in her eyes?

She stood up, suddenly ashamed of where she'd let her thoughts roam.

Theodore hadn't looked at her with love. He was milk drunk.

She was a food bank. That was all it was and all it was going to be.

She stood and took Theodore to the crib. She laid him down, slowly and gently to keep him sleeping, then tiptoed across the room. At the door, she turned and looked then returned to his bed and covered him with the small blue sheet.

"From here on out, you're on your own, little man."

With one more look, she tried to memorize every one of his features. She bent down and placed the softest and subtlest kiss of her life on the sweet down of his forehead.

Then she turned and quietly shut the door behind her.

CHAPTER 26

A week later, Lucy decided to walk the dogs farther out on the property, past where she'd gone before. It wasn't as if Suki would be expecting them back any time soon. She rarely left her room here, just like back in the city. Lucy didn't know if she was depressed or just hormonal, but it would've been nice to have more than the midwife to talk to occasionally.

The housekeeper had been there earlier and had put together a meal to be popped into the oven later. She wasn't a source of companionship, though. She only spoke Spanish, and Lucy had already forgotten the few words she'd learned in the tenth grade. She was down to *hola* and *buenos días*—oh, and *margarita*—and the conversation went nowhere.

Even if they could have communicated, Lucy was pretty sure that Ian had paid the woman to keep her mouth shut. She acted scared to breathe and avoided even eye contact. When the baby could be heard crying, Lucy saw her tense up as if she wanted to go and intervene, but she never did.

Lucy also stayed away now. The one night she'd gone to him, it had messed with her mind for a week. Suki would have to figure it out on her own.

Bentley stopped to pop a squat, and Lucy held her breath. That was one smell that would wreak havoc with her system.

Bailey was eager to get going, and they started walking again, but before they could get much farther, Lucy heard a horn blow. It sounded as if it was coming from near the front gate. She hurried back that way, but it took her a few minutes, and a white delivery truck was pulling away.

"Come on, guys. He's about to leave." She tried to wave at the driver, but he kept going and was gone by the time they got to the gate.

He'd left a package. In block letters across the side, it said Mirror-Pak Universal Do Not Lay Flat.

Ian hadn't mentioned that he had anything coming, but it appeared to be a boxed-up painting.

"Oh, shit."

Lucy saw that the box was damaged. One corner was ripped open, showing the brown paper wrap inside. She also saw a bit of white slip showing, so she reached through the fence and pulled it out to find it was a customs slip. In the sender's field, it read César Collazo.

That sounded very familiar, but Lucy couldn't quite place it. The country of origin was Uruguay. And the value was listed at two hundred dollars.

She tucked the slip into her pocket and headed for the house to tell Suki so she could get the new code and open the gate.

"Suki," she called out when she entered through the front door.

After she released the dogs, they headed to the kitchen for water, and Lucy went to Suki's bedroom door. She was about to knock but heard something from within.

She put her ear to the panel.

Someone was crying. And it wasn't the baby.

Lucy quickly backed away. She didn't know the woman well

enough to comfort her, even if she had been the kind of girl's girl who was good at that stuff.

"I hate you!" she heard Suki call out, then something slammed against the other side of the door. The baby erupted into an ear-splitting cry.

It startled Lucy, and she jumped back farther, lost her balance, and crashed to the floor. She hit hard, cussing instantly when her hip made contact with the hardwoods.

The door was snatched open, and Suki stood there, her face tear streaked and her hair stringy and wild. The baby was on the bed, his little fists red and pumping back and forth in a tantrum.

A phone lay on the floor inside the door—obviously the item that had been flung.

Lucy rolled to a sitting position, one hand on her throbbing hip. "What the hell's going on in there, Suki?"

"What are you doing standing outside my door. Eavesdropping?" Suki asked, crossing her arms over her chest.

"Why yes, Suki, I'm okay. Thanks for asking." Lucy glared at her then got herself onto all fours then to her feet again. "Your concern is overwhelming. Oh my God. I'm going to have a hell of a bruise."

"You're invading my privacy," she declared, sniffling back tears.

"No, I wasn't. There's a package outside the gate, and it looks like a painting. I was coming to tell you to open the gate so I can grab it before it rains. It says it's a César Collazo."

"I don't have the code."

That was strange. Lucy had thought that Ian would let Suki have it for emergencies.

"Okay, then, call Ian."

Suki looked pointedly down at the phone, which was obviously broken, judging by the shattered screen and the chipped corner.

Lucy couldn't believe Suki's childishness.

"Why would you do that? Do you have another phone? Or another way I don't know of to get in touch with someone? What if your baby gets sick?"

Suki shrugged, but more tears came.

Lucy sighed. "Suki, can we talk? I mean, like real people?"

"I do talk like real people."

For the first time, Lucy heard an accent in Suki's speech, but she couldn't place it. It was slight, but it was there. Looking more closely at her, she realized that Suki looked as if she'd been crying for a long time, not just having a sudden outburst.

Going against her normal tendency to avoid physical touch, Lucy crossed the distance between them and held her arms out. "My big sister used to tell us that there was nothing a hug couldn't make better. I'm pretty sure we are the only ones here, so it looks like I'm your only option."

Suki stared at her for a few seconds then burst into sobs and retreated to her bed, where she flopped down face-first into a pillow. The baby immediately stopped crying and watched her.

Lucy was beyond shocked. The tantrum and now this? Suki didn't show emotion. Ever. She didn't know what to do. Then she decided to keep up the Taylor act and do what her sister would have done: either leave her alone or press on.

Suki had spent enough time alone. It was time to try something different.

"I'm coming in, Suki. Not to invade your privacy but to comfort you. I think you need someone to talk to, and I'll be that person if you want."

Suki shook her head emphatically in the pillow, her sobs increasing. "No. I can't."

Lucy sat down on the bed and tentatively laid her hand on Suki's back, first in only a light touch then rubbing it in a circular and, she hoped, comforting circle.

"I might be able to help but not if you don't tell me what's wrong."

Nothing.

"Well, let's check on your phone, then." She went to the doorway, picked up the phone, and touched the home button. "It lit up, Suki. I don't think it's as bad as it looks."

Suki's sobs subsided, and she turned over and sat up. "Doesn't matter. I can only call Ian. I am sick of Ian."

Lucy looked puzzled. "What do you mean?"

"I mean—I can't call anyone but Ian. It's blocked. It only allows communication for specific contacts. He's the only contact in it."

"He set up parental controls on your phone. Why would he monitor who you call? You're his wife, not his child." This was bizarre. Lucy could understand that Ian didn't trust her to keep their situation completely confidential, but why Suki?

The other woman began to sob again and shook her head. "No. I'm not his wife or his child. I'm his sister."

Her words stunned Lucy silent, but it made sense. She'd never seen the two of them act like a couple. To the contrary, they had never touched one another in front of her, and Suki didn't even appear to enjoy being in his presence. There was not a single photo of them as a couple in their penthouse or in this home either.

But his sister?

"Look, I don't know what kind of sick con you all are running, but I just want him to give me my money so I can go."

Suki let out a harsh laugh that cut off suddenly. "Don't be stupid. You are as much a prisoner as I am. Just like me, he has no plans to let you go. He knows you could come back later and try to claim the child. I had talked him into trusting you, but now you have snooped at the painting, and that can hurt him later. He probably saw you on the camera."

"The painting? What do you mean?"

"The one at the gate. The César Collazo."

When she said the name, Lucy suddenly realized why it had

looked familiar to her on the slip of paper. César Collazo was the name the paisley-suit guy had mentioned at the cocktail party the first night she'd gone out of Lucia. He'd said Collazo's works brought in seven figures.

So why was the slip filled out with a value of only two hundred dollars?

Her mind was piecing things together, but it was still a tornado of bits and pieces, nothing making sense.

"I'm not following."

"Ian is not a reputable art dealer and consultant, Lucy. The art is his front for helping the big boys launder money out of Ukraine. Our so-called marriage helps his image as a wealthy family man. He and my father have gotten away with it for years. Now my father thinks people might start getting suspicious that we are still only a couple. Your son completes the picture."

Lucy was floored. Suki's story was getting crazier by the minute.

"I don't know what you're talking about, but he can't keep me here. That's kidnapping."

Suki nodded. "Tell that to my mother. Or to my fiancé, Agustín, both in Ukraine. I haven't spoken to them in three years. They bought Agustín's silence with the first death."

"Death?"

"Yes. His sister. Told him one word gets out about my fate, and his mother and father will be next. Don't you see? There's nothing I can do. There's nothing *you* can do."

Lucy stood and began pacing. "Is your name even Banfield?"

"Of course not. But we have perfectly forged documents."

Now Lucy knew why she wasn't allowed to use her phone or the internet.

She was mad at herself. She'd walked into Ian's life and presented him with the perfect pawn: a young woman who had come to the city with no ties to family or friends. She'd played right into his sick hands. She'd worked with him!

She felt suddenly cold.

She was an accessory to crime.

If Taylor had thought shoplifting was a big deal, she was really going to flip her lid about money laundering. Lucy stopped pacing. "And who are the *big boys*? Please don't say what I think you meant."

Suki nodded slowly.

"Oh my God. The mafia? Shit. Shit shit shit. The mafia don't play." Sweat popped up on her upper lip.

"I know," Suki said. "Why do you think I haven't tried to run away? There's nowhere for me to go, or I would be gone. This is the Russian mafia, and they have people everywhere."

Lucy felt sick. "And the baby? What of him? You don't want him?"

As though on cue, the baby began to wail again.

Suki picked him up and moved him back and forth in her arms, bounced him, then stood and began walking. He looked as if he was ready for a crying marathon.

She looked guilty as she rearranged him against her shoulder, her moves awkward and clumsy. "Yes, I did. I mean, I do want him. I agreed because I thought a baby would make me less lonely for Agustín. But it only makes me miss him more. The baby reminds me of the life we could've had together, but I will adjust, and I'll learn to be a better mother."

"Why are you telling me all this now, Suki? Aren't you afraid of Ian? What if he finds out you've told all the secrets?"

"I'm very afraid of Ian. And my father. But I am also tired of being lonely. I need more than a baby, Lucy. I need a friend."

⁕

LUCY SAT at one end of the couch and Suki at the other, balancing the baby in the crook of her arm. He was almost asleep after nearly an hour straight of crying. His wails had settled into little hiccups while he fought to keep his eyes open.

"Okay, tell me more about how Ian cleans money, Suki. I'm pissed, and I want to know how involved I am before I figure a way out of this mess. But I can promise you this: he's not keeping me here."

Suki shrugged. "It's not as complicated as you'd think. There are many ways to do it. One time, he bought a very high-end piece for a million dollars at an auction in Geneva. He had it moved to storage in a free port."

"What is that?"

"A high-security storage space near an airport. Then he sold it for ten million to an anonymous buyer, who picked it up from there. He cleaned the first million and made a ton of money without moving the painting an inch, all cash sale from the space he used as a tax haven."

"And what about Jorge? He's a real artist. What did Ian plan to do with his work?"

"The work won't be valuable for years, but Ian can claim to have discovered the artist and sell it now for big cash to his cronies around the world. Later, he buys it back at a higher price. Then the money has gone back and forth and is clean."

Lucy put her fingers to her temple. The baby's cries, along with the realization of her bad situation, were giving her a major headache. "I don't understand any of this."

"Because you aren't a criminal."

That made Lucy laugh. "I always thought I was, but now, I see I'm Mary Poppins compared to your family."

"The painting you found at the gate—I guarantee that it wasn't shipped through legal channels. It was probably smuggled in. The shipping invoice will be false too."

The baby got a burst of energy and began to cry again, sending a bolt of fresh pain into Lucy's head. "Let me think," she said, leaning back on the couch.

Suki took the opportunity to hum to the baby until he was back to hiccups then could no longer stay awake.

"Thank God. You did it," Lucy said, opening her eyes. "Now, let's pray he stays asleep when you put him in the crib."

"I'm not moving. I'll stay right here until my arms fall off."

Lucy got up and pushed a throw pillow under Suki's elbow to help support the weight of the baby's head.

"I know I don't look like I know what I'm doing, but I used to hold my sister's newborn. Before we left, I mean," Suki said, her voice wistful.

"What is your sister's name?"

"Iana. She had a little girl. I sewed the birth outfit."

"Oh, you can sew?" Lucy had never seen her doing any sort of hobby. Or anything at all.

Suki nodded. "I used to. I made her a long shirt and embroidered the symbol of Rozhanytsi on it."

"What is that?" It was surreal that she and Suki were having a real conversation. Lucy wanted to keep her talking. There was a lot she needed to figure out, and Suki had the intel.

"Rozhanytsi are the goddesses of human fate. They appear when children are born and decide their fates."

"Did one appear at the labor?"

"No," Suki said. "At least, I didn't see one. But I was too busy comforting my sister to notice. Her labor was difficult."

Lucy wished she had had one of her sisters with her during the labor.

"Is your sister still in Ukraine?"

Suki nodded. "Yes. She is in a marriage arranged by my father."

"Ukraine has arranged marriages? Isn't that a bit outdated?"

"It's rare now, but my family is very traditional, and my father does nothing that doesn't further his goals for the future. My sister and I are assets, like any other possession to him. He would never let one of us marry a man of our own choice.

Unless it was someone who he knew could further the family fortune."

"Your American accent is nearly perfect. How long have you and Ian been in the States, concocting your fake life?"

"I have had an English tutor since I said my first words. We've been here more than ten years now." A tear slid down Suki's face. "Agustín has probably married someone else by now."

"That's easy to find out. You spend most every day alone, so why haven't you reached out to him? Or your mother? Your sister. Surely, you can trust her."

"I can trust Iana with my life, but I will not jeopardize hers and her daughters' by trying to communicate with her. Same with Agustín. He must protect his family."

"It sounds like you're talking about the Dark Ages," Lucy said.

Suki sighed. "It is true that Ukraine has a history fraught with political turbulence and violence. Corruption at every corner. However, it is also a country full of good people, and in many ways, we are as forward as Americans. If I had been born into a different family, I would still be in Ukraine, married to Agustín, with his children surrounding me, living a normal life. It was my fate that I should be born to a father involved in crime. Ian, too, though he has grown up to be just like him. So different than the brother I once knew."

He sounded like a psychopath. Now, a lot of his personality quirks made sense to Lucy.

"Didn't he ever fall in love and want a real wife? Not his sister pretending?"

"You mean you can't tell?"

"Tell what?"

"Ian doesn't like women that way. His preferences lean toward the more masculine. That was another reason he didn't want to stay in Ukraine."

"Does your father know he's gay?"

"Oh God, no. Ian would rather die than tell him. My father

would disown him immediately. Same-sex couples are allowed in Ukraine, at least technically. But they have no rights like they have here. The Family Code of Ukraine has not changed with the times. Same-sex couples cannot get married or inherit each other's property. They can't visit each other in hospitals and can't adopt or raise children together. My father expects Ian to produce an heir to the family one day. That was another reason to adopt Theodore from you."

"Ian cannot keep you here, Suki. This is America, not some Third World country. What about political asylum?"

"Lucy, have you ever been in an abusive situation?"

"Not one I couldn't find a way out of."

"Then you can't possibly understand. Ian has connections all over the world. As many or more now than our father. I can't run. Without money, I can't hide. If I tried, it would only be a matter of time before they found me, and then the punishment would be dear."

"But he's not living as his true self here either."

"Oh, but I think he has plans to do so one day. Ian is smart like a fox. My father may think he has Ian in his pocket forever, but I think my brother is planning his own exit. I know without a doubt that he is hiding money that my father knows nothing of."

Lucy's mental wheels were turning, and when the baby startled in his sleep, she felt her stomach sink. "And Theodore? Is he only a ruse, or what do you think he means to do with him if he puts his exit plan in place one day?"

"He'll take him. Ian told you that I was the one who wanted a child so much, and I did think a baby would help me, but it was really him. He has been obsessed with being a father. He will mold Theodore into the son he's always dreamed of. His heir to all the riches he's storing up."

The statement sent a chill up Lucy's back. She had no reservations about same-sex couples raising children—but knowing what she did now, she saw that Ian would never be a fit father.

What kind of man could he be if he was willing to steal his sister's happiness? Her entire future?

"You look worried," Suki said. "Even if Ian leaves this life to create another, he'll take me with him because I know too many of his secrets. I will always protect Theodore, but Ian would never hurt him. He will treat him like his most prized painting."

Lucy hoped she was right about that. In the meantime, she had to find a way out, and she wasn't going without some sort of compensation.

"I'm just thinking. Ian mentioned he had ten thousand dollars here that he could give me and send me on my way. Do you know where it is?" Lucy hated to leave without the full fifty thousand, but she wasn't going to wait around to find out if he would hold up his end of the bargain. Her gut told her to get out and do it quick.

"No, but I'm sure it's in his office. He keeps the door locked."

"There must be another key around here somewhere."

"Okay. Let me put Theodore to bed, and I'll help you look."

"I'll start. Meet me in the kitchen." She left the room quickly, hoping that Suki could manage to get the baby into his bed without starting his motor again. She didn't know how much more crying she could take on top of everything else right now. She needed to think.

In the kitchen, she started with the drawers, moving from one to the other and rummaging through them, looking for keys. She found one, but it ended up fitting the back door. She tucked that one into her pocket, though once she was out, she didn't expect to ever return.

Suki joined her, and they moved into the bedroom that Ian used. Lucy took the closet while Suki claimed the nightstands.

Ian's closet was immaculate, his clothing hanging in color-coded clusters. A dresser held a line of watches on a spindle. The shoes on the rack gleamed as though never worn outside. He didn't keep any clutter or secret items like most people hid away in closets, so it only took her a short time to complete her search.

"Nothing," she said, coming out to stand by the bed.

"Same. Just a bunch of art books."

They both took on his bathroom, but they came up empty there too.

"What about the garage?"

"Might as well." Suki led the way.

"Too bad he doesn't just put it over the doorframe like my dad always did in our house," Lucy said.

"Did you check?"

"No way would it be that simple." Still, Lucy went to the office door, reached up, and ran her hand along the top of the frame. She felt something and pushed it off, catching it with her other hand. "Well, I'll be damned."

She held the key up.

Suki grinned. "I'm so glad we don't have to search the garage. He's got tons of stuff out there."

Lucy used the key and opened the door.

Suki went in first and opened the small closet. "I'll look here."

Lucy went to the desk.

It held a computer, and she thought first about sending a message to Taylor—maybe even asking for help. She could see it now: *Dear sister, please come get me. I'm involved with the Russian mafia and being held against my will.*

Taylor would laugh, thinking Lucy was acting like a fool. Then she'd delete it.

No, Lucy wasn't going to get her family mixed up in this. She'd never let them know how dumb she'd been to get herself into such a disastrous situation. And the baby—that was a secret she planned to take to her grave.

She opened the lap drawer and immediately saw the battery for her phone. The first person it occurred to her to call was Jorge. But that was out of the question. She slipped the battery into her pocket. Next was the deep file drawer, and she flipped through the hanging folders, looking for cash. She saw many invoices and receipts for art and notes for future sales.

She pulled out one folder, curious to see if she recognized any of the names of those who had made deals with Ian.

A name stood out on the cover page on a sheaf of papers in a see-through pouch.

"Who is Sakura Lia Banfield?"

"Me. Why?"

Lucy held the pouch up. "It's a life insurance policy. Five million dollars, with your name listed as the insured."

CHAPTER 27

*T*he irony of Lucy's recommendation to Suki wasn't lost and would probably have been a psychoanalyst's wet dream if they had known about the tragedy of her childhood.

"A fire?" Suki said.

They were back in Suki's room, lounging on the bed, eating big bowls of ice cream. They were trying to brainstorm how to get Suki and the baby out along with Lucy. Considering the circumstances, they were both remarkably calm. The baby was in his crib, the house was quiet, and it was nice having someone to talk to after so many months of loneliness. Suki was turning out to be a decent person now that she wasn't following orders to stay away from Lucy and keep her mouth shut. Ian had feared they'd get together and something might slip out, according to Suki.

If he had been a fly on the wall now, he'd be having a stroke. Oh, the mutiny.

"Yes. We are so far out that it would take a long time for the fire department to get here, and the house will be nothing but ashes by that time, I hope."

"There must be bodies found for him to think we died. This

isn't a movie, Lucy. What do you want to do, go rob a graveyard? Then the DNA wouldn't match."

Lucy shrugged. "I know, but wouldn't it be great just imagining Ian standing there, looking at his precious safe haven, burnt to the ground?"

"No, it wouldn't. He is already going to be enraged if I run away. I don't want to poke the dragon any more than I must. If we can even get out."

She was right. Lucy needed to keep her spiteful side from ruining everything.

"We *can* get out, Suki. That's not the problem. The fence is only eight feet high, so it's easy enough to scale if we get something to climb on then drop down on the other side. The real problem is where do you go from here? I will have a better chance to disappear because he doesn't even know where I came from, but you have a baby you're going to have to hide too. That's not going to make it easy to blend in. Especially without money."

She was beyond livid that they hadn't found any secret stash of cash. If Ian had ten thousand in the house, it must be in the best hiding place of all time, because after they'd found the life insurance policy, they'd spent four hours turning every room upside down, looking for money.

Suki wasn't a bit surprised at the life insurance policy. According to her, Ian was cold enough to kill her and collect on it, too, especially because he would come out of everything looking like a grieving widower who would valiantly take care of his young son alone. Talk about movie fodder—he should have been a producer himself.

Lucy couldn't wait to leave it all behind, especially the persona of Lucia Leighton, and go back to being just Lucy Gray without any connections to the Banfields, New York City, or the Russian mafia. She wasn't going to get her big payday or her houseboat, but at this point, she was going to be lucky to get away with her life.

She was very disappointed in herself. This wasn't the first time she'd been cheated out of a deal, and it probably wouldn't be the last, but she had no one to blame but herself. She should've gotten the money up front before giving birth. Now she'd leave here with only what she'd earned from being Ian's assistant— a measly six grand or so—plus the money she'd taken from Taylor.

She turned to Suki again. "Do you have any money of your own at all?"

"Not more than about two hundred. He doesn't let me have much. No credit cards or bank account either."

"He's a piece of work, isn't he?" Lucy wouldn't be able to let them go off with nothing. She could be ruthless to a point but not enough to leave a woman and baby on the run and penniless. "I have some money. Not a lot, but you won't have to leave broke. I'll share."

"Thank you. But I don't think I'll be going anywhere."

"What do you mean? You can't stay with him. He's obviously planning your death."

She shrugged. "Maybe. Or it could be just in case I decide to stop cooperating."

"Don't be ridiculous. This is no way to live."

"If I can't have a life with Agustín, it doesn't matter anyway."

She said it so matter-of-factly, backing it up with another bite of ice cream, that Lucy fully believed she meant it.

"Suki, you listen to me. You never know. If you'd married, you might not even be with him right now. Men come and go, and you can't depend on them. You must be self-reliant and know your value isn't tied up in who you marry or who you don't. It's in who you have the self-confidence to become."

"That's easy for you to say. I would be starting with nothing."

"Let me ask you something. Do you love that big penthouse apartment in the city?"

Suki shook her head. "No. I hate it."

"What about all the fine clothes and shoes and the pricey bags you have stacked up in your closets?"

"Ian picked all of it I don't want it."

"See, you already know that money cannot bring you happiness. Starting over is something many people would be envious of. You can create who you want to be. Like Ian created who *he* wanted you to be. And me to be. But this time, you get to decide."

"But I've never—"

Lucy held her hand up to stop Suki. "Think positive. Look at starting over with nothing as a windfall. If Ian was able to get both of you papers to start over as the Banfields here, then you know you can get papers to be someone else. You are gorgeous and you are smart, so you're starting off with tools that many don't have. Use them to your benefit, and it'll get you somewhere."

"I don't have any idea how to be on my own," Suki said. She set her ice cream down on the nightstand. "I'm afraid. How have you managed? You've told me nothing about yourself. Where you're from. About your family."

Lucy set her bowl down too. It was time to get serious. But they needed to focus on Suki's life, not hers. There would be time for that later.

"I have an idea, Suki, but it would mean that you'd have to be braver than you'd ever been in your life. Since you don't really seem to care what happens to you, it's time for you to focus on revenge. And we'll make our move tonight. We can't chance that Ian will come in the morning."

Suki suddenly looked more interested, as though revenge appealed to her. Lucy wanted some revenge of her own too. Ian had played her like a fiddle, and Lucy hated being played. She would love to see him squirm. Or at least know she'd helped make it happen.

Time to reel her in.

Lucy scooted closer and took Suki's hand. "Listen to me.

Your father and brother basically stole your life. You can't contact your lover. You've lost the relationship with your mother and sister. You're an island to yourself, without resources. Don't you want Ian to pay for that? Or do you just die off and let him win?"

Suki only paused a moment before her lips turned upward ever so slightly.

"What do I have to do?"

※

LUCY LAID a hundred-dollar bill on the counter and took the key from the night clerk. It was nearly two o'clock in the morning, and she was exhausted after riding in the car too long, followed by too much walking while looking over her shoulder. Lucy had ended up carrying the baby most of the way, since Suki had complained incessantly about her aching feet and tired arms, not acknowledging that Lucy had recently given birth and had her own issues going on. Fortunately, the child had been calmed by the car ride and walking and hadn't stirred.

Now Suki waited outside with him, hidden around the side of the building. One woman checking in during the night was nothing out of the ordinary, but two women and an infant would be memorable. It was unlikely that they could be tracked to the small no-tell motel, since the taxi driver had dropped them off at a local coffee shop and they'd walked the mile from there, but she wanted to take every precaution she could.

"Checkout is at ten." He was already back to staring at the screen of his phone, which he propped on the mound that was his belly, his pupils going huge at whatever he watched.

"Ten? Why so early?" Lucy asked.

"If you want it later, it's ten an hour extra." He looked up briefly, challenging her.

"No, that's fine." She mentally scolded herself for even asking.

Every extra word to him could be something that triggered his memory if Ian came around, questioning.

She went out the door and around the corner, relieved to find Suki still sitting on the curb, the baby sleeping soundly in her lap even though Suki's body looked rigid and uncomfortable.

"Everything okay?" Suki asked, her eyes wide as she looked from side to side then back at Lucy.

"Yep. Just fine. Let's get into the room. You take the baby, and I'll handle your suitcase and his bag."

They were supposed to have been limited to only one bag each to travel fast and light, but Suki had insisted that there were things she couldn't leave behind. She'd packed a backpack for the baby and a rolling suitcase for herself in addition to her large purse.

Lucy had left everything behind other than her money and what she'd brought to New York in her backpack on that first day. She wanted nothing to remind her of the stupid trap she'd fallen into. And as soon as she could offload Suki and the baby, she would eagerly put it all behind her.

"I'm worried about the dogs," Suki said as she followed Lucy through the parking lot.

"The housekeeper will be there in the morning and will see the note. After that, Ian will make sure someone is with them all the time. You know he loves them too." Lucy wished they hadn't had to leave the two behind. She'd become quite attached to them during her confinement when they had been her only friends. But dragging along a baby was hard enough and made them stand out. Adding a duo of expensive French bulldogs would put a target on their backs wherever they went, and poor Bent had a bad knee that would slow them down.

"Can you believe this place still has real keys?" As luck would have it, the room was located on the far side of the motel, as far from the office as they could get. Once they got there, she used the key and flung the door wide.

"Ugh," Suki said, moving past her. She gingerly sat on the very edge of the bed, the baby still in her arms as she looked around, her face in a disgusted grimace.

"Yeah, not a penthouse, for sure. But it'll do for tonight. Here, I'll make him a cradle," Lucy said. She'd stayed in worse, though it would've been nice to have two beds. She hadn't wanted to stir up any curiosity by asking for a double room. She went to the dresser, pulled out a drawer, and set it on the floor next to the queen bed. Then she grabbed a dingy pillow and tucked it into the drawer.

Luckily, they hadn't had to scale the fence and chance dropping the baby. Suki had found their security company's phone number in Ian's desk and had called and told them she'd forgotten the code and needed it reset. Lucy had put her battery back into her phone long enough to call a taxi, and then they'd been on their way.

"Are there clean towels? We could cover the pillow," Suki said, grimacing at the stained pillowcase.

Lucy went to the bathroom and came back with a scratchy towel. She smelled it. It was technically clean but had seen better days. "I'll put it on top, then you can sandwich him between his own blankets."

They both worked to settle Theodore in, moving quietly to not wake him. Somehow, he'd found his thumb, and other than making a few sudden sucking noises, he didn't even stir when Suki set him in the drawer.

When they were done, Lucy felt light with relief. Maybe she could get some sleep.

Suki went to the bed and sat down heavily, her shoulders slumped. When she looked up, her eyes shimmered with tears. "I'm afraid."

"Don't be," Lucy sighed, feeling the fatigue all the way to her toes. "We've already done the hardest part. You're out, and he has no idea where to look for you."

Suki didn't look convinced. "What will become of us? Theodore and I?"

Lucy sat down beside her. "I don't know, but I can promise you this: once you realize you don't have to be tied to anyone and can walk away at any time, you'll feel powerful. But remember, Ian and your father will look at Agustín first. They'll think you will try to get back to him. You cannot contact him in any way."

She looked solemn. "I know. I would never put him in that danger."

"Good. Remember, that life must be done with. You'll start a new one. And I can tell you this much: broken women grow into warriors. You'll be just fine."

"I'll be poor." She sniffled then waved her hand around the room. "This is what I can expect going forward?"

Lucy bit her lip until she tasted blood. It wouldn't do to show her irritation. "You said you didn't care about that, Suki. Your family's money is tainted and will only bring you trouble. You can earn your own once you decide what you want to do with your life. You'll get help along the way. The feds won't leave you floundering and take the chance you'll mess up the investigation."

Suki shrugged. "I guess you're right."

"I know I'm right. Now, we need to get to bed and rest while the banshee is sleeping. You go ahead and wash up. I'll watch him."

Suki went to the bathroom and closed the door. A few seconds later, Lucy heard the shower running. She listened for a moment then went to Suki's suitcase and laid it on the bed and unzipped it.

There were a few manila folders in the netted area. She and Suki had gone through Ian's file cabinet and grabbed the ones that could be valuable later. One held copies of invoices—records of paintings sold with details of buyers and shipping locations.

That was the one Lucy wanted in her own possession. It was like Ian's Rolodex of criminal clients. If Lucy had learned nothing else over her New York fiasco, it was that no one could be trusted. She needed collateral as a backup for her own safety.

She stripped the folder of the papers and stuffed them down into her own backpack. She'd make a copy of them as soon as she could get away for an errand then return the originals before she left Suki at a shelter.

After she took some papers from another folder and put them into the empty one to keep it from standing out, she sifted through the suitcase to see what else Suki had brought.

She found a photo of Suki posing with a young man's arm snugly around her. In the picture, she wore a much longer hairstyle. She looked fresh-faced and gazed at him adoringly.

They appeared to be in love. Obviously, it was Agustín.

Lucy hoped that Suki would heed her warning and leave him alone. Contacting him would bring nothing but trouble.

The rest of the suitcase was packed with mostly clothes and makeup, with a few pairs of shoes. Lucy picked up a Nike sneaker and ran her hand down into the toes. There was something in there. She pulled out a wad of money.

It wasn't the money that Lucy had given Suki either. She flipped through the wad and saw that it was all hundreds.

She went to the other shoe.

Another wad.

Her heartbeat pounded in her ears, and a jolt of pain traveled through her jaw. She carefully unclenched her teeth and quickly searched the rest of the suitcase. She found twenty stacks of cash banded with tags that marked them as $1000 each, all hidden in several places.

The blood rushed into her face.

Suki wasn't as innocent as she'd portrayed, obviously.

Where had she even gotten the money? There was no way Ian would have given it to her.

And the bigger question was why she hadn't told Lucy about

it. She'd said she had none. And if she'd lied about that, what else was she lying about?

Was she even committed to their plan?

Lucy had laid it all out for Suki. They would get on a Grey-hound, and after changing buses in several cities and small towns, they'd settle in one that had a women's shelter that would take in Suki and the baby.

Once they did that, Lucy was going to go the opposite direction, and Suki was going to reach out to the FBI. The feds would literally salivate over a money-laundering whistleblower who had evidence to back up her claims.

Lucy had promised to help her decide what information to hand over first. The plan was to dole it out gradually as they bartered first for Suki and the baby to be put in a safe house and then for help starting over with new identities. The feds would get all they needed but only when Suki had her new life started.

They'd solidified the details, and Lucy had given Suki three thousand dollars of her own money, which now turned out to not be much compared to what was socked away in the suitcase.

Lucy was risking her own life to help Suki, and there was nothing worse than risking her neck to help someone and then finding out they couldn't be trusted.

Quickly, she tucked everything back into the suitcase, including the wads of money, zipped it up, and put it back on the floor.

The shower was still running, and Lucy went to the door. She was about to knock when she heard Suki talking.

She put her ear to the door.

Suki wasn't in the shower. Or if she was, someone was in there with her. "Sorry" was the only word she caught at first. Then she heard Suki give the name of the motel.

Lucy had a sudden thought and hurried to her bag. She unzipped the small top pocket and reached inside, where she'd put her phone and the battery.

They were gone.

Suki was a liar. Not only that, but she was also a coward. After all their talking, planning, and running, Suki hadn't even lasted one night before calling Ian to come get her and the baby. The fact that Ian had a multimillion-dollar life insurance policy on her obviously didn't faze her.

Then why should Lucy care?

She sprang into action. First, she tossed Suki's suitcase back onto the bed. She was going to take what was rightfully hers then spend the next two minutes getting the hell out of there before Ian showed up. But if there wasn't an opportunity to do it, she needed the money more than Suki did. Something told her that Suki might be able to save herself by begging forgiveness from her brother, but he'd have no mercy on Lucy for taking Suki and especially the baby. In that case, she needed collateral.

CHAPTER 28

*T*aylor leaned back on the new bench that Sam had finished that morning. He stood at the end of the dock while he tossed the ball out into the water for Diesel. After he'd spent a week at her place fixing Diller's car, he'd insisted on leaving Diesel with her full-time for security until she got some cameras installed on the property.

He came back and forth every couple of days to visit.

"Ready... go!" He tossed the ball farther out then turned to Taylor. "I don't think it's possible to wear him out. At least not before my arm is done for."

"Agree."

"You doing okay?" He looked worried. "Not too talkative tonight."

"Yeah." She looked at her phone and couldn't help releasing a long sigh.

When she was in high school, she'd written an essay about a poet named Henry Van Dyke. One of his quotes that she'd included had always stuck with her throughout the years but never more so than now, as she watched her phone more than ever before, waiting for the call from Montana to tell her when they'd go to trial.

Time is too slow for those who wait and too swift for those who fear.

One week had turned into two then three.

During that time, she'd gone back to life as it was before she'd known Cate was alive. The only difference was that every few days, she talked to Adele, who was just as nervous waiting for the call. Her dad didn't have any idea they'd gotten this far with the case, so he wasn't asking too much. Cecil waited for Taylor to bring it up, for he knew her stress level was high and that she'd tell him if anything had changed.

Sam had let her know he was there to talk if she needed him, but he wouldn't pry.

Between being busy at work, training Deputy Kuno, investigating some small-time burglaries with Shane, and then spending time with Diesel, she'd hoped her days would pass quickly, but she still found herself glancing at her phone dozens of times a day to see if she'd somehow missed the call.

She was both eager for and afraid.

Diesel brought the ball back, and Sam plucked it from his mouth then tossed it again. He came and sat down next to Taylor.

"Thank you again for this bench, Sam. It's nice to have out here. I sometimes bring a chair, but if the wind gets up, it blows into the water."

"You're welcome, and you don't have to worry about that happening with this thing. I used heavy-duty bolts to secure it."

"Are you staying over tonight?"

"No, I need to get back. I don't think I told you, but we are shutting the shop down. Dad needs me to help pack up."

"You didn't tell me that. Why are you closing it?"

He shrugged. "Too much competition. There're half a dozen shops in our town, and he's tired of fighting for business. Says he's ready to retire and spend his days fishing."

"What will you do? I figured you'd take over the business when he retired."

"I was thinking I might open my own garage from scratch."

"Oh. Why not take over and build from what you already have?"

He looked at her. "I was thinking of doing it here, in Hart's Ridge."

Taylor didn't reply at first. She could see that he was very interested in her reaction. Thus far, they were still only friends. Admittedly, there were sparks, but her life was too tumultuous right now for anything more. Sam seemed to respect that. Who knew? Maybe he wasn't interested in her that way. Taylor wasn't even sure.

At work, Shane was closer to making a move than Sam was, and she wasn't open to that right now either.

She didn't know what she wanted.

Life was confusing, and right now, she needed to focus on her family.

Diesel climbed out of the water and onto the dock then shook himself all over, sprinkling them with lake water.

They both shielded their faces and laughed.

"Why Hart's Ridge?" she asked after Diesel flopped down between their feet, finally exhausted.

Sam leaned back and crossed his arms, his gaze on Diesel.

"Because of that brute, for one thing. You aren't ready to let him go, and I just can't walk away from him. If we live in the same town, it'll be easier to share him."

Guilt washed over her. She couldn't continue holding Diesel hostage.

"Sam, I know he's your dog, and I need to let you take him."

"No, not right now. Let's get this whole Cate thing behind you first. It's not only that. There's a need for another good mechanic here. Mr. Diller has already gotten me two more small repair jobs. He says it's hard to find an honest garage these days. I can do that here and build a good business at the same time, without all the competition I have in my town."

"What does your dad think about that?"

"He's fine with it. He's just glad I haven't reenlisted. That's his worry, and he's thrilled to have me anywhere within a few hours' driving time."

"Have you already looked at garage space? Or somewhere to live?"

"No. First, I wanted to float the idea by you. Make sure you didn't think I was some kind of stalker or something."

He grinned at her, and it sent little butterflies circling in her belly.

Her phone rang, and she pulled it from her pocket. When she saw the Montana number, her eyes widened, and she showed it to Sam.

"Take it. I'll go."

"No, stay. I'm nervous." She put her hand on his thigh to keep him from getting up. When he relaxed, she let go and hit the button then popped up to pace the dock.

"Hello?"

"Taylor, it's Jan and Hensley. Are you sitting down?"

"No. Should I be?"

"Yes, definitely. If you're driving, I need you to pull over."

Taylor sat down on the bench and waved at Sam to stay. "I'm not driving, and I'm sitting now. Tell me."

"Cate was sent to the county jail to await trial, but based on the new evidentiary discovery, the prosecution team declined to defend the conviction."

"What does that mean?" Taylor could feel her pulse pounding in her chest.

"It means there won't be another trial, and as soon as the paperwork is filed, Cate will be released on her own recognizance. Probably in a few weeks at the most!"

Suddenly, Jan's voice faded, and all Taylor could hear was a roar in her ears, as though she were standing next to a raging waterfall.

Sam squatted in front of her, his hands suddenly on her shoulders. "Are you okay?" he asked, his eyes full of concern.

She gripped the phone so hard her fingers ached.

"Taylor? Taylor?" Jan's voice came filtering back in.

"I—I'm here, Jan. Sorry. Could you repeat that last thing you said?"

"I said we won! Cate will be free!"

Taylor could hear Hensley in the background, screaming congratulations.

"Have you told Cate yet?"

"No. We have a meeting set up for tomorrow. We wanted to tell her in person, so you got to hear it first. Congratulations, Taylor. You did what you set out to do. Now go—celebrate with your family!"

She hung up without Taylor knowing if she'd said goodbye.

Jan was wrong.

Taylor hadn't set out to free Cate.

There had been much more to it.

She'd set out to find out if her mother was guilty.

CHAPTER 29

*E*xactly twenty-three days later, Taylor sat at her kitchen table with Adele and looked into the living room, taking in the scene. Anna and Pete sat on the couch, their two kids between them. Jo and Levi lounged on the floor in front of the television, a news channel playing unwatched.

All talk was centered around catching Cate up on family events.

As for the children, they weren't fazed that they'd suddenly gained not only a grandmother but a great-grandmother.

The only missing piece was Lucy. She still hadn't checked in, and Taylor had no way to reach her. It was sad that this was all happening without her, but it was Lucy's own fault.

The first hour of the urgent family meeting that Taylor had called was tense. They'd all gathered, and before she could even hint at why they were there, Cate had arrived with Adele. The introductions had been like something out of a bad reality show, but Taylor had known no other way to do it than to just pull off the Band-Aid.

Both Anna and Jo went through several emotions, including shock and then anger that their dad had kept Cate a secret for so many years. Before the anger could get out of control, Adele had taken the lead, explaining to them how Cate had thought the secrecy the best way for them to have a semi-normal childhood.

Adele had shown a side that Taylor hadn't known she had: fierce and protective, stepping into the role of a matriarch who wouldn't stand for nonsense, especially when it came to Cate and all she'd been through.

None of them had been brave enough to inform their grand-mother what their childhood was really like. At least not there, in front of their father.

Pete wanted all the legal details, finally interested in some-thing about their family and the ex-con mother-in-law he had never known he had. In his curiosity, he'd forgotten to behave as if he was better than everyone else and would be ashamed of the skeleton in his wife's closet, though most likely, that would come later. Anna followed his lead, not surprisingly, and it helped that though Cate was fresh from behind bars, she had a certain aloofness to her that came across as a more cultivated personality.

Her jaw was no longer wired shut, but it was still sore, and she wasn't talkative.

Taylor's dad had taken up his favorite chair, his arms crossed as he scowled at Pete's constant questions. He kept stealing peeks at Cate, and Taylor wondered where their relationship stood in all this. Or was there any relationship to wonder about? As for his past friction with Adele, Taylor didn't see any evidence that those feelings remained. They weren't overly friendly with each other, but they were polite.

Cate sat in the old, worn rocking chair next to her dad, Diesel at her feet. He'd decided she was his best chance at nonstop belly scratching and tasty morsels from the feast they'd cooked earlier that day. He had received most of what was on her plate. She hadn't eaten much, probably still in a state of shock at her new reality. She hadn't tried to shower the kids with attention either.

It was going to take time, and she seemed more comfortable with Diesel.

"Sounds like they disassembled every piece of evidence the state had," Pete said.

"They sure did. And Jan's experts on fire science said the initial reports were all wrong," Taylor said. "The original fire marshal testified that the fire was hotter because a liquid accelerant was used, but controlled experiments in the last few years have proven that fire from accelerants doesn't burn hotter. The heat level depends on what is being burned."

"Your lawyer was genius for subpoenaing the test data used by the ATF back then," Pete said.

"As well as all the related documents," Taylor said.

"Then how do they think the fire happened?" Jo asked.

"An electrician testified that the electrical wires that ran between the roof and the drop-down ceiling tiles in the trailer were overloaded, causing a small electrical spark early that morning. With the limited oxygen up there, the spark smoldered and produced carbon monoxide that built up in the ceiling. When it got hot enough, one of the tiles burned and dropped to the floor."

"That was what woke me," Cate said, looking up. "It had to be."

"Probably," Taylor said. "Then the carbon monoxide filled the room, and Robert died within minutes."

Her dad sighed long and heavily, and Taylor could see Cate's eyes fill with tears.

"Kids, go outside with Diesel for a few minutes," Anna said.

They were all quiet until the door closed behind them.

"Did Robert suffer?" Anna asked. "I always wondered."

"No, he did not," Taylor said. "The new experts agree on that. He had no burning in his trachea or his lungs, so that showed he had stopped breathing long before the fire got hot."

"I still play it over and over in my mind," Cate said, her voice soft as she stared at her feet. "I have for twenty years, always wishing I'd have done something different. That I'd woken up earlier or, I don't know—done anything that would've stopped this tragedy."

"It's not your fault," Taylor said.

"I remember feeling paralyzed when I realized the flames were blocking me from the hallway to him. I've thought all these years that I wasted valuable time. Time that could've saved him. It was surreal. One minute, life is fine, and the next, people are holding me down and telling me I can't go in and get my little boy."

She ended the statement on a ragged sob.

"He was gone by the time the flames were there, Cate," Taylor reminded her again.

"You suffered all that guilt while you were also trying to survive the nightmare of prison," Adele said. "It's just so sad."

"It was all a bunch of bullshit was what it was," Jackson said, slamming his fist against the arm of the chair. "There wasn't a single witness that saw her set the fire or ever heard her talk about doing so. There wasn't even evidence that she or I had ever purchased a liquid accelerant, and there wasn't a trace of accelerant found on her nightgown. How could she have been splashing something around and not gotten any on her?"

"And no motive, right?" Pete asked. "Life insurance?"

Jackson shook his head. "No. We could barely afford our regular bills."

Taylor nodded. "Even more stunning than all that was that the prosecution's original reports showed that yes, kerosene was detected on the floor samples from the living room, which wasn't a surprise because that was where the kerosene heater was located. But the tests from the bedroom floor were negative for anything. There wasn't any liquid accelerant or kerosene detected back there. Jan found that there was a report that showed negative, but someone had crossed it out and changed it to positive."

Her sisters both drew in shocked breaths.

"That's criminal," Pete exclaimed. "That ATF agent should be held accountable."

"Well, currently, he's being held in an assisted-living ward, and his dementia won't allow him to ever testify about what happened or to be held responsible," Taylor said.

"It's a damn shame," Adele said. "At a time when your mother's world was destroyed, she should've had a community rallying around her. Instead, she was victimized by the system and the supposed experts who framed her just to further their careers."

"So, Kinley got to just walk into a fire scene and make up whatever the hell he wanted to and send my wife to prison for twenty years," Jackson said. "How is that justice?"

Taylor could feel the waves of anger coming off him. It was going to take a long time for him to come to terms with it.

Cate stood. "I think I'll go outside and watch the kids play for a bit. I can't get enough of the feel of the evening air on my skin."

They watched her slowly cross the living room and go out the back door.

"She doesn't want to talk about it anymore," Jo said.

Pete stretched and yawned. "I hope she will find a way to get over this. Maybe use her story to raise public awareness, because you never know when you'll find yourself on a jury, listening to some expert spouting junk science and taking away someone's life."

No one said anything. They all needed to find a way to get over it, and Taylor wished she had the guts to insist on family therapy, but she could just see how that would go. They were a family that had always worked to bury their emotions, trek through their pain, and hide it from others. A therapist would have to be a miracle worker to do anything with them.

"Damn, would you look at that," Jackson said, pointing at the television. "Another one."

The channel was on world news, and a camera zoomed in on a huge house that was cordoned off with police tape.

A dressed-up journalist stood in front of the house, broad casting solemnly. "Sources say the homeowner, Theodore Ian Banfield, age forty-two, was shot and killed in his bed. He was an art dealer, and many valuable art pieces were taken in the home invasion. The only other victim was his wife, Sakura Lia Banfield, and she was not injured. More details to come, but while the investigation is ongoing, we want to highlight the rising statistics of home invasions in America and what you can do to protect yourself."

"What you can do is stop letting some people get filthy rich while others can't feed their families," Jackson said to the TV. "New York. A bunch of gussied-up folks with no more sense than their mama gave them. He probably splattered photos of his collection all over social media. Of course, he was going to get robbed. He invited them in!"

Taylor heard a car on the gravel and got up to look out the window. She saw a taxi pull up, but the kids blocked her view of who got out.

Before she could get to the door, it opened, and Cate stepped through. "Look who I found," she said. "Lucy made it after all."

Lucy followed, bewilderment on her face at finding all of them there, staring at her.

Jackson jumped out of his chair. "Lucy, we have something to tell you."

Lucy turned to Cate. "I'm sorry, but I didn't catch who you were."

"This is going to be a shock, but there's no easy way to say it, Lucy. I'm your mother. Cate." She looked apologetic as she said the words. When Lucy didn't respond with anything but an open mouth, she turned her attention away from her face. "And who is this you have with you?"

Lucy looked down with a surprised expression, as though she'd forgotten she was carrying something. "Wait—you said you're my mother?"

Jackson took Lucy's arm. "I can explain."

Taylor went to them. "Lucy, before you start to get upset—"

Lucy laughed. "Oh, I'm not upset. After what I've been through for the last eight months, nothing can surprise me, even my dead mother coming back from the grave. But here, Taylor, hold your nephew while someone tells me what the hell is going on."

THE END

READY FOR MORE HART'S RIDGE? YOU can get book three, IN MY LIFE, at the following link:

DOWNLOAD *IN MY LIFE*

HART'S RIDGE **used to be such a quaint, peaceful little town, but when a much beloved family is hit by a senseless tragedy, Deputy Taylor Gray won't stop until she finds the ruthless killer.**

WORKING a murder case is hard enough, but when she is also trying to navigate a new relationship, not lose her dog, and keep her own family straight, Taylor realizes she may have taken on more than she can handle. Something has got to give.

Deputy Taylor Gray is a young woman carrying the world on her shoulders as she does her best to solve mysteries (each inspired by a true crime) as well as fight to piece her fractured family back together. What will it take to convince her to step back and figure out what *she* needs?

In My Life **is book three of the new Hart's Ridge mystery series, written by Kay Bratt, million-copy best-selling author of** *Wish Me Home* **and** *True to Me.*

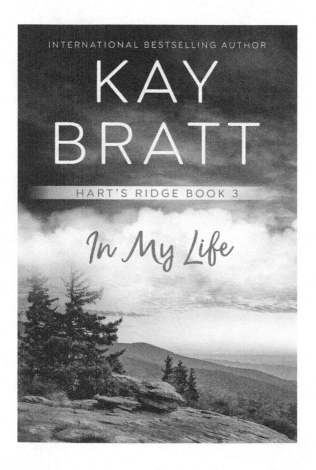

DOWNLOAD *IN MY LIFE*

PLEASE JOIN my monthly newsletter to learn more about the Bratt Pack and me, and to be notified of new releases, sales, and giveaways! Get to see what my feisty little Chorkie, Hazel Bea Bratt, has to say in her own article, Bea's Bytes. YOU CAN JOIN KAY'S NEWSLETTER HERE.

an article from the paw of a feisty chorkie

BEA'S BYTES

Hi Everyone!

Every month I have a little something to say, and I can't promise it will be nice. I'm the Queen Bea of this pack and what I say goes. Sometimes I spill a little tea, as we say in the South.

Come find me on my Pack Mama's Newsletter!

Hugs and Sloppy kisses!

xo Hazel Bea

FROM THE AUTHOR

FROM THE AUTHOR

Hello, readers! I hope you enjoyed the second book in the Hart's Ridge series. I enjoyed creating Lucy's character, because if you have a family of sisters, you know there's always that one who finds herself in and out of a lot of trouble. I am one of three sisters (with one older brother) and can relate to some of the feelings that Taylor has when it comes to being the eldest daughter and how that dynamic creates a certain self-imposed responsibility.

The plot line with Cate was inspired by the true story of Kristine Bunch, who languished behind bars for more than seventeen years after she was charged with setting the fire that tragically claimed the life of her three-year-old son, Anthony.

Cate's story is fictional and is not written to be exactly like the real travesty that Bunch suffered at the hands of unscrupulous so-called experts. However, Bunch's story inspired me to bring light to the injustice of the wrongful convictions of many prisoners who are still behind bars. Since 1990, there have been more than 2,500 confirmed exonerations with proof presented of abuse of power and lying about evidence. While I believe in our judicial system, there are always going to be some bad actors who manufacture evidence or work to hide facts that can prove someone's innocence, to further their own agenda.

I look forward to bringing you the next book, *In My Life*, in which Taylor is entrenched in the investigation of a triple murder while, at the same time, she is trying to piece together her fractured family. I have so much more to tell you in this series, and you will get to know each sister in a much deeper way.

You can download the next book in the series, *In My Life*, right now at this [link].

Can I ask a favor? I'd be overwhelmed with gratitude if you'd care to post an honest review for this book. On Amazon especially—and BookBub and Goodreads if you're feeling exceptionally generous. It's a big ocean of books out there, and authors need all the help they can get to be more visible. Reviews help improve that algorithm. Please recommend it to your bookworm buddies too!

And lastly, if you are a long-term fan, I want you to know I appreciate your picking up this book, which is a bit of a detour from my usual stuff. If you are new to my work, thank you for taking a chance, and I hope I didn't let you down! Come find me in my private Facebook readers' group, Kay's Kindness Krew, where I'm known to entertain with stories of my life with the Bratt Pack and all the kerfuffles I find myself getting into.

Until then,

Scatter kindness everywhere.

Kay Bratt

AUTHOR BIO

Writer, Rescuer, Wanderer

Kay Bratt is the powerhouse author behind over 30 internationally bestselling books that span genres from mystery and women's fiction to memoir and historical fiction. Her books are renowned for delivering an emotional wallop wrapped in gripping storylines. Her Hart's Ridge small-town mystery series earned her the coveted title of Amazon All Star Author and continues to be one of her most successful projects out of her more than million books sold around the world.

Kay's literary works have sparked lively book club discussions wide-reaching, with her works translated into multiple languages, including German, Korean, Chinese, Hungarian, Czech, and Estonian.

Beyond her writing, Kay passionately dedicates herself to rescue missions, championing animal welfare as the former Director of Advocacy for Yorkie Rescue of the Carolinas. She considers herself a lifelong advocate for children, having volunteered extensively in a Chinese orphanage and supported nonprofit organizations like An Orphan's Wish (AOW), Pearl River Outreach, and Love Without Boundaries. In the USA, Kay served as a Court Appointed Special Advocate (CASA) for abused and neglected children in Georgia, as well as spearheaded numerous outreach programs for underprivileged kids in South Carolina.

As a wanderlust-driven soul, Kay has called nearly three dozen different homes on two continents her own. Her globe-trotting adventures have taken her to captivating destinations across Mexico, Thailand, Malaysia, China, the Philippines, Central America, the Bahamas, and Australia. Today, she and her soulmate of 30 years find their sanctuary by the serene banks of Lake Hartwell in Georgia, USA.

Described as southern, spicy, and a touch sassy, Kay loves to share her life's antics with the Bratt Pack on social media.

For more information, visit www.kaybratt.com.